# LO
# VOYAGE

A gripping crime thriller full of twists

PAULINE ROWSON

*The Art Marvik Mysteries Book 3*

JOFFE BOOKS

Revised edition 2023
Joffe Books, London
www.joffebooks.com

First published by Fathom in Great Britain in 2020

This paperback edition was first published
in Great Britain in 2023





Cover art by Dee Dee Book Covers

ISBN: 978-1-80405-823-7

*For all those who work at sea.*

# CHAPTER ONE

*Monday*

Marvik stared across the dark, deserted stillness of Newtown Harbour on the Isle of Wight, his thoughts troubled. Only the gentle slapping of the sea against his boat and the rustle of the reeds on the April breeze disturbed the silence. He hadn't felt like sleep, which was why he was on his motor cruiser drinking a beer instead of in bed in his cottage close by.

His head was throbbing, not just from the wounds incurred in combat while on service in the Marines but from the bombshell that Detective Chief Superintendent Crowder, head of the National Intelligence Marine Squad and his occasional boss, had tossed in his lap at the end of March: that the murder of Sarah Redburn — whom he'd met only once in a steamy café in the Dorset coastal town of Swanage — was possibly connected with his parents' deaths in the Straits of Malacca in 1997 when he'd been seventeen. He didn't see how it could be and Crowder had refused to elaborate, which wasn't unusual, because Marvik's role in the National Intelligence Marine Squad was to go into a mission cold with the minimum of information, to ask questions, stir up trouble and provoke a killer into the open. Was Crowder giving him another mission? To find Sarah's killer? It couldn't be his parents' murderer because they had died in an underwater tremor while diving. It had been an accident. Or so he had thought. But if Crowder wanted him to undertake the mission then why not come right out and say it?

The trill of his mobile phone pierced his thoughts, shattering the silence and causing him to start. Perhaps this was Crowder calling him now, he thought, reaching for his phone, but then Crowder only ever used the specially designated mobile phone he'd given Marvik. He wouldn't call him on his personal one. It had to be Strathen then, his close friend and former Marine colleague who he worked with in the Squad, but it wasn't. Surprised, Marvik saw the caller was Helen Shannon, a woman he had met back in February on his first mission for the Squad, when he and Strathen had been detailed to discover who had killed her sister in 1997. The same year his parents had died, he thought, answering her call, wondering what had prompted her to ring him, and so late. It was just before midnight. He hadn't heard from her since finding the man who had murdered her sister.

'I need to see you, Art. When can you get here?' she curtly demanded.

'I'll tell you that when I know where you are,' he asked, curious by the summons.

'Sovereign Harbour Marina, Eastbourne.'

That was on the mainland, about sixty nautical miles to the east. He had a powerful motorboat but it would still take him about two-and-a-half hours to reach there. He headed for the helm. There was no need for him to return to the cottage. It was locked and he always kept provisions and a change of clothes on board in case he had to leave in a hurry — a product of his service training. His laptop computer was also with him in his rucksack.

'What are you doing there?' he asked as the engine throbbed into life.

'Didn't you say never to trust mobile phones?'

He did. Mobile phones could be easily hacked so whatever she had to say was something sensitive, and something she was afraid of if her tone of voice was anything to go by. She sounded frightened and Helen didn't scare easily. His concern deepened. He made for the deck. 'I can be there by three a.m.,' he answered with the phone crooked under his chin as he loosened the lines.

'Can't you make it sooner?' she asked, disheartened.

'Are you OK?'

'I wouldn't be calling you if I was,' she snapped.

'I'll be there as quick as I can.'

'See that you are.'

'Where shall I meet you?' But he was speaking to a dead line. That was typical of Helen, he thought, casting off. Bluntness was her customary style.

Within minutes, he was in the Solent heading east with only the lights of the buoys and the city lights of Portsmouth on the coast to his left to puncture the darkness. There was no moon or stars to guide him but he didn't need them. His night-vision was excellent and the equipment on his boat was the latest state-of-the-art technology. Even if it hadn't been he'd still have been able to navigate the English Channel. This was child's play compared to the night ops he and Strathen had been engaged in on far more perilous seas.

He'd thought of Helen often since February, as he was sure Strathen must have done, although neither of them had mentioned her. It had been their first mission after being invalided out of the Marines, he on account of a head injury which he still bore the scars of on his face and Strathen because of the loss of his left leg just above the knee incurred during the conflict in Afghanistan. Marvik again wondered why she had called *him*. Why not Strathen? He also had a powerful motorboat, which was moored at the Hamble close to where he lived, near Southampton. But perhaps Helen felt closer to him because of their shared danger while travelling the coast on his boat in February in search of her sister's killer. Or perhaps she had already tried Shaun and, getting no answer because he was engaged on one of his private security consultancy projects, she'd rung him.

Marvik was tempted to call Strathen but he thought he'd wait to see what Helen wanted and, if truth be told, he was glad of the action — remarkably his throbbing head was easing. He opened up the throttle. He had plenty of time to consider what it was that had panicked her into calling him. From what he knew of Helen, she wasn't the panicking kind. Was she in trouble? He hoped not. But it sounded very much like it. What sort of trouble, though? Did she think he was the only person who could help her out of it? She didn't know the full details of what he did but she did know he was often engaged on assignments that involved risk.

Ruminating over what was disturbing Helen, though, and why she had summoned him was pointless. He'd find out soon enough, so he let his thoughts return to Sarah Redburn's murder. He might have dismissed Crowder's claims that her death was connected with his parents in 1997 but for the fact that he'd discovered a notebook in Sarah's belongings which had belonged to his father. It was a small, dark blue hardcover book with blank pages in the front, while the rest of the pages had been torn out. Taped to the inside back cover was a three-and-a-half-inch floppy disk with his father's handwriting on it: *Vasa*, the name of Marvik's parents' research vessel.

Marvik couldn't fathom how it had got there when all his parents' papers had been catalogued by the solicitor after their deaths and placed in his safe-deposit box in a bank in London. And he was certain that Sarah had never known or worked with his parents, his father a leading oceanographer and his mother a renowned marine archaeologist. True, Sarah had also been a marine archaeologist, but he'd researched her background and could find no connection between her and them. She had heard of them, but then so had everyone in that field of expertise.

He'd placed the notebook and floppy disk in his safe-deposit box in London two weeks ago. He didn't have the hard drive at his disposal to open the ancient computer disk but Strathen did. He hadn't mentioned it to him yet, nor, in fact, even to Crowder. He'd wanted time to check out a few things for himself first. The black expanse of sea spread out before him as he recalled his conversation with the retired solicitor's clerk he'd visited earlier that day.

'It was a tragic accident,' Bell, a lean, bald man in his early seventies with steel-rimmed spectacles shielding restless grey-blue eyes had said in a precise manner as Marvik sat opposite him in the neat, small retirement apartment in Lymington on the south coast. There was no sign of a Mrs Bell physically or photographically. Perhaps Bell was a bachelor. It was of no consequence to Marvik. 'Everything was listed and a copy of the contents given to Mr Colmead and to yourself,' Bell had told him.

Michael Colmead was the managing partner at the Southampton based legal firm that had managed his parents and now his own affairs. Marvik had contacted Colmead last week and asked him about his parents' research papers. Colmead had passed him on to Bell, but had reassured Marvik that Bell would only reiterate what he was telling him. It seemed that Colmead was correct.

'Were you alone?' Marvik had asked Bell.

'No. Mrs Rathan assisted me. Sadly, she's no longer with us. Is there something wrong?' Bell's high-domed forehead had creased with concern.

Marvik had said there wasn't and had given Bell what he hoped was a reassuring smile which hadn't quite hit the spot, perhaps because his scarred face always seemed to make him look sinister even when he didn't mean to be. He'd said, 'I was just curious because something has turned up belonging to my father and I wondered where it had come from.'

'He might have given it to someone before his death, a friend or colleague, perhaps?'

But who? Not Sarah Redburn, as far as he was aware. She had gone straight from school to Southampton University, where she'd gained a BA (Hons) in Archaeology and an MA in Maritime Archaeology. She'd had no living relatives. Her mother had been laid to rest in 1998 in the same cemetery as Sarah had been three weeks ago. Her father's body had been consigned to a watery grave eleven weeks after she'd been conceived in 1979. After graduating she'd worked as a maritime archaeologist for English Heritage and for various consultancies in the UK.

Bell had said that their task of cataloguing everything had been undertaken a month after the accident in July 1997. Marvik knew what Bell was implying — that anyone could have entered their house on the Isle of Wight or broken into the boat before then and helped themselves, except as far as Marvik was aware there had been no forced entry of either and no one else had had keys to the house or boat except him and the solicitor. But how did he know that for certain? He'd been at boarding school miles away and had had minimal contact with his parents since being despatched there very much against his will at the age of eleven. For all he knew, they could have dished out keys to neighbours, cleaners and friends — anyone, in fact, except relatives. Neither his mother nor his father had had any of the latter or, if they had, no one had come forward after their deaths, which had been covered by all the professional magazines and by newspapers both home and abroad, along with glowing obituaries. The scattering of their ashes at sea according to their wills had been a very private affair with just him, his guardian, Hugh Freestone, the solicitor, Colmead, and Fred Davington, a diver and the only crew member on their boat when they had died.

As the coast of southern England sped past him, he thought he knew so little of his parents' life; once at boarding school he had rarely seen them. Before that he'd led a nomadic existence with them on board *Vasa*. It seemed, looking back, to have been sun-filled and happy. But memory could play tricks, as Langton, the army psychiatrist, had told him. *The least remembered is usually the most accurate. Memory is very malleable; it's dangerous to think that it is a perfect picture of the past. It's not.*

Where did he go next with his enquiries? But he knew the answer to that as the lights of the small but busy port of Newhaven drew near. It was quiet now. No fishing boats and no ferry sailing to Dieppe in France at this time in the morning. Soon he would be at Eastbourne. He needed to speak to Colmead again and visit his bank in London to trawl through the catalogue that Bell and the late Mrs Rathan had compiled. He also needed to know what was on that disk.

As Eastbourne approached, he turned his thoughts to the present and Helen. The lock to the marina was looming. Making his way through it, he caught sight of Helen pacing up and down on the pontoon. She was wearing the dark-mauve sailing jacket he'd bought her in Weymouth in February. Her hair was still purple but longer, blowing across her narrow-featured face, and she still favoured Doc Marten boots, black tights and a skirt. In the low-level lights he could see all too well the anxiety etched on her angular features. It bothered him. He threw the line to her, which she caught expertly, but instead of tying off she held on to it and leapt on board.

'I thought you were never going to get here,' she said with feeling.

'I came as quickly as I could.' It was just before three a.m.

'Well, what are you waiting for?'

'We're leaving?'

She nodded and glanced over her shoulder.

'It's not often I take hitchhikers,' he said, smiling, but she didn't return it. Her green eyes still sported the same heavy, dark make-up, but they were ringed with fatigue.

'For God's sake, Art, can we go?' she cried.

He swung the boat around and headed out of the lock, disturbed by her evident distress and keen to know the cause of it. He noted that she made sure to stay below as they went through the lock. Only when the marina was behind them did she emerge. He could feel the tension in her slender body as she stood beside him at the helm. She made no attempt to explain her actions or tell him what was worrying her. Marvik said nothing. She'd tell him when she was ready but he knew that, whatever it was, it had to be something substantial to have rattled her this much. There was no hurry, except he had no idea where she wanted to go. He was heading west. He'd put in at Newhaven, the nearest port with marina facilities.

After several more minutes had passed, she said, 'What does a girl have to do around here to get a coffee?'

'You know where everything is. And while you're at it, make one for me.'

'I'm not your skivvy.'

'Never said you were,' he muttered as she disappeared below to the galley.

He remembered the cold February days and nights he'd travelled with her on board along the south coast in a bid to find her sister's killer. She'd had a tough time in the past. Her father, who had served in the army, had been killed in the Falklands War when she was eleven and her mother had died of multiple sclerosis not long before her sister, Esther, had been murdered. Like him, she'd been left without family at the age of seventeen, but unlike him she'd had no money and none of the stability and comradeship that the Marines had provided for him. They'd faced danger together and Helen had stood up to it well. She was not easily scared, so whatever had frightened her in Eastbourne had to be significant, but he began to wonder if it was real.

He knew a great deal about the emotional and psychological symptoms of trauma and Helen was exhibiting them in bucket loads. She was edgy, tired, anxious and afraid. Perhaps her telephone call to him had been a cry for help. All the horror of her sister's brutal death, which had been recently dredged up, refused to cease tormenting her. She was lonely and desperate. He was the only person she could reach out to for help. He knew how that felt. There had been no one he could turn to when his parents had died. No one he could trust or that he felt would understand his sense of isolation. The Marines had been his salvation, the rigorous training, the comradeship, the shared danger, the focus on the missions. The adrenaline surges had made him feel alive. The missions had given him a sense of purpose and a feeling of self-worth despite sometimes witnessing appalling brutality which had saddened and sickened him. For a long time he hadn't cared whether he lived or died. Injury, incapacity and failure had been his biggest fears and he'd faced all three. He'd thought he'd come to terms with them but he knew he hadn't, not completely.

The smell of coffee wafted up to him. Though Helen might look and behave tough and resilient, it was just a front. Behind the facade was a fragile woman with a broken, sorrowful past. Perhaps she was on the verge of a mental breakdown. Whatever it was that had driven her to call him, it was clear she needed help. Maybe he shouldn't have left her alone so soon after the trauma of facing up to her sister's murder, but it had been her decision to go away.

She put a mug of coffee on the table behind him and clutched hers with both hands. They were almost at the entrance to Newhaven Harbour but Marvik stopped the boat and dropped the anchor. She'd discarded the sailing jacket and was wearing a black zip-up fleece which sported a logo and a name he didn't recognize — Aquamarine Cleaning. She saw him looking.

'It's a boat-cleaning company. I work for them, that is I did until last night. Yeah, I decided I liked boats after being force-fed them with you and Shaun. Been doing any more of that James Bond stuff lately?' she asked, sipping her coffee.

'Some,' he said, lightly thinking of his last mission.

She eyed him closely. 'And Shaun? You still working with him?'

'Yes.'

She nodded, as though he'd given her the correct answer, and resumed, 'I lost my job in that crummy call centre near Southampton on account of not phoning in or showing up for work when we were, well, you know, finding Esther's killer.'

'Did you tell them what had happened? They might have been sympathetic.'

She snorted derisively. 'You must be kidding! The management doesn't know the meaning of the word and I certainly wasn't going to tell them my personal business. I was glad they sacked me — or rather, before they could I told them they could poke their rubbish job. The lease on that crappy house was up and I decided to go to Eastbourne.'

'Why there?'

'Why not?'

Marvik let that pass. After a moment, she expanded.

'I saw this job advertised online for a telephone sales clerk in a book wholesalers. I was offered it and started almost immediately. I got myself a small flat, a shitty bedsit actually, but the job was so dull that I thought I'd prefer to be dead. Then one of the tenants in my building said the company he worked for, Aquamarine Cleaning, was looking for people to clean boats. I said I'd had plenty of experience on boats. Well, it wasn't a lie.'

It certainly wasn't.

'I went for the job, Ian Bradshaw, the boss, said he'd already filled the vacancy. I thought that was it but the next day I got a call from him. He said someone had left and would I like to start, on a trial basis — casual to begin with. I chucked in the sales job — well, walked out actually. They didn't stop me and I started at Aquamarine the next day. That was a fortnight ago yesterday.'

She took a draught of her coffee. Marvik thought she was using the time to gather her thoughts and, from her expression, they didn't seem to be pleasant ones.

She continued, 'It was going OK. Then, yesterday afternoon, Ian Bradshaw said he'd like to see me. He said he thought I had potential and all that crap. Yeah, the only potential he was interested in was between my legs. Like an idiot, I believed him and agreed to meet him on his boat. OK, so I was naive,' she tossed at him as though he'd spoken. He didn't think his expression had betrayed his thoughts.

'Bradshaw tried it on and I told him to sod off. He said I was sacked. I said I wouldn't want to work for a wanker like him anyway. I left the boat but as I turned on to the pontoon heading back to the boardwalk I heard these two men on board one of the boats talking.'

She swallowed her coffee before continuing. 'One of them said, "It's dealt with. The target's been taken out". The other man said, "How?" The reply was: "You don't need to know that. Don't worry, there'll be no comeback".'

Marvik frowned. 'Are you sure you heard this?'

'Of course I'm sure! I wouldn't be telling you otherwise.'

'It wasn't a television you heard?'

'OK, so you don't believe me.' She made to rise but the confines of the table prevented her.

Marvik said, 'I didn't say that. I'm just exploring possibilities.'

'I'm not stupid, Art. I can tell the difference between real speech and a TV programme.'

'I'm sorry. But that sort of language implies—'

'A murder, I know. Why do you think I called you? You're in the Marines.'

'Not any longer.'

'Anyway, I must have made a noise or they had a feeling someone was on the pontoon because it suddenly went quiet. I got scared. I didn't fancy being the next target so I dived on to the boat beside me, opposite them. It was a fishing boat. I climbed inside the locker along the side of the cockpit and hid.'

She took a breath. Marvik could see she was reliving the fear of it. Her hands were gripping the sides of the cup, her purple varnished nails were bitten to the quick and he noticed there was a sliver of blood on the right-hand sleeve of her fleece. His concern for her deepened. There was still the possibility that she had fabricated this story. Or perhaps she genuinely believed she had heard these men and dived on to the fishing boat because her mind had told her she had to find a way of making contact with him and Strathen.

She sniffed. 'I felt a movement on the pontoon and heard footsteps. I didn't even dare to breathe. I was terrified they'd find me. Then I heard one of them say, "All clear. Must have been the wind or a bird". I stayed put until I heard them leave the marina.'

'On foot?'

'No, by boat. Two boats left.'

'What time was this?'

'About nine thirty. It could have been later. It was dark. I climbed off the fishing boat and walked to my flat, and I'm telling you it's a bloody long way from that marina stuck out on the edge of town to Harold Road where I live. I didn't want that shit-heap Bradshaw to come after me or those men to turn back in their boats and follow me, but I got the feeling I *was* being followed.'

'Go on,' he encouraged when she faltered.

'I thought I must be imagining it. I told myself that it was a legacy of my days with you. Perhaps you trained me too well. But when I got to the house I still felt as though someone was there. I let myself into my flat and went to the window. There was someone hanging about in the doorway of the opposite building. It spooked me. I wasn't going to stick around to find out if I was going to be another "target". I got out quick. I thought about knocking on Gavin's door. The guy who I work with. The one who lives in the same building as me. But I didn't. I climbed out of the window on to the fire escape. It comes out into a small backyard and there's a side entrance leading around to the front next to a convenience shop. I made for the seafront. I thought the only people who would believe me would be you and Shaun. So I called you.'

What did Marvik make of her story?

'I'm not making this up,' she hotly declared, misinterpreting his silence.

'I never said you were.'

'You look as though you think I am.'

'Were those two boats on the pontoon when you went on board Bradshaw's boat?'

She frowned as she tried to recall. 'I wasn't really taking any notice. I didn't hear them arrive, so they must have been.'

'What time did you arrive on Bradshaw's boat?'

'Just before nine o'clock.'

So if they had been there what had the occupants been doing for ninety minutes while Helen was on board with Bradshaw? Taking out this target? Or perhaps one of them had.

'Did you get the name of the boats?'

'Oh, yeah, I climbed off the fishing boat and asked them. 'Course I didn't.'

'OK, so we'll get them now and their arrival and departure times.' Marvik let up the anchor.

'How?'

'We go back to Eastbourne.'

'But it's nearly four o'clock.'

'Which means the night-duty lockkeeper and the marina night-duty manager will still be there and can tell us.' He started the engine and began to swing the boat round.

'You still don't believe me, do you?'

'What were the boats like?'

'They were both modern motor cruisers. One was larger than the other but they both had a fly bridge, sleeker than this boat and Shaun's, the flashier speedboat kind. The type you where you sit on deck and sip a gin and tonic, or so I'm told. I've never had the chance.'

'Did they have canvas awnings over the cockpits?'

'Yes, both of them, dark blue. I didn't see the men so I can't give you a description.'

'We'll check it out. Then we'll go back to your flat and make sure no one's staking it out.'

'Don't bother. You think I've cracked up. Just drop me off then you can bugger off. I can see I've wasted your time.'

But Marvik ignored her.

# CHAPTER TWO

*Tuesday*

'Two boats came in last night within ten minutes of each other just after seven thirty,' the lockkeeper relayed over the radio as Marvik entered the lock.

Helen flashed Marvik a look that said, *See, didn't I tell you.*

'The first, *Merry Maid*, was a Sealine F46.' Which Marvik knew to be a large and expensive motor cruiser. 'The second was a Princess 45, called *Sunrise*.' Equally large but possibly not as pricey. 'They locked out at nine thirty-five p.m.'

That bore out what Helen had said. The lockkeeper didn't have the boat owners' names but the marina duty manager might be able to give them that information. Marvik thanked him and moored up where he had picked up Helen earlier. He asked her to remain on board while he made for the marina office. 'Just in case one of those guys did see you and returns and starts asking questions about you.'

'If he does then he'll soon be able to identify me.' She pointed at her hair. 'And most if not all the marina staff know me, given that I work here.'

But she did as he asked and stayed put. Perhaps fatigue was finally wearing her down. Marvik was back within a few minutes.

'James Colbourne was the skipper on the *Merry Maid* and George Marwell on *Sunrise*, but the duty manager only saw Colbourne — heavy-set, muscular, about forty. He said he was meeting Marwell and they'd only be staying for a short time. They paid cash.' Marvik had spun a yarn that he had been due to meet them but had been delayed, hence his very late arrival. He didn't mention that he'd locked in earlier and the man in the marina office didn't query it. He probably hadn't noticed, or, if he had, thought it not his place to pry.

So far, that corroborated Helen's story, and the payment of cash, while not necessarily suspicious in itself, added a little more credence to what she had said. There was still the possibility that she had invented the conversation as a cry for help. He'd also paid cash for the berth and had told the duty officer that he wasn't sure how long he'd be staying.

Marvik asked Helen where Bradshaw's boat was moored.

'Just down there.' She pointed to a pontoon that was not far from where Marvik was moored, adding, 'And those other two boats were just farther along from yours, almost opposite the pontoon where Ian Bradshaw's boat is.'

'Let's take a look.' Marvik was keen to see the layout because something Helen had told him earlier didn't quite add up.

They set off along the pontoon. Across the marina, the restaurants and shops were shut and only a few lights glimmered in the houses and flats surrounding them. Insomniacs or early risers, Marvik thought. There was no one on board any of the boats they passed and only the sound of the wind rattling the halyards on the yachts disturbed them.

The pontoon where Bradshaw's boat was moored formed a T-junction with the one Colbourne and Marwell had been on. They turned on to it and Helen halted by a sizeable motor cruiser three boats down on the left-hand side facing out on to the marina, not on to the boardwalk to their far right. It was a modern four berth cruiser with a fly bridge and, from what Marvik knew of these boats, had two cabins. It was about ten years old. He didn't know how long Bradshaw had owned it but Marvik estimated it would have set him back about eighty thousand pounds. As he had expected, the boat was shut up.

'Was Bradshaw on board when you arrived?'

'Yes, the canvas awning was open and he came up on deck.'

'You called out to him?'

'No. He must have heard me. He had a glass of red wine in his hand and offered me one as I climbed onboard. I don't much go for the stuff, but it was on offer and he was the boss. Then he asked me to take a seat in the cabin. Big bloody mistake, because then I was stuck behind a fixed table on a bench seat and you know how awkward it is to get out from them on a boat, quickly. The slimy toad came and sat next to me, started pawing me. I told him to keep his hands to himself.' Her brow furrowed as she obviously recalled the incident.

'And did he?'

'No.' Her face flushed and she glared at him. 'I scratched the bastard's face and while he was cursing and trying to fumble for a handkerchief or tissue I managed to slide out of the seat at the opposite end. He was furious, calling me names. I threw a few choice ones back at him, but I had to get past him to get off the boat and he grabbed me as I tried to get round him, so I spat in his face and kicked him in the shins. He let go of me, told me I was fired. I said that was fine by me — I wouldn't work for a tosser like him anyway. Then he laughed and said he wouldn't shag me if I was the last woman on earth. I told him to go screw himself because no one else would want to. I left.'

'Did you look back at his boat when you were on the pontoon?'

'No. I just wanted to get away. I was angry with myself rather than him.'

Marvik headed back towards the T-junction. Helen fell into step beside him. It was only a short distance. Marvik turned left and halted where the two boats with Colbourne and Marwell on board had been moored up. The berths were currently empty. 'OK, so you walked past the boats in the direction of the quayside and the marina office.'

'I was about to when I heard the word "target". It made me think of you and of Esther.' She sniffed and looked away then back up at him. 'Then they suddenly stopped talking. I freaked. That's the boat I climbed on to hide.' She pointed at the fishing vessel to her left.

Marvik nodded but his mind was racing as he again considered something that had occurred to him earlier when she had first told him about the conversation. The movement of the pontoon caused by Helen's footsteps coming from Bradshaw's boat would have made this pontoon gently rise and fall. It must have been felt by those two men on board one of their boats and warned them that someone was approaching, so why had they continued talking? Had they thought it was just the wind over the water in the marina that was causing the movement? Perhaps. Or perhaps they'd been so engrossed in their conversation that they hadn't noticed until the movement ceased when Helen stopped and one of them heard or sensed someone outside. Had she really heard anything? Was Ian Bradshaw's pass at her genuine? Or had she fabricated both? Perhaps she'd seen the boats arrive and had spun him the kind of story she knew would appeal to him. Or perhaps she hadn't been able to repel Bradshaw's advances and something more had happened on board his boat and she was too frightened and too ashamed to tell him. It would explain why she hadn't gone to her work colleague Gavin Yardly's flat, because she couldn't face telling him that Bradshaw had raped her. Marvik tensed. His stomach knotted. If that was true . . . If Bradshaw had laid so much as a finger on her he'd beat him to a pulp.

'Are you up to walking?' he asked. He didn't want to hail a taxi and chance that Helen might be recognized if it came to a police matter, and he was going to have to personally deal with Bradshaw.

'Yeah. Good job I left my stilettos at home,' she joked with a tired smile. She looked exhausted but Marvik knew Helen wouldn't admit defeat.

They struck out towards the centre of the town, taking the most direct route which was along the deserted promenade. Marvik tensed at the thought of Helen walking this route last night, worried, scared, angry at Bradshaw, perhaps even traumatized by what had happened *if* it had happened. And maybe she had been too scared to stay in her flat, afraid that Bradshaw would come after her, which was why she wanted someone with her now when she returned to it. Helen was tough and streetwise but the toughness could be just an act to hide her vulnerability, and being streetwise was no protection against brute force.

They walked in silence. He wondered what Helen was thinking but didn't ask. Maybe she wondered what his thoughts were. It would have been difficult for him to explain because mixed up with his concern for Helen were thoughts of Sarah and the fact that her last address had been nearby and her last maritime archaeological project a wreck just off Beachy Head four miles to the west. But she had finished that and had been about to embark on a new project in Gibraltar when she'd been diverted into pursuing research of a more personal nature — that of her father's disappearance — when Marvik had met her in Swanage. Shortly afterwards she'd been killed. But it hadn't been here that he had discovered his father's notebook — it had been in a house where she had stored her possessions, not far from London. A house where he had almost been fried alive and Sarah's possessions destroyed. Had the arsonist been after him or the notebook? Maybe both, but there had been no further attempts on his life, so perhaps Crowder was wrong. Or perhaps the arsonist was biding his time.

'My flat in Harold Road is just off the seafront, down there.' Helen's voice broke through his thoughts and he followed her pointing finger to a narrow street that ran alongside an Italian ice-cream parlour and coffee shop on the corner. They crossed the deserted main road. The side street gave on to a broader one that ran east to west, parallel to the main promenade.

'I told you it was a select area,' Helen muttered facetiously.

He smiled briefly as they walked the length of the grimy road with nothing to disturb them except the litter blowing in the gutters and the occasional sound of a car on the seafront. Harold Road was a mixture of decaying terraced houses interspersed with ugly low rise flats, five-storey Edwardian houses which had long passed their glory days and shabby shops, many vacant with 'to let' boards in the windows but a few still operational — a launderette, a cycle shop, a Chinese takeaway and, as they progressed farther westward, the modern convenience store Helen had mentioned, with a small car park, and beyond that a café on the corner.

'Home sweet home,' she announced, waving a hand at the dilapidated Edwardian house next to the convenience store, which was closed. It was the end one of a terrace of four set back from the pavement with what had once been front gardens but which were now paved over for vehicles. Only one car, a rusty old Ford, was parked at the front of the house.

'Not mine,' she said, reaching for her key as they climbed the six stone steps to the scuffed and scarred door. A light shone dimly from the basement window, but aside from that, the building, like its neighbours, was in darkness. Discarded crisp packets, sweet wrappers, paper coffee cups and polystyrene takeaway food cartons swirled around the forecourt. Three black wheelie bins lined the coloured stone-patterned path. The house occupied five floors, which included the basement and attic rooms.

'I'm on the third floor at the front. That's Gavin's flat.' She pointed to the one to her left on the ground floor. She made to switch on the hall light but Marvik put a hand on her arm. He had already retrieved his torch from his rucksack.

She rolled her eyes as if to say *more James Bond stuff* but he thought she seemed edgy, which was natural if he was correct about what she had been through. No one was watching the house and no one had followed them. It was still dark — the sun wouldn't rise for another hour.

The torch's powerful beam swept the grime-laden, dusty hall with its smell of dirt and stale food. He didn't like to think of Helen living in such a place, coming here after a day's work. It was enough to make anyone despair. Ahead, the narrow corridor led to a door — to another flat, he assumed — while halfway down the corridor, which contained a bicycle and a pushchair, steps led down to the basement flat where the sound of a fretful baby was coming from. Even to his untrained ears, it sounded hungry.

Helen made to speak but he indicated to her to keep silent. She shrugged and followed him up the stairs to the third floor. No one disturbed them. There she took a key from the pocket of her jacket. Marvik couldn't explain why but he felt uneasy. Was Helen's apprehension and tension rubbing off on him? Her breath was coming a little faster and she seemed to be holding back. Something smelled wrong and it wasn't just the drains. The door was intact; there was nothing to indicate it had been forced. And nothing to show that anyone lay in wait for them behind it but, just as he had on past operations, he knew instinctively that there was danger.

As she made to open the door he took the key from her hand and moved ahead of her, blocking her way, thrusting back the door so it crashed against the wall. No one was behind it. He stepped inside and let his torch play over the room. Its beam froze as it alighted on the body of a man lying on the floor. Swiftly, Marvik turned, pulled Helen in and placed his other hand across her mouth, causing her to start violently. Still holding her tightly, he kicked the door shut behind him and ran the torch over the bundle on the floor.

'Is that Ian Bradshaw?' he asked quietly as the beam of light fell on the wide, staring, sightless eyes.

She nodded.

'You won't scream?'

She shook her head. He withdrew his hand.

'I never scream,' she said indignantly, swallowing hard. 'But I do swear. Holy shit.'

# CHAPTER THREE

'Stay where you are,' Marvik commanded.

'I wasn't about to go and make a cup of tea,' she quipped. 'Sorry, always flippant when I'm scared, as you probably remember.'

He crossed to the body. There was no need to check for signs of life because the bloody gash across the throat told Marvik that Bradshaw was dead. His mind was racing with scenarios. Maybe she had lied to him about going to Bradshaw's boat and Bradshaw had come here, attempted to assault her and she'd killed him? But Colbourne and Marwell had been real, although not necessarily their conversation. It was possible that Bradshaw had followed Helen back here and, drunk, had tried again to force himself on her. Or perhaps she had returned willingly with him, plied him with drink and drugs and then slit his throat. The self-harming knife wounds on her wrists he'd seen when he'd first met her in February flashed before him, along with the sliver of blood on her sleeve he'd noticed on the boat earlier, but surely there would have been more blood on her if she'd killed him.

His torch picked out the spattering of blood around the body, on the chairs either side of it and on the floor close to the electric fire where it had spurted when the artery had been severed — the pumping of the heart had literally sprayed the blood. Even if Helen had slit his throat from behind — and there was no other way from what he could see of the wound that it could have been done — there would still have been blood on her, some splashes on her upper clothing and fine blood spots on her lower clothing and shoes when the blood splashed on to the floor. The carpet was threadbare and hadn't soaked up the blood. But she could have changed and dumped her bloody clothes in a bin somewhere and cleaned herself up in a public toilet while waiting for him to arrive at the marina. Bradshaw had got into this flat somehow and the only way he could have done so was with a key he'd been given or she'd let him in. The lock on the door was intact.

Roughly, he pushed such thoughts aside and concentrated on the corpse. He was careful to avoid stepping in any of the congealed blood and leaving footmarks but knew that even if he avoided doing so there would still be traces of him left in this room for the forensic experts to find. He moved the left leg only slightly and noted that rigor hadn't yet reached the feet or lower leg. Rigor could occur from two to four hours after death and last for up to four days depending on the manner of death and the temperature. The room was cold. The windows were shut and the April weather had been unseasonably chilly, slowing down the process of rigor mortis, and he could see that Bradshaw was a heavy-set man — running to fat — which would further slow it down.

'What time did you leave here?' he asked quietly while his ears were attuned to the slightest sound from the hall.

'About eleven o'clock or just after. I didn't stop to look at the clock — there isn't one anyway and I don't wear a watch.' She bit at the fingernails of her right hand. Her eyes seemed incapable of leaving the body.

It looked to Marvik as though Bradshaw had been dead for about four hours, maybe five, which would put his death very close to when Helen said she had left here. Had she done this? Even if she had found super-human reserves of strength out of anger and desperation, she couldn't have put a knife around this man's throat and slit it from behind — not unless he had been sitting in one of the chairs in front of the small fireplace and she'd come up behind him while he was drugged. But then the body would be either in the chair or it would have slipped or been pushed forward on to the floor in front of the grate, whereas it was lying on its back behind the two shabby, grimy, threadbare chairs in front of the five-bar electric fire, the head towards the door, feet facing into the room. Helen could never have moved him. And the blood spatter didn't match with him having been seated. There would have been more arching around the fireplace and over the wall. There was also no evidence of any kind of struggle, unless the room had been tidied.

'Did you draw the curtains?'

Her eyes flicked towards the window. 'No. At least, I don't think so. I just wanted to get out. Do you think he followed me?' She scowled at the body.

Marvik caught the sound of a distant siren. 'Get some things together.'

'But . . . OK.'

He heard her moving about as he adroitly searched Bradshaw's pockets. There was a driver's licence in a wallet with a photograph. There were also credit cards and a membership card to the Grancha Casino. Marvik didn't know it or where it was situated, but then he wasn't a gambling man.

Wiping the cards, driving licence and the leather wallet clean with a tissue, he replaced them in the dead man's pocket. Then, patting the pockets of Bradshaw's sailing jacket, he located a set of keys on a fob that carried the Jaguar emblem. He hadn't thought the rusty old Ford in front of the house had been Bradshaw's but neither had he seen a Jaguar parked along Harold Road. He stuffed the keys in his pocket and did likewise with Bradshaw's mobile phone as the sound of the siren drew closer. It could be an ambulance. A fire engine had a slightly deeper tone. It could be going anywhere. It was unusual that it was sounding this early in the morning when there wasn't much traffic to negotiate. And, as if reading his thoughts, it stopped. Perhaps it had reached its destination.

He quickly surveyed the room, keeping his torch low. 'Bring your passport.'

'We're going abroad?' she asked, surprised.

'You never know.'

'But shouldn't we report him . . . this, to the police?'

'Only if you fancy spending a couple of days in a police station being questioned.'

'Not bloody likely.'

She opened a drawer and rummaged around for a passport while throwing some things into her rucksack. The streetlight afforded them further illumination over and above the torch. Marvik didn't want to risk switching on the light and alerting anyone either within or outside the building to their presence. He took in the surroundings. There was nothing on the mantelpiece above the fireplace and nothing personal displayed in the depressingly dreary room. The single bed was made up, and beside it a small cabinet with a lamp. Opposite the bed and to the right of the door was a small television, and on the other side of the door was a chest of drawers with a mirror on it and then a wardrobe. The room was neat. Nothing was out of place, unless you counted the body on the floor. The kitchenette was directly opposite the door, with a sink, a cabinet underneath it, another cabinet to the right next to the cooker and a fridge to the left of the sink. On top of the cabinets was a kettle, a toaster and a couple of mugs. He crossed over to them. They hadn't been used, or if they had they'd been washed. But he didn't think Bradshaw had sat and supped tea with his killer. Again, he wondered if Helen could have drugged him, then washed up the mugs. There was no bathroom, which meant that Helen must share one with the other tenants. It was probably farther along the corridor on this floor.

He played the beam of his torch over the smoke alarm on the ceiling to the right of the door. It didn't look as though it had been tampered with. A single pendant lamp hung from an elaborate ceiling rose in the centre of the room. Then, crossing the room, he turned his attention to the bedside light.

'What are you doing?' she asked.

He threw her a look.

Her eyes widened with disbelief. 'Who the hell would want to watch and listen to me?' Then her expression darkened and she glared at the dead man. 'Unless that creep . . .'

'He wasn't. There aren't any devices.' No one was after Helen. It was just his training kicking in. And his training was telling him that the police siren that had started up again was much closer. His instinct was telling him it was heading here. And his gut was telling him that, for some reason he didn't know or understand, Helen had been framed for the murder of her boss.

He crossed to the window where, standing to the side of it, he peered down into the street. There was no one loitering in a darkened doorway and no one suspicious walking past but, just as Helen had said, he sensed someone was there. No, he *knew* they were. His eyes travelled over the squalid block of flats opposite. He couldn't see anyone observing this room or the building but that didn't mean they weren't.

He turned away. 'Cover your hair.'

'Eh? Oh.' She threw the hood of her sailing jacket over her head.

With one last glance, he registered exactly how the shabby bedsit looked, the position of the body and where everything was, as though taking a photograph. His visual recall was a great gift when he wanted it to be and a curse when he didn't. He'd had to perfect a technique of mentally switching it off to prevent it from recalling every minute detail of the horrifying sights he'd witnessed in the Marines. Silently, he closed the door. The siren had ceased, which meant the police must be close by or drawing up outside. The baby had stopped crying.

Swiftly, he indicated the landing window which came out on to the fire escape. Helen nodded and made for it behind him. Once there, he lifted it open. It gave a soft screech but no one came to investigate. He indicated to her to climb out after he'd made sure no one was waiting for them below in the dark backyard. Stealthily and quickly, they descended the iron steps. The yard was bounded by a high wall at the rear and to the right. To the left was a gate which led, as Helen had described, into a narrow alleyway running between the house and the convenience store next door. He could hear the whirr of the refrigeration unit of the chillers inside it. Marvik went ahead of her. At the entrance, he paused in the shadows. The police car was parked, silent, no flashing blue lights. Two police officers were at the front door, one male, one female. The female was talking into her radio while her colleague was pressing a buzzer. Marvik couldn't see which one but he knew the officer stood no chance of it being answered. Was this visit just coincidence? He didn't think so. His eyes again scanned the road, and then the block of flats opposite. A curtain twitched. That didn't mean much — the occupant might have noticed the police car and was curious to see what was going on.

From the shadows of the alleyway, Marvik watched as the officer pressed another buzzer and, after a delay, the door opened. He could hear Helen breathing beside him. Then both officers stepped inside. Marvik seized the opportunity, nodded at Helen and jerked his head to the right. They walked speedily towards the café on the corner and the main road. When he reached the junction, Marvik glanced back but there was still no sign of the police officers or anyone following them.

'Do you think Ian Bradshaw was the target I heard those men talking about?' Helen asked as they came out on to the deserted seafront.

'They'd already left the marina,' Marvik answered, scanning the road and noting that only a few cars were parked in the bays adjacent to the promenade. One of them was a Jaguar. He made towards it.

'They could have ordered someone else to do it,' Helen suggested. 'But why would anyone want to kill him?' she asked, baffled.

Marvik pressed the fob on Bradshaw's key ring and the flashing lights of the sleek new Jaguar responded.

'Do you know where Bradshaw lived?' he asked, opening the passenger door and examining the contents of the glove department. Nothing but the usual car-related documents.

'Not here, if that's what you mean,' she answered, quickly catching on. 'He has an apartment at the marina.'

The car documents confirmed that. Did Marvik chance going there before the police? Not with Helen though, and he didn't think he'd find anything there that could help him.

'Ever been inside it?'

'No,' she vehemently declared. 'And I've never been in that, either,' she added, pointing at the car.

'Good.' No fingerprints or DNA.

Bradshaw would have known Helen's address from her employee records. All he had to do was wait long enough for her to arrive home. He'd parked here because an expensive car like this would stick out like a ruddy great beacon for thieves and joyriders in Harold Road. Maybe Bradshaw had been afraid his car would be vandalized or stolen if he left it there.

There was nothing on the seats and only a rug, a Barbour jacket and a box of empty wine bottles ready for the recycling bin in the boot. He zapped the car locked.

'Is he married?'

'Divorced and no kids, or at least none as far as I know.'

'We'll walk back to the marina.'

He could see she was exhausted but she made no complaint, as he knew she wouldn't, and she knew as well as he did that they couldn't risk taking a taxi. They were too easily identified, him with his scarred face and she with her purple hair. The police would put out a call for Helen. The connection would be made between Bradshaw and her — that of employer and employee — and maybe someone would report seeing her go on board Bradshaw's boat last night or the marina CCTV would pick her out. The police would consider that Helen and Bradshaw had been lovers, they'd rowed, he'd followed her home and she'd killed him — the exact same scenario that had crossed his mind. The police had no former knowledge of Helen or her background but they'd make certain to get the latter and that bothered him. There was another scenario, too — an even more worrying one. It wasn't long before Helen voiced what had already occurred to Marvik; he'd hoped she wouldn't have got that far yet but she was no fool — quite the opposite — and now that the initial shock was wearing off her mind was working, despite her exhaustion.

'Was that knife across Ian's throat meant for me?' she said quietly.

Marvik threw her a glance. She looked thoughtful and bewildered rather than scared.

'If I hadn't been spooked enough to leave the flat that might have been me lying on that floor, dead.' She pushed her hands in her pockets and hunched her shoulders. 'Maybe I'm the target those guys were talking about.'

Marvik couldn't see why she should be, but then neither could he see why Bradshaw would have been. Unless . . . He said, 'Is there anything you've heard or seen while working on the boats that might have been suspicious?'

'No. It was all pretty boring and damn hard work. Gavin and I just got on with cleaning. The owners weren't on board. We'd pick up the keys from the office and drop them back there. Occasionally an owner would arrive and say he was pleased. There's usually only minimum supplies and personal belongings on the boats we clean. It's not like cleaning someone's house.' She threw him a nervous look. 'The man who killed Esther—'

'Is dead.'

'Are you sure?'

'Certain.'

'And the man falsely convicted of her murder?'

'Is a Christian and would no more seek revenge on you or anyone else than fly to Mars. And you didn't falsely convict him, Helen. He's living abroad, and yes, I'm sure.' He wasn't, but he was positive that Terrence Blackerman had nothing to do with this. He heard her sigh heavily. It turned into a yawn, which she didn't bother to hide.

'Were there any boats or visitors you wondered about — that you felt there was something not right about?'

She quickly caught on. 'Drug smuggling, you mean, or bringing in illegal immigrants? I've never seen or heard anything but I wouldn't put it past Bradshaw to have been mixed up in something illegal. I must have been mad to agree to go on his boat. Maybe the killer saw me and thought I was in league with him. How did the killer get into my bedsit? I didn't leave the door unlocked.'

'Maybe Bradshaw got there first,' Marvik said.

'You think I let him in.' She halted and rounded on him.

'Someone did; the door wasn't forced.'

'You think I killed him!' she cried incredulously. 'You believe I'm capable of that! And I thought I could trust you. Well, that just proves what shit taste I've got in people.' She made to turn round but Marvik gripped her arm.

'No, I don't think you're a killer but the police might. You had a motive — he tried it on with you. You rejected him. You also had the opportunity — he was in your flat. And you had the means, a knife, which could have come from the kitchen drawer. I didn't see a knife lying around but it might have been under the body or you could have taken it away and ditched it in the marina before I met you. But,' he quickly added as she was about to explode in protest, 'neither I nor the police, if they've got any sense, could see you having the strength to overcome Bradshaw while he meekly stood or sat as you slit his throat before pushing him on to the floor and turning over his body.'

'Well, thanks for that,' she said with heavy sarcasm. After a moment, he felt her body relax. He let go of her arm and they walked on. A drizzling rain had begun to drift off the sea.

Marvik said, 'But Bradshaw could have been drugged and you could have had help?'

'And who was my accomplice?' she tossed at him, her anger making her walk faster. Marvik didn't mind that.

'Gavin Yardly.'

She threw him an amazed glance. 'You're nuts. Gavin! Why would Gavin want to kill him?'

'Because he lives in the same house as you. He got you the job and he works with you.'

'So?'

'Maybe Gavin found you struggling with Bradshaw in your bedsit and decided to defend your honour. Or he killed Bradshaw in a fit of jealous rage when he found you together.'

'That's bollocks and you know it!' she cried, but there was despair in her voice and in her eyes. 'Gavin will tell you there's nothing between us. He's not even my type — he's a bit nerdy, nice guy, quiet, thank God. I hate people who witter on about nothing or only talk about themselves. And he's years younger than me. Just ask him.'

That's what the police would be doing soon.

'Jesus, this is a mess.' She glared at him. Marvik watched the fury slowly fade from her face, replaced with bewilderment. 'I can't think straight.'

'Then don't.'

'But what are we going to do?' she pleaded.

'First, we're going to pay a visit to Bradshaw's boat.'

'Why?'

'Because I want to check that it is as you left it.' She eyed him suspiciously again.

'And yes, I believe you, Helen, when you say you stormed off it. But there might be evidence of someone else having been on board after you left.'

She grunted acceptance of this and fell silent, which lasted until they reached the marina, although a few times Marvik thought she was about to speak then changed her mind.

He checked several times to make sure they weren't being followed. They weren't, and no one was waiting for them at the marina. The boardwalk was deserted and there was still no one moored up next to him. The wind was whistling through the masts and the drizzle was becoming heavier. As they turned on to the pontoon, Marvik said, 'Did anyone see you waiting for me to arrive?'

'I don't think so. I didn't see or speak to anyone. I called you from the seafront and when you said it would take you about two-and-a-half hours to arrive I sat in one of the shelters for a while then slowly walked towards the marina. There was nowhere open, otherwise I'd have had a drink and a warm up. I walked past the Martello Tower and around to the lifeboat station where I knew I'd be able to see you approach. I didn't think anyone else would be coming into the lock at three in the morning so when I saw the lights of a boat I hurried to the marina and let myself on to the pontoons. I have the security code.'

Their conversation had taken them to Bradshaw's boat. Marvik unzipped the awning. He climbed on. Helen followed suit. The teak deck was clean. There was a white plastic table with white vinyl seats around it, and a small fridge. He opened it, making sure to cover his fingers. Inside were two bottles of beer and a can of lager. Ahead was the helm. He crossed to it and, using Bradshaw's boat key, turned on the ignition. According to the chart plotter, Bradshaw had last used his boat nine days ago on a trip west along the coast to Brighton. Marvik unlocked the hatch and climbed down into the cabin. To Marvik's right was a wood veneer table and around it pale blue vinyl seating. On the table was an almost empty bottle of red wine and two glasses.

'Is this where you were?'

She nodded. 'And that's my glass but I didn't drink all that wine.'

Marvik picked up the glass Helen had indicated. There was a trace of lipstick around it. He wiped it clean and replaced it in the cabinet in the galley opposite. Then he wiped the bottle and the table and seat where she had sat. 'Don't want to make it too easy for the police to say you were here with the boss.'

'Shit.'

'Did anyone know you were coming here? Gavin, for example?'

'No. He wasn't in work yesterday. And when Ian asked me to meet him here, we were outside the office, so Glenda — she's the manager — didn't hear. Ian could have told her, I suppose, but he probably didn't.'

'And the office is where?' Marvik ran his fingers around the seat and in the creases.

'The other side of the marina, by the car park.'

Marvik played his torch over the floor, looking for any jewellery or possibly a button. He found a small stud earring. 'This yours?'

'No.'

He pocketed it anyway. He could wipe the boat clean but that would only make the police more suspicious. But now, if they picked up Helen's prints there was nothing to say that she had been on board last night. She could have come on board at any time.

He entered the forward cabin.

'I certainly didn't come in here,' Helen hotly declared, looking at the bed.

There was a casual zip-up man's jacket lying on it, nothing in the pockets, some men's clothes in the lockers and men's toiletries in the toilet and shower cubicle. No women's items. He checked again for any jewellery but there was nothing. 'OK, let's go.'

He locked up after ensuring he hadn't left his prints anywhere. The police would discover from the paperwork in Bradshaw's apartment and from his office manager that he owned a boat. At some stage they would come here. They might think it irrelevant to his murder. They might talk to the marina staff, but by the time their enquiries reached here, the night-duty manager and night-duty lockkeeper would have left. But they would talk to Bradshaw's office manager, Glenda, and discover that Helen had worked for him. What would she tell them about Helen? wondered Marvik.

It didn't look good for Helen. There might not be enough evidence to actually charge her but the police would seek it. He could contact Crowder and ask for his assistance but this wasn't a mission and Marvik didn't want Crowder to think he couldn't handle it alone. It would make him look weak, and Marvik wouldn't countenance that.

His precise recall and slightly obsessive nature confirmed that everything on his boat was exactly as he had left it. He hadn't really suspected anyone breaking into it but it paid to be cautious. He asked Helen to cast off and immediately got the boat underway, instructing her to stay below as they went through the lock. He didn't have to explain why. Once they were safely out of sight of the marina she came up on deck. Her face was harrowed, her eyes sunk in dark hollows made even deeper by the heavy make-up.

'Where are we going?'

He needed to buy Helen some time. He needed to put some distance between her and the dead man until he could find out who had murdered him and why. There was only one place to go and one man who could assist them. Strathen. Marvik made for the Hamble.

# CHAPTER FOUR

*Tuesday, 10.30 a.m.*

'I've checked the usual satellite tracking data of vessel movements for the area around Eastbourne last night and there are no leisure craft fitting the time of those two boats leaving the marina,' Strathen said. The expression on his rugged face was neutral as always but Marvik knew he was as worried as himself about what had happened and how it implicated Helen.

He was alone with Strathen in the operations room of his apartment with its computers, hard drives, plasma screens, whiteboards, telephones and fax machine. Marvik had called him on the way to the Hamble and had quickly brought him up to speed with events, giving him only the bare facts. Strathen's voice had registered concern when he'd said he'd set to work right away. Marvik didn't know what security consultancy projects Strathen was working on but knew he would postpone them or work around them for Helen.

It had been just after nine when Marvik had moored up at Hamble marina and he and Helen had walked the short distance to the Grade II-listed whitewashed manor house set behind secure gates in spacious landscaped gardens. It bordered on to the Solent and a small dinghy park where Strathen kept a canoe. His large, sturdy motor cruiser was kept in the marina. Strathen had made them breakfast. They hadn't discussed what had happened. Helen looked too tired and Marvik wanted to speak to Strathen in private. She had requested a shower and Marvik had urged her to sleep. She looked as though she'd like to refuse but it was clear she was dropping on her feet. He also needed sleep, but first he was keen to discuss his findings with Strathen and to hear what Strathen had discovered.

Strathen said, 'I might be able to pick up their movements recorded by one of the intelligence satellites,' which Marvik knew not even private maritime security consultancies could access. It was used by the intelligence agencies and, unless Strathen could encrypt his access, his location would be identified. But then Strathen was an expert computer hacker and cyber analyst and could circumnavigate even the most supposedly secure systems without being traced. It had been part of his job in the Marines.

'Why meet in the marina if they didn't want to be noticed?' Marvik asked. 'They had to call up the night-duty lockkeeper and give the name of their boats.'

'Which could be false, as are probably the names given to the marina night-duty manager, unless Colbourne travelled from Newcastle at the age of eighty-six and Marwell returned from Thailand where, according to his social media profile, he is currently on holiday. They clearly don't want to be found but, as you say, Art, why choose such a public location for a meet unless the target was there? But if he or she was, it can't have been Bradshaw or Helen because they were both alive when Colbourne and Marwell left.'

'And there's something else that doesn't add up.' Marvik handed Strathen the SIM card which he'd extracted from Bradshaw's mobile phone while heading for the Hamble and while Helen was making coffee. He had viewed its contents before throwing the phone in the sea. 'Take a look at the photographs.'

Strathen reached for a mobile phone and slotted in the SIM card. 'Why didn't the killer take the phone?' he asked.

'It can't contain anything incriminating, unless he deleted it and replaced it in Bradshaw's jacket.' The police would apply for Bradshaw's phone records and, if there was a number that Bradshaw had called which was connected to the killer, Marvik knew it would be dead like Bradshaw — just as the last text message sent to Sarah Redburn asking her to meet on the beach below Ballard's Point had proved to come from a mobile phone number that was no longer in existence. The killer had used a basic pay-as-you-go phone, which had been purchased for the express purpose of luring her to that location in order to kill her.

Marvik continued, 'The last call Bradshaw made was on Monday at five twenty p.m. There's no name against the number but it was to a local landline.'

'I'll check it out.'

Bradshaw had made three other calls on Monday, including to his business, Aquamarine Cleaning, and he'd received two local calls, both from mobile numbers, the names and numbers of which meant nothing to Marvik. He'd also sent and received some texts but nothing on Monday. There was no call or text to or from Helen. And although Bradshaw could have deleted them, Marvik thought it unlikely there had been any.

'It's the photographs rather than the calls that I find interesting.' Marvik recalled what he had seen. Pictures of a jowly man with a flushed face and flabby body, about early fifties with sunglasses perched on his short, slightly balding dark hair, with smallish eyes and a wide mouth with full lips smiling into the camera. It was difficult to put that man with the corpse he'd seen on Helen's bedsit-room floor but not impossible. All the photographs, about twenty in total, were of Bradshaw either beside his Jaguar or on board his boat. Some of those on the boat had been taken on the Continent judging by the blue sky and azure seas, but others were closer to home, along the Sussex coast with the Seven Sisters white chalk cliffs in the background. Some had been taken in the marina, and in what to Marvik looked like Brighton and Chichester marinas. What was interesting, though, was Bradshaw's choice of companion in the boat pictures. All were women — five different ones — and all were leggy blondes, about early to mid-thirties with shapely figures and small bikinis, while Bradshaw sported a beer gut over lurid shorts and a hairy chest in some snaps and in others a loose-fitting, brightly patterned shirt over shorts but always with a glass of wine, champagne or a beer bottle in his hand and his arm around the woman, who was laughing and nestling in close to him. Bradshaw obviously thought he was a fine figure of a man judging by the smile on his face and the women clinging to him, but in Marvik's opinion he was far from that. Perhaps he had a magnetic personality. Maybe he was charismatic, generous and humorous, although Marvik was more inclined to believe Helen's version of Bradshaw — bluff, groping, exploitative and possibly violent. But should he? Whatever Bradshaw's character, he had been brutally murdered and no one deserved that, although Marvik had reservations on that score. He'd met some evil bastards in his life and a quick death, even a violent one, was more than they deserved.

Marvik saw surprise on Strathen's face. Interpreting it, he said, 'Yes, I wouldn't have said that Helen was Bradshaw's type either. The women he's groping in those pictures are the opposite of her.'

'Maybe he thought he'd go for something completely different.'

Marvik looked dubious.

'Or he thought she'd be a pushover,' Strathen added more seriously. Keeping his voice low, he added, 'There is a vulnerability about her despite her manner.'

Marvik knew that. Just as there had been a vulnerability about Sarah, although she had been a completely different personality to Helen — quiet and shy, but then perhaps Helen's brusque manner and bluntness hid a shyness, and the heavy make-up and dark clothes were designed to keep people at bay.

Strathen said, 'Helen is not Bradshaw's usual type so either he was trying it on or he was told to get and keep her on board his boat, only she declined to play ball.'

'And there's something odd about the conversation she overheard on the pontoon.' Marvik relayed his thoughts about the movement of the pontoon and how those men must have felt it and yet they had continued talking. 'If, as she says, they were talking about murder they would have been fully alert to a fish swimming under the boat let alone someone walking on the pontoon. They'd have shut up, so either they're incompetent or—'

'They *wanted* Helen to hear,' Strathen said thoughtfully. 'Maybe Bradshaw *was* the target. He was ordered to do as you said, Art — get Helen on board his boat after being spun some yarn about her, but the real reason was because she was to be framed for his murder. Someone knew her background. They could make it look as though she was unbalanced.'

Marvik was disturbed by that idea. It had occurred to him, but the more he thought about it the less it fitted. 'If that's the reason, surely they'd have found an easier way of killing Bradshaw to fit her up, *if* they needed to. Slitting someone's throat is not the most common way women kill.'

'But she has tried to cut her own wrists at some time,' Strathen insisted solemnly. 'And her medical records will show that. It might be why that method was chosen.'

Marvik didn't like the idea any more than Strathen did.

Strathen continued, 'Whoever is behind it thought that because of her past history it might look more natural for her to resort to using a knife as a murder weapon. And if they knew her medical history then it's someone who knows her or went to the trouble of discovering it. Bradshaw could have been killed for the sole purpose of framing Helen.'

'Perhaps there's a connection between Helen and Bradshaw that she's not told us about. Maybe they go way back. Or there's someone in Helen's past who is intent on destroying her for some reason. If she is being framed then what's the betting someone will find some of her blood-spattered clothes? She could be the "target" Colbourne and Marwell were discussing as in the target being fitted up for murder instead of being killed. What did they say? "It's dealt with. The target's been taken out". That could have been *being* rather than *been* and they sounded pretty confident there would be no comeback. They'd arranged for someone to watch her flat for her return, knowing that Bradshaw would follow her back there because he'd been paid to. Only she decided to leg it and that could also have been arranged.'

'The shadowy figure she saw in the doorway opposite and the sense she was being followed.' Marvik sat, considering this.

'The killer might have stashed some of her blood-spattered clothes under the sink, where naturally she wouldn't have looked when you told her to bring some with her.'

Marvik heard the shower stop.

'Alternatively, maybe she did kill him. Could she have done it?' Strathen posed.

'No,' Marvik firmly replied. 'She didn't call the cops while I was inside her flat with her. And the timing of their arrival fits much more neatly with her being framed.'

'I can't see her as a killer either, unless severely provoked or defending herself. If she'd killed him I think she'd have come right out with it and told us. She's not one for hiding things.'

But did they really know that? Marvik wondered. Everyone had something to hide. He hadn't mentioned finding that disk in Sarah's belongings to Strathen or to Crowder. But he knew he would have to mention it to the former if he wanted to explore what was on it. It wasn't his reluctance to trust Strathen that held him back but his fear of what he might discover on it. And he despised his cowardice. At one time he wouldn't have given such an emotion so much as a toehold, let alone a bloody great grip.

Strathen's voice pierced his tired thoughts. 'I haven't got much on Bradshaw, only that he's been running Aquamarine for two years. It's only one of his businesses under a holding company called Frankline Pace, registered address West Quay, Newhaven. He owns a yacht brokerage called Antara, which has offices in Newhaven, Eastbourne and Brighton, and a property company called Medlowes based in Eastbourne. He was doing well — good turnover and healthy profits. His death has been reported on the news and the Internet. But the name hasn't been released. Maybe the police are still looking for the next of kin, or perhaps they're just playing it close to their chests. Nothing about looking for Helen yet. But that might get leaked.'

The police would be questioning the tenants and one of them could put out on the Internet the fact that the body had been found in Helen's bedsit.

Marvik said, 'The police might not be the only ones looking for Helen.'

'She'll be safe here.'

Marvik knew that. He also knew that he didn't have to spell out to Strathen that the killer might be looking for her in case he thought she could identify him.

He wondered what the police would make of not finding Bradshaw's keys and mobile phone on the body. Would they suspect the killer had taken them, and that killer to be Helen? They would have obtained Bradshaw's car registration from the vehicle licensing database by now and probably discovered his car parked on the seafront. Strathen would copy the information on Bradshaw's SIM card across to his own phone or to his computer, and then destroy the card so that it wouldn't be traced.

Marvik rose and stretched himself. 'I've got to get back to Eastbourne and start asking questions.' But he also needed sleep. Strathen offered him his bed, which Marvik gratefully accepted. Helen was in the spare room. He managed to grab five hours. Then, after a shower, shave and a change of clothes, he made himself a sandwich and took it into the operations room. It was late afternoon and the weather was closing in, but that didn't worry him. He was ready to go. But first he needed to see what, if anything, Strathen had turned up while he'd slept.

'The police announced at midday that they're looking for Helen Shannon and Gavin Yardly, who they'd like to talk to in connection with the death of Eastbourne businessman Ian Bradshaw,' Strathen said.

'Yardly?' Marvik said, surprised. 'Then he wasn't in his flat.'

'Apparently not. And that last number Bradshaw called is a pay phone just off Eastbourne promenade.'

This didn't look good. The speculative scenario Marvik had spun earlier about Gavin Yardly possibly being Helen's accomplice who had killed Bradshaw out of jealousy now seemed to be carrying more weight.

Strathen said, 'I can't find anything on Yardly on the Internet. Either he doesn't use social media or he does but under another name.'

'Maybe Helen knows.'

'Knows what?' she said, entering. She looked less harrowed. Her make-up was in place and she'd changed her clothes, but still sported her customary black.

'If Gavin Yardly used social media?' said Strathen.

'No idea. Why do you want to know that?'

'Because he's missing.'

She looked confused. 'He can't be. He was in his flat.'

'When?' asked Marvik.

She sat at one of the three desks in the operations room and pushed a hand through her hair. 'Actually, the last time I saw him now I come to think of it was Thursday. We cleaned a boat belonging to a guy called Colin Prior. He was visiting the marina and wanted a quick job done. We finished at about five o'clock. I returned to the office.'

'Without Gavin?'

'Yes. He stayed on board with Mr Prior, who inspected our work. Gavin returned to the office ten minutes later. He said everything was OK. Mr Prior signed our worksheet. I went into town. I assumed Gavin went back to his flat. He wasn't at work on Friday. I didn't know he was taking a day off so I knocked on his door as usual but there was no answer. We always went into work together, by bus.'

And perhaps one of the tenants would have told the police that, which would again reinforce the theory that Helen and Gavin were more than just acquaintances or work colleagues.

Helen was saying, 'When I got to the office, Glenda told me that Gavin had booked the day off. He didn't say anything to me about it. I thought he must have forgotten to tell me or that perhaps it was personal and he didn't want to explain. Not that I'd have asked him to.'

'Did you see him over the weekend?' asked Strathen.

'No.'

'Was that usual?'

'Yes. Although sometimes we'd bump into one another in the hall. And I saw him go into the library once, about two weeks ago.'

'And on Monday?'

'Again, I knocked on his door. No answer. I thought maybe he had decided to stay over somewhere. Glenda was moaning like hell about him when I got to work. I don't know why she was complaining when all she does is sit on her arse, answer the phone and dole out the jobs. I had two boats to clean — one I did in the morning and the other in the afternoon. It took me longer because I was on my own. It was when I was leaving the office that Bradshaw crawled out of the woodwork, the creep. Sorry, I know he's dead but . . .' Her troubled glance swung between them. Resting on Marvik, she said, 'What you said on the seafront this morning about Gavin being my accomplice — you don't think the police will believe that?'

'Is there anywhere he would have gone? Did he speak to you about friends or family?'

She was shaking her head. 'There must be some perfectly reasonable explanation for why Gavin's not around. He can't have anything to do with this. He certainly couldn't have killed Ian. He's the least likely killer you could come across.' A shadow touched her eyes. They both knew she was recalling the man who had been falsely convicted of her sister's murder, a naval chaplain. She was looking increasingly worried.

'Have you been in his apartment?' Marvik asked.

'No.'

'Has he been in yours?'

'Yes, twice.'

Marvik exchanged a glance with Strathen.

'So? There's nothing wrong with that, is there?' she declared, seeing their glance.

'Not if you've spring-cleaned the bedsit since his visit.'

'And why should I do that? Christ, you mean fingerprints and DNA and all that crap? But that doesn't mean anything.'

'Not on its own,' Strathen interjected.

'Thanks, you're a great comfort.'

'When was Gavin in your flat?' Marvik asked. 'How recently?'

She took a breath. 'The first time was about a fortnight ago. He wanted to borrow a tin opener. He said his was busted and he couldn't be arsed to go out and buy one that night. It was quite late, about ten o'clock. The second time was the Sunday before last. He asked me if I had a postage stamp. It was about nine thirty. He said the shop next door had run out of stamps and he wanted to post a letter that night. I assumed it was for a birthday card or something like that, and perhaps he'd forgotten to send it on time because I couldn't see why he didn't just send whoever it was an email or a text.'

'Perhaps the recipient didn't have a computer or mobile phone,' suggested Strathen.

'Is there anyone left like that!' But she quickly continued, 'I guess it could have been for a child or elderly person. He didn't say and I didn't have a stamp. There's no one I need to send a birthday card to, or any other type of card. I asked him the next day, the Monday before last, if he'd posted his letter OK and he said he had. He'd gone out and found a convenience store that had some stamps.'

Strathen said, 'Did you hear any sounds coming from his flat over the weekend?'

'I didn't really take any notice. I went to the launderette on Saturday and walked along the seafront on Sunday. Another riveting and action-packed weekend,' she said, a slight bitterness showing through her flippancy. She was embarrassed by her loneliness. Marvik saw Strathen's jawline tighten.

Marvik's phone rang. But it wasn't his own or the basic mobile phone that Strathen had christened their mission mobile. It was the phone issued to him by Crowder for his assignments with the National Intelligence Marine Squad. And there was only one reason why Crowder was calling — he had a mission for him to undertake. Marvik cursed silently. That was the last thing he needed now when both he and Strathen should be devoting all their time to assisting Helen. But he had to answer the call and he knew he wouldn't be able to refuse a mission. If he did it would mean the end of his work for the National Intelligence Marine Squad and he didn't want that. With a glance at Strathen, who had immediately grasped the situation, Marvik quickly stepped out into the hall.

'I'll meet you on board your boat in half an hour,' Crowder announced without preamble. 'Come alone and be ready to leave the Hamble immediately.'

Marvik rang off. Crowder had known where he was and that he was on board his boat, despite not being able to track it because Marvik had never engaged the Automatic Identification System. But as he and Strathen had discussed earlier, there were other means of tracking and identifying craft, both air and seaborne. Computer systems were available to defence and the intelligence agencies, which Crowder would have access to.

'I've got to go,' he announced, returning to Strathen.

Strathen knew what that meant.

'I've no idea how long I'll be away.'

'You're walking out on us?' Helen asked incredulously.

'Shaun will take care of you. Give me your keys, Helen.' To Strathen, Marvik said, 'I'll contact you when I can.'

Helen opened her mouth to speak, then closed it again. Marvik saw the disappointment in her eyes that he interpreted as betrayal. Whatever the mission, he would just have to resolve it quickly. Until then, he'd have to rely on Strathen to keep Helen safe.

# CHAPTER FIVE

'Helen Shannon,' Crowder said without preamble, startling Marvik. It was the last thing he had expected to hear from the solemn, square-set man in his mid-forties seated in front of him across the table on the lower helm deck.

Crowder placed a black canvas briefcase on the table. The wind had risen and was gently rocking the boat. The afternoon was drawing in fast because of the heavy cloud rolling in from the west. The visitors' berths were empty except for Marvik's boat and the one Crowder had arrived on a moment ago, a twenty-five-foot powerful modern motor cruiser. Marvik had no idea where Crowder had come from but it couldn't have been far to have reached him within half an hour.

Marvik also didn't know where Crowder was based, although he suspected London. Neither did he know who was on the rest of Crowder's team. He and Strathen had not been introduced to them. Their roles, in whatever mission Crowder assigned them, remained secret. There were police officers who could possibly identify both him and Strathen from their involvement in two successful missions for the Squad but there was no reason why they should. And Crowder had made sure that their identity was kept secret and they weren't required to give evidence in any court proceedings.

Marvik held Crowder's stare, trying to read what was behind the deep brown, serious eyes, but his expression was as inscrutable as ever.

'Helen *is* with you and Strathen,' Crowder stated.

'Yes.' Marvik saw no point in denying it. 'I assume you know that the police are looking for her and why?'

'Yes.'

'Are you going to give them her location?' Marvik asked stiffly.

'Not unless she killed Ian Bradshaw and has confessed it to you, or you believe her to be a killer.'

'Neither. But she could be in danger from the killer. Do you know who that is?'

'No. But I'd like to.'

'Then the mission is connected with Bradshaw's death?' Marvik asked, relieved. His pulse quickened.

'Yes.'

'Because of Helen?' he asked, puzzled.

'No, because of Gavin Yardly.'

That was Marvik's second surprise of the afternoon. He eyed Crowder keenly. 'He's missing.'

'Not any more, he isn't.'

Marvik quickly caught on. 'His body's been found.'

'Yes. The news hasn't been released but it soon will be. The current thinking is suicide as a result of being consumed with remorse after killing Ian Bradshaw.'

'Motive?'

'I don't think you need me to tell you that.'

Marvik didn't. It was exactly as he and Strathen had discussed. 'Gavin killed Bradshaw in a jealous fit of rage because he found him with Helen.'

'That's one version.'

'And the other?'

'They both killed him.'

Marvik tensed. 'Why?'

'To steal from him.'

Marvik thought of the mobile phone and keys he'd taken from the body. Perhaps that had been a mistake. But surely the police couldn't think Helen and Gavin had killed for the sake of a mobile phone. Bradshaw's credit cards and wallet had still been on the body and he didn't think anyone would have had the opportunity to enter Helen's flat and lift them after he and Helen had left and before the police arrived. But then he rapidly reconsidered. It was possible. Someone, the killer or the person who had tipped off the police — who could possibly be the same — could have been inside one of the other flats, an empty one perhaps, or in Gavin's flat and then slipped up to Helen's after they'd left by the fire escape. Marvik asked if the wallet had been found on the body.

Crowder confirmed it had, which was something of a relief to Marvik. But Crowder added, 'No keys, though, so perhaps Helen and Gavin took them and entered Bradshaw's apartment in order to steal from it.'

'I doubt it,' Marvik said tautly, but made no mention of taking the keys himself.

Crowder didn't press him but continued, 'Gavin Yardly's body was discovered just after two o'clock this afternoon, thirty minutes before low tide, on the shore between the Birling Gap and Flagstaff Point, under Bailey's Hill.'

Birling Gap was about five miles to the west of Eastbourne and could be reached by road, sea and by foot along the cliff edge of the Wealdway and the South Downs Way.

Crowder said, 'A walker spotted it and called the East Sussex police. They will, of course, put out an appeal for anyone who might have seen Yardly between twenty-two hundred hours on Monday — the approximate time when Bradshaw was killed — and when his body was discovered.'

Marvik quickly assimilated this. 'Why didn't anyone find him earlier?'

'Because his body was only revealed as the tide went out. And low tide before this afternoon, as you know, was two a.m. There were no walkers at that time in the morning to spot his body in the dark.'

Marvik's brain teemed with thoughts. 'Why, then, if he threw himself off the cliffs after killing Bradshaw, wasn't his body swept out to sea on high water at seven twenty-seven?'

'Because it was weighed down with the kind of weights you and Strathen use to keep fit.'

Marvik raised his eyebrows at this unexpected and curious piece of news. Cynically, he said, 'So Yardly killed Bradshaw, bought some weights today—'

'Or had them in his flat.'

'Walked nearly seven miles to the Birling Gap, carrying these weights, unless he owns a car?'

'He doesn't and he doesn't have a driver's licence.'

'So he walks, and then with these weights stuffed down his trousers—'

'In the pockets of his jacket.'

'Throws himself off a cliff.'

'People do strange things when desperate, and suicidal people aren't thinking rationally.'

'Like you believe that,' scoffed Marvik. 'Yardly's body was put there after low tide in the early hours of this morning or maybe even late last night because it doesn't sound like the Gavin Yardly Helen described. I doubt he'd even know what a weight looked like.' But someone did — his killer.

'She mentioned him, then.'

'Only because I asked her about him.' Marvik studied Crowder closely. How much did he know? Probably a great deal more than he would reveal. Marvik knew the rules. His role was to start from scratch with only basic information. To go in, start asking questions, stir things up, take risks and provoke the killer into making mistakes, including sometimes making attempts on his life. One such attempt in March, though, hadn't been linked to the mission he'd been on, or so Crowder claimed, but to his parents' deaths at sea and his father's notebook. Marvik's meeting with Bell from the solicitors' office yesterday morning now seemed like a lifetime ago.

He said, 'Bradshaw tried it on with Helen on board his boat on Monday night. She told him where to get off and left. As she was heading back for the marina she overheard two men on board another boat talking about taking out a target. That target could have been Bradshaw.'

'It was more likely to have been Gavin Yardly.'

Marvik was taken aback. 'Why Yardly?' His interest deepened.

'Bloodstained clothes and trainers have been discovered in his flat. The blood will probably match Bradshaw's. That doesn't mean he killed Bradshaw.' Crowder hastily added, 'The killer could have worn Yardly's clothes and shoes to carry out the attack.'

'And then deliberately walked around the body, stood in the blood that spurted from the artery and wiped the weapon he used on Yardly's clothes. Has it been found?'

'Not yet.'

Marvik thought this was no amateur.

'Have they found a phone on Gavin's body?'

'No, but that doesn't mean he didn't have one or that Helen didn't contact him.'

'She didn't.' But Marvik was beginning to wonder if, when the police obtained Yardly's mobile phone records, it would show a phone number that could be linked to Helen. Maybe one from a call box close to the property or at the marina. Not that that would prove she was the caller.

Crowder was saying, 'The discovery of Gavin's body and his identity will be released to the media once the East Sussex police have the autopsy findings and can locate a next of kin, which might prove difficult because, very much like Helen Shannon, Gavin has no family. They will pursue the theory that Yardly, either alone or aided and abetted by Helen, killed Bradshaw. Yardly, unable to live with what he had done, committed suicide and Helen has gone on the run from the police.'

'While in fact Gavin Yardly was killed and Helen and Yardly were set up for Bradshaw's murder.' Thank God Helen had had the sense to call him.

'Yes. Because what the police don't know is that, shortly before his death, Yardly sent a letter to GCHQ.'

The postage stamp! Writing to the Government's Communications Headquarters in Cheltenham was hardly normal practice unless he had been applying for a job. And perhaps that was what Gavin Yardly had been doing in the library — job hunting. GCHQ worked with MI5 and MI6 and its American equivalent, the National Security Agency, to combat terrorism, drug trafficking and other serious organized crime, as well as providing intelligence support to help protect the military. He and Strathen had liaised with them on many operations. But if Yardly had been job hunting then Crowder wouldn't have been interested in him, and Yardly could hardly have been killed because of that.

'Saying?'

'That he'd located the *Mary Jo*.'

'And that is?'

'A salvage towing vessel that disappeared in the North Atlantic in July 2003.'

'And he was killed for passing on this information?'

'It looks that way.'

'Which means Gavin's killer must be someone working within GCHQ or an employee who passed the information on to someone they knew on the outside.' And Marvik knew that would be a serious breach. 'Or someone within the intelligence services,' he added, remembering the language Colbourne and Marwell had used.

But Crowder suggested otherwise. 'Not necessarily. Gavin could have told someone about this letter before or after he posted it.'

'You mean Helen? He didn't, but the killer won't know that. She said Gavin asked her for a stamp nine days ago on a Sunday night but that she has no idea what the contents of the letter were or even that it was a letter he wanted to post.' Helen was in even greater peril than he'd realized. 'For Yardly to have been fitted up for Bradshaw's death he must have been decoyed somewhere — possibly on Thursday night, the last time Helen saw him. He wasn't at work on Friday or Monday and Helen claims he wasn't in his flat at the weekend. For the frame-up and suicide theory to work he must have been held captive until he could be dumped on that shore. If the letter was posted a week ago last Sunday, it would have been collected from the post box on Monday and delivered to GCHQ by Wednesday latest. Why wasn't Yardly located and questioned by GCHQ then? Or killed then?'

'The letter arrived on Thursday even though it had a first-class stamp on it. There was some delay. That's being investigated.'

'You mean it might have been tampered with in the post?'

'It seems unlikely but not impossible. Yardly didn't give an address or contact number in his letter. It was treated dismissively, thought to be a prank.'

Marvik raised his eyebrows disbelievingly.

Crowder's lips shaped a brief, knowing smile. 'It was Saturday before it reached someone in authority who decided to look up the *Mary Jo*. It was a salvage tug, of no significance and nothing to say it, or the letter mentioning it, posed any threat to security. There was no need for an immediate alert. But instructions *were* given for Gavin Yardly to be traced. It soon became clear that he wasn't active on the Internet, or if he was then he was very careful, very clever and very experienced.'

'Which made the powers that be at GCHQ take more notice.'

'Yes.'

'They dug more deeply into the *Mary Jo*.'

'Yes.'

'And found there was more to its disappearance than they'd thought.'

Crowder unzipped the case on the table and withdrew a manila folder. He took two photographs from it. Both were of ships, one a sizeable cruise liner but clearly not a modern one, the other a salvage tug, the *Mary Jo*.

'The cruise ship in that picture started life as the MS *Lyudmila*. It was a small Russian cruise ship built in Volkseigener Betrieb Mathias-Thesen-Werft shipyard in the Baltic port of Wismar — which in 1961 was in communist controlled East Germany — for the Soviet Union's Baltic Shipping Company and was launched in 1964. It was named after a famous Russian sniper in the Second World War and was one of many built there between 1958 and 1964. The *Lyudmila* was built with greater hull strength and stability than a normal vessel of this type in order to enable it to navigate through broken ice. In its heyday it took wealthy Russian tourists on Arctic cruises.'

Crowder's words struck a chord with Marvik. The Arctic had been his father's area of expertise and his passion. It had been where he had met Marvik's mother while on a joint expedition with Norway in 1989. His father, Dan Coulter, had been engaged in a study on ocean turbulence and the development of underwater robotics, his mother on a team working on charting wrecks. Eerika had been thirteen years his junior. They'd married seven months later. Marvik thought fleetingly of the floppy disk before bringing his full concentration back to Crowder.

'The *Lyudmila* was also built to be used as a troopship if necessary, which meant it had unusually large storage areas and was equipped with powerful deck-lifting gear able to transport armoured vehicles on board if required. We believe it was built to carry approximately eight hundred passengers, although that number was never confirmed. It's documented that she spent some time in the 1970s on the Leningrad to Montreal route, calling in at Helsinki, Copenhagen, London, Quebec and Montreal. Records show she stopped off at Bremerhaven during the summer months. She was a popular choice for Finnish passengers sailing to London and to Canada.

'As the cruise market expanded and with greater global competition, not to mention the oil crisis in 1973, things became more difficult, and in 1979 the Soviet Union decided to withdraw it from service. She sat in Murmansk shipyard for six years with everything inside her intact, including murals, ornamental structures and balustrades made of bronze and silver. The Chinese expressed an interest and in 1985 bought her but quickly resold her to a Norwegian shipping line in 1987 without even moving her. She was renamed the *SS Celeste* and moved to the Lloyd Werft Bremerhaven shipyard, where she underwent renovations to be put back into service, once again cruising the Arctic and the fjords. The interior was re designed and renovated, the storage areas converted into cabins and public areas and she resumed service in 1991. She was successful for some time but again the competition began to bite. Slowly she lost the cache of being for wealthy cruises and became a bargain cruise ship. She began to develop several mechanical failures, causing delays and breakdowns, until in 2000 there was a boiler explosion on board and she was towed into St John's, Newfoundland, where she stayed. The shipping company failed to pay the port bills and she was confiscated and sold in 2003 to a British company for salvage, Helmsley Marine, based in Newhaven, East Sussex.'

So now they were back closer to home. Newhaven was about thirteen miles along the coastal road to the west of Eastbourne.

Crowder continued, 'Helmsley Marine, using their salvage vessel the *Mary Jo*, were to tow her from St John's to the UK to be broken up. This was around the same time that thirteen rusting American warships were to be transported to Hartlepool for dismantling. Environmentalists, and some of the people of Hartlepool, were none too pleased about that. The obsolete American warships were labelled toxic ghost ships because of the hazardous substances on board, including asbestos, heavy diesel, mercury, lead-based paints and polychlorinated biphenyls, more commonly known as PCBs.'

Marvik interjected. 'Most ships, if not all built in the 1960s contained asbestos. Had it been stripped out of the *Celeste*?'

'No. It also contained PCBs and radioactive materials in the smoke-detection systems, but the people of Hartlepool and the media were focused on the American warships, not a cruise liner. It didn't attract any attention. The *Mary Jo* never arrived in Newfoundland and has never been found. That is, it hadn't until Gavin Yardly claimed to have discovered it.'

'The authorities must have tried to locate it in 2003.'

'They did. The Canadian Coast Guard searched for it after it failed to arrive. There was no Mayday call and they found no wreckage or bodies. It was assumed it went down in heavy seas. It had no Automatic Identification System but it did have a beacon, only no one picked it up. If it could have been tracked by satellite there might have been a chance of finding it, but there was no satellite sophisticated enough then to do so, and once the trail goes cold and it's lost it can stay lost for ever, especially in the Arctic.'

And Marvik knew that better than anyone, not because of his experience in the Marines but because his parents had spent their working lives looking for lost ships. He'd thought they had died trying to find one.

'How did Gavin Yardly find it then?'

'*If* he did?'

'He didn't give you the location?'

'Yes, but it's not there now. We're looking for it.'

Marvik almost said *a bit late for that* but didn't. 'You think he lied?'

'It's possible.'

If he had, there was a reason for it. 'What happened to the *Celeste*?'

'It was sold on to another marine salvage company, Almbridge, also based in Newhaven, who successfully towed it out of Newfoundland and transported it to India to be dismantled, which it duly was.'

'Do Helmsley Marine know that Gavin Yardly claimed to have located the *Mary Jo*, their missing tug?'

'Both the owners of Helmsley Marine, Martin Elmsley and Duncan Helmslow, are dead. Elmsley died in 2001 and Helmslow in 2004. The company was acquired by Almbridge in 2004. No one has told Alec Royden, the owner of Almbridge, or Meryl Landguard, the widow of the salvage master on the *Mary Jo*, Timothy Landguard, that Gavin located it.'

Marvik knew that was his job. To ask questions, stir things up and see what transpired. He said, 'Did Gavin have a computer?'

'He might have done but none was found in his flat. Meryl Landguard lives in a village called East Dean, which lies to the west of Eastbourne and north of the Birling Gap.' He passed over the folder with the photographs of the vessels and Meryl Landguard's address.

'And the other crew members?'

'The second officer was Simon Warrendale, the engineer was Peter Goodhead and the final crew member was Lewis Chale. Strathen will find their details in the marine accident investigation report on the *Mary Jo*.'

'And information on Gavin?'

'Aged twenty-nine, born and brought up in Hastings on the coast. His mother worked in a supermarket. She died in 1999, and his father worked on railway maintenance at nights. He died in 2006. Gavin left school at seventeen with qualifications in maths, computer science, English, music and art. He went to Hastings College to study A-levels in computer science, music technology and maths and achieved top grades. After that he drifted around, picking up jobs here and there: bar work, cleaning, labouring, some IT support work — anything he could get. He moved to Eastbourne, took that flat in Harold Road eight weeks ago and started working for Ian Bradshaw six weeks ago. He was a loner, didn't make friends easily. A handy profile for a killer.'

'Do the police know where Gavin was from Thursday?'

'In his room, brooding, preparing to kill Bradshaw.'

But Marvik didn't believe that for an instant and neither did Crowder. Somewhere in the town a CCTV camera might have picked up Yardly's movements, but would the police bother looking? Not if the evidence showed they had Bradshaw's killer in the mortuary.

He followed Crowder up on deck, but as Crowder made to disembark, Marvik said, 'Why did Gavin Yardly write to GCHQ with this information? Why not MI5 or the National Crime Agency?'

'Perhaps he was making a point.'

And Marvik could conjecture what that was. In fact, it could be two things. Gavin had managed to penetrate the government's satellite system and was showing how clever he was, or that someone within or connected to GCHQ had been involved in what had happened to the *Mary Jo* in 2003 and subsequently in the murders of Gavin Yardly and Ian Bradshaw. It was his job to discover who that was and why.

He cast off and headed for Eastbourne. Tomorrow morning he'd start by talking to the widow of the master of the *Mary Jo*, Meryl Landguard.

# CHAPTER SIX

*Wednesday*

It was just after eight thirty when Marvik pressed his finger on the brass bell of Meryl Landguard's house. Its metallic clang echoed inside the substantial red-brick detached property, set back from the road and approached via a gravel drive. There was a white Audi parked outside the detached double garage with a child seat in the back.

He'd taken a taxi from the railway station at Eastbourne but had asked the driver to drop him off on the main road a couple of hundred yards from the turning to East Dean. The house hadn't been difficult to locate. The village was small and many of the houses were spread out along the road that led south to the Birling Gap and the coast.

Last night, on arrival at the marina, he'd called Strathen on the mission mobile, a very basic, old model very much like the one Crowder had given him. Both were functional for text and calls only, although there was also a torch and a radio. But there was no access to the Internet on either phone, and therefore no location identifier and no phone contract so no records for anyone to peruse. He'd brought Strathen up to speed with events, after which Strathen had said he would get what he could on the *Mary Jo* and its crew. Helen would see if she could dig up more on Gavin Yardly, which Marvik thought unlikely because if GCHQ couldn't find it then it was doubtful Helen would, except she had known Yardly, and Crowder could have been withholding information.

Marvik's thoughts turned to Meryl Landguard as he again rang the bell. It would be upsetting for her having the past and her husband's tragic death dragged up, made even more traumatic by the fact there had been no body to bring back home and lay to rest. No finality about it. At least he'd had that with his parents' deaths.

He heard the clip of footsteps in the hall and steeled himself to meet a woman who had been grieving and wondering for years about the fate of her husband. He wasn't sure how he envisaged her but a smartly dressed, slender woman in tight-fitting black trousers and a multi-coloured top answered the door. She was in her late fifties with highlighted short blonde hair and a fair, clear and relatively unlined skin. Her eyes looked troubled as they flicked to Marvik's scars on the right-hand side of his face. The door closed a fraction. He'd already decided to begin by seeing if Gavin Yardly had approached her with the news that he'd located her husband's lost ship. Hastily, he said, 'I'm sorry to disturb you, Mrs Landguard, but I wondered if you could help me.'

Thinking he was a door-to-door salesman, she said crossly, 'I'm not interested,' and made to close the door, but then it registered he had used her name.

Quickly, Marvik followed up with, 'I think you might know or have met a friend of mine, Gavin Yardly.'

Her shock at hearing the name was evident. Her body stiffened and she blinked hard before frowning and saying crisply, 'I've never heard of him.'

Oh, but she had. So why deny it? 'I believe he might have contacted you about your late husband, the master on the *Mary Jo*.'

Her lips tightened. Her alarm swiftly turned to wariness but Marvik also detected fear in her pale blue eyes, perhaps because she didn't want painful memories dredged up. Her voice was hard when she said, 'I have no idea who you are talking about and I have nothing to say to you about my husband or the tragedy.' She made to close the door but was halted by the arrival of a car which drew to a stop in a flurry of gravel. With interest, Marvik noted the name emblazoned on the side — *Medlowes*, along with the words *Letting and Property Management*. Strathen had told him that Medlowes was one of Bradshaw's companies, along with Aquamarine Cleaning and Antara Yacht Brokerage.

Meryl Landguard addressed Marvik sharply. 'I'm busy. I need to see to my grandson. Now leave.'

'Of course.' But Marvik merely stepped aside as a woman in her early thirties retrieved a bawling child from the rear of the car. He recognized her instantly as one of the women in the photographs on Bradshaw's mobile phone, only this time she was wearing a lot more than a bikini. She was dressed smartly in a tight-fitting black skirt and red jacket, underneath which was a crisp, white open neck shirt.

'I can't get him to settle,' she said, handing over the squirming child to Meryl Landguard and barely glancing at Marvik. When she did, she showed no curiosity about him being there. She looked too tired and seemed to be in too great a hurry to worry about anything more than offloading her child. Her eyes were red-rimmed from lack of sleep, probably because of her fretful baby but perhaps also because of her boss and lover's death, if those photographs on Bradshaw's phone were anything to judge by. Her fair-skinned face was drawn. Meryl Landguard's expression wasn't exactly softening either as she took the little boy in her arms. Marvik got the impression she'd liked to have thrust him back and told the younger woman what she could do with her child. Grandson he might be, but Meryl Landguard seemed a most reluctant grandmother. Marvik sensed the tension between the two women.

'I'm late. I have to go,' the younger woman said tetchily. She tossed Marvik a dismissive glance before hurrying back to her car.

Marvik addressed Meryl Landguard. 'I realize it must be upsetting for you but I'd like to talk to you about the *Mary Jo* when it's convenient.'

'Well, it isn't and it never will be. I have nothing to say to you or to anyone else about it.' And with that, she slammed the door on him.

He stood for several moments staring at it and listening to the cries of the baby, which seemed to increase in volume. Obviously the *Mary Jo* was a sensitive issue as far as Meryl Landguard was concerned, understandably so. She didn't know who he was. He expected her to be wary but why so hostile? She'd given him no time or encouragement to introduce himself. And why hadn't she been curious as to why he was asking about her husband's vessel all these years later or how he knew about it? And she hadn't asked him why he was enquiring about a man called Gavin Yardly.

He turned south out of the driveway and began to walk towards the Birling Gap and the coast. Was the younger woman Meryl Landguard's daughter or daughter-in-law? What had they rowed about or was their relationship always so cold and antagonistic? It was none of Marvik's business, but the fact that the younger woman worked for Bradshaw was. And he knew where to find her. First, though, he was keen to see where Yardly's body had been discovered.

It was a little over a mile to the Birling Gap. He walked briskly along the road through the rolling green countryside with only a few cars passing him. Soon he was entering a large car park to the right of a sharp bend in the road which led up to Beachy Head before going on to Eastbourne. There was only one car parked in it. He crossed the gravel towards the sea. It was high tide and he could hear the waves crashing on to the shore. A handful of coastguard cottages stood to his left. Once there had been seven; now there were only four, and those would one day crumble over the cliff edge just as other buildings and land had disappeared here over the years. It was a long time since he'd been here walking the Downs and many years since he'd been moored out at sea on his parents' boat. He couldn't remember why they had been here. Perhaps for the same reason Sarah had — exploring one of the many wrecks that had been dashed to pieces on these shores over the years.

He crossed to the top of the steps and stared out to sea. There wasn't a single boat in sight. In the last two days he'd passed this way four times by sea, once on his way to meet Helen, then with her on board before heading back to Eastbourne, when they had discovered Bradshaw's body, then making for the Hamble, and again yesterday evening returning to the marina at Eastbourne. The marina staff were too polite and too used to the ways of the strange and often erratic behaviour of yachting types, due to the weather and tides, to query his frequent comings and goings. They had heard the news of Bradshaw's death but had nothing to add to what Marvik already knew, when he had delicately questioned them, and no one he had spoken to had made any connection between Bradshaw's death and Gavin Yardly or Helen.

Marvik turned away from the sea. The land around him was owned and managed by the National Trust. To his left was the shop, visitors' centre and café, all closed with a notice saying they opened at ten a.m. To his right and the east was the coastal path up to Beachy Head, a well-known spot for suicides which Gavin had shunned, or rather his killer had. And to the west and Marvik's left was Crowlink and the path over the Seven Sisters chalk cliffs where, just below Bailey's Hill, Crowder had said the body had been found. There were a few houses on the upward approach to the clifftop so someone living, or staying in them if they were holiday homes, might have seen Gavin, but Marvik thought it unlikely. He was convinced Gavin's body had been taken ashore by boat.

He struck out for the clifftop to the west. He'd consulted his Ordnance Survey map last night and had checked the distance between the flat where Gavin had lived and the place where his body had been found. He'd been correct when he'd said to Crowder it was seven miles. Gavin could have walked here but not at night and not carrying weights. And if he had done so in the daytime and thrown himself over the cliff, someone could have seen him, unless of course it had been very early morning. There was no one around now and it was just after nine a.m.

He came out on the clifftop and walked the short distance to Bailey's Hill, where he stopped and, in the blustery, cold April wind, peered down at the grey stones. There was nothing to indicate a body had been found there. Marvik gazed out to sea again. Still no shipping or boat movements on the grey, choppy waves of the English Channel. This would have been an isolated spot when Gavin and his killer had arrived.

Whoever had killed him could simply have dumped his body in the sea, but that would have meant he might never have been found and therefore the police couldn't assume suicide. They might have believed that Yardly was on the run. The killer had wanted Yardly to be found and for it to look like suicide so that Bradshaw's murder could be neatly tied off. If Gavin was the 'target' Helen had overheard Colbourne and Marwell discussing then he was dead *before* Bradshaw was killed. Maybe that didn't matter because the time of Gavin Yardly's death would be difficult to pinpoint once the body had been exposed to the sea and the air. Or perhaps when Helen heard them say 'it's dealt with', Gavin was being held somewhere by one of them until Bradshaw was killed. That made some sense because, according to the lockkeeper, those men had been in the marina for two hours. What had they been doing during that time? Sitting on their boats waiting for Bradshaw to arrive with Helen? Or had one of them been in the marina while the other had gone to kill Gavin at the place he was being held and had then returned to his boat, by which time Helen was on board Bradshaw's boat or just leaving it?

Marvik returned to the Birling Gap and this time took the coastal path east towards Beachy Head. He set off at a brisk pace, ignoring the ache in his leg, a legacy of a former mission in the Marines. It would take him just over two hours to walk back to Eastbourne.

He wasn't at the peak of his fitness levels — his leg wound saw to that — which depressed him, but he wasn't far off it and he'd fared better than Strathen, even though his array of expensive and ground breaking technological prosthetic limbs meant that Strathen wasn't far behind.

He mulled over what Crowder had told him. Had Gavin Yardly simply stumbled on the discovery of the *Mary Jo* by accident? But if so, why report it to GCHQ? What did he know about the *Mary Jo* and its disappearance? Marvik was hoping Strathen would have some answers later that morning after locating and reading the marine accident investigation report.

He wondered how long Gavin had been looking for the *Mary Jo*. Perhaps it was only recently that he'd gleaned some information about it, much as Marvik had done about his parents' deaths, although he had no proof that it was anything other than an accident. His thoughts flicked to Sarah Redburn. Perhaps she had deposited other research material of his parents elsewhere. Neither her former boyfriend nor her previous boss had known of any but then she might not have told them. And what of Gavin Yardly's research into the finding of the *Mary Jo*? In addition to writing to GCHQ, had he backed up his information on a USB stick that his killer had taken along with his computer? Or perhaps Gavin had backed up online and the information was waiting for someone to access it with an encrypted password. The killer could have extracted that password from Yardly, though, before killing him.

What might have happened to the salvage vessel on her last voyage? The obvious answer was that it had run into bad weather and had been overwhelmed by heavy seas before having the chance to send out a distress signal. He'd be interested to know what the weather had been like on the day in July 2003 when it had vanished. But why was that salvage vessel so important? Why had Gavin been killed because of it? Why hadn't anyone else located it? Maybe they had and Gavin Yardly wasn't the only person to have died as a result. Other deaths could have been arranged and put down as suicide. If so, this killer was clever and experienced, and that made him highly dangerous.

It was late morning by the time Marvik reached the town. He quickly located Medlowes, which wasn't very far from Harold Road, and just off the seafront. It was a small office sandwiched between a Turkish restaurant and a shop selling what appeared to be every kind of bead and button on the planet. Medlowes' windows displayed a range of accommodation and it was open for business as usual. As he pushed open the door he had wondered if it might be closed out of respect for its owner, or because the police had requested it, and that the woman he was seeking would be working in a back office behind the closed doors. But she was sitting at a desk towards the rear, and her name plate on the desk told Marvik she was Karen Landguard. A man in his late twenties with sleek-backed gelled hair was sitting at a desk at the front of the office.

Karen Landguard looked up from her telephone conversation as he entered. It took her a moment to register where she had seen him before, at Meryl Landguard's, and when the penny dropped a scowl flashed across her face that had a hint of concern in it. Hastily, she terminated her conversation and, rising from her desk, reached Marvik at the same time as the man in the light grey suit too tight for him addressed him.

'Can I help you?'

'I'll deal with this, Danny,' she cut in abruptly and tossed Marvik an irritated glance. Her voice was hard when she said, 'Are you from the police? We've already told you everything we can.'

'I'm not the police.'

She looked anxious and perplexed. Glancing back at her colleague, Danny, she stepped towards the door, expecting Marvik to follow, which he did. 'Then what were you doing at my mother-in-law's? And why have you followed me here?'

she asked, keeping her voice low. He could see she was trying to work out who he could be.

'I wondered if you might be able to tell me more about the *Mary Jo*.'

Her astonishment was quickly surpassed by her relief. He guessed she'd been worried that he'd somehow found out about her affair with her boss, if those intimate photographs of her with Bradshaw on his mobile phone were anything to judge. Perhaps she suspected her husband of hiring a private detective — him — who was now intent on blackmailing her in exchange for his silence. He wondered if the police had told her that Bradshaw's mobile phone was missing. How had she reacted to that news if they had? She was uneasy, yes, and she looked as though she wasn't sleeping, so perhaps she was fretting that the phone and its photographs might be discovered.

But if so then she could simply tell the police that she had enjoyed the occasional business trip with Bradshaw on his boat and they were entertaining clients. In a bikini! Maybe. And Bradshaw wasn't around to contradict her. There was also no need for the police to speak to her husband. He had no connection with Bradshaw or his murder.

She said, 'The *Mary Jo* happened a long time before I met Stephen, my husband, and he never talks about it. Neither does Meryl. Why are you interested?'

'A friend of mine was researching it — Gavin Yardly.'

Just as her mother-in-law had shown shock at hearing the name, so too did Karen Landguard.

'You know him?' Marvik quickly asked and watched the hesitation cross her face. Would she deny it, as her mother-in-law had done, or tell the truth?

'He's one of our tenants,' she answered warily.

She'd used the present tense, indicating Gavin's name still hadn't been made public by the police, or if it had she'd had no time to check the news or the Internet. Marvik hid his surprise at this new piece of information. He said, 'Medlowes own the property where Mr Bradshaw's body was found?'

'Yes. Among others in the town.' She studied him, perplexed and with continuing unease. 'The police asked me about your friend but I have no idea where he is. Have you spoken to them?' Then she registered what he had said. 'Why would Gavin Yardly be interested in the *Mary Jo*?'

That was something Marvik very much wanted to know. 'Did Mr Bradshaw ever mention it?'

'Of course not,' she confidently replied. 'Why should he? Now, I have work to do.' She made to turn but Marvik forestalled her.

'I'm sorry about your boss's death. I didn't think you would be open.'

'The police said we could carry on. There are still tenants to help and properties to let and manage.'

'But no boss to pay you.'

'The accountant is handling all that,' she stiffly replied. 'Now—'

'I'd like to talk to your husband about the *Mary Jo*. Where can I contact him?'

She eyed him, panic-stricken. 'You can't. He works in London.'

'I can call him and arrange to see him.'

'I can't give you his number without asking him first.'

'Fine, I'll give you my mobile number.'

'I don't think . . .' But he held her gaze and, after a moment, she pursed her lips, spun round and marched back to her desk to retrieve her mobile phone, obviously deciding that it might be the only way to get rid of him. She punched the number in as he relayed it to her, and his name.

Danny interrupted them. 'I've got to show that prospective tenant around the Cruikshank's property.'

She tossed him the car keys. Danny threw Marvik a curious glance before leaving.

The phone started ringing. She was the only one there to take the call. Picking up the receiver with a defiant yet troubled glare at Marvik, she announced with false brightness and a slight tremor in her voice, 'Medlowes Letting and

Property Management, Karen Landguard speaking, how may I help you?'

He stood for a while, wondering if he should wait for her to finish the call and then press her further, but perhaps letting her stew for a while to grow more perplexed about his arrival and enquiries would yield better results, although he wasn't sure what she could tell him except more about her boss and her mother-in-law.

As he made for the door, he didn't think the latter would have confided in Karen Landguard from what he'd witnessed earlier. Besides, he knew where to find her. He also knew that Strathen would be able to discover where she and her husband, Stephen, lived and probably where Stephen Landguard worked. Marvik wouldn't wait for her to pass on a message to her husband to call him because he knew she wouldn't deliver it anyway. But, as he turned, glanced back at her and caught her anxious glance, he took heart in the fact that she had given him some new and revealing information, because he now knew how Ian Bradshaw had entered Helen's flat.

# CHAPTER SEVEN

He bought a takeout coffee, a toasted bacon, lettuce and tomato sandwich and, finding a vacant seat on the promenade in a sheltered position, called Strathen.

'The police have released Gavin Yardly's name as the man found dead on the shore and asked for any witnesses who might have seen him on the cliff edge to come forward,' Strathen said as soon as he came on the line.

'When did they release it?'

'Half an hour ago on the eleven thirty news.'

Long after he had spoken to Meryl Landguard. Marvik told Strathen that the property in Harold Road was owned and managed by Medlowes, adding, 'It explains how Bradshaw got into Helen's flat. The fact that he was her landlord as well as her boss could make her sound more culpable for his murder in the eyes of the police. Bradshaw could have had a set of Helen's keys in readiness before seeing her on his boat on Monday night, in case he felt like dropping in from time to time. But the keys weren't on his body and they're not on his key ring so the killer must have taken them after he killed him. What's more, Karen Landguard works for Medlowes and she's one of the women who feature in the photographs on Bradshaw's mobile phone. Ask Helen if she knew Bradshaw owned that building and if she recognizes Karen Landguard.'

Marvik held on and ate his sandwich while Strathen did so. After a couple of minutes, he came back on the line. 'Helen had no idea that Bradshaw was behind Medlowes — he never mentioned it — but she recognizes Karen Landguard as the woman who showed her the flat. She hasn't seen her since signing the tenancy agreement. Helen's monitoring social media now that Gavin's name's been released to see if anyone picks up on it and comments.'

'Meryl Landguard claims Gavin never approached her but she's lying. Karen's also holding something back but that could just be the fact she was in a relationship with Bradshaw and the last thing she wants is her husband and mother-in-law finding out about it. What did you get from the marine accident investigation report?'

As Strathen began to speak, Marvik finished off his coffee and sandwich.

'The report doesn't throw a great deal of light on what occurred because there was no wreckage to examine. The *Mary Jo* was a salvage tug owned by Helmsley Marine, built of steel construction in the Netherlands and registered there in 1992. It was acquired by Helmsley in 2000 and was inspected two weeks before it left Newhaven on 15 July 2003 for Newfoundland to tow the *Celeste* to Britain for recycling. Everything was certified as being sound. The master, Timothy Landguard's instructions were to meet another tug owned by Tagline in Newfoundland. Together they were to tow the *Celeste* out into the North Atlantic and, if necessary, assist in towing her to Britain. The *Mary Jo* was expected to arrive at Newfoundland on the 19 July. When she didn't show, Tagline tried to make contact with the master. They only got silence. The weather on the crossing was fair, with wind speed of four knots. The wave height was moderate and visibility good. A depression had moved north-east along the eastern seaboard until it merged with another weather system to the east of Newfoundland, and although it continued to deepen it was heading towards Iceland and away from the *Mary Jo*. It changed direction towards the southeast in the direction of the *Mary Jo*'s passage but that was *after* she was expected to reach port. The last contact from the *Mary Jo* was made by Landguard, who radioed to Helmsley on the 16 July to say everything was OK. She was last seen by a cargo ship on the same day. Although the report gives an open verdict, and there are no reports of a large sea swell, it's suggested that a freak wave is a possible cause for its disappearance. The crew were all experienced seamen.'

Marvik rose and tossed his coffee cup and sandwich wrapper into the waste bin as Strathen continued.

'Timothy Landguard was an experienced salvage master. He'd worked on projects for various marine salvors in Singapore, Australia and Canada before joining Helmsley in September 2000. Before that, he was master on container ships and car carriers. As Crowder told you, the salvage officer on the *Mary Jo* was Simon Warrendale, aged thirty-four, a marine engineer cadet who had progressed through the ranks to second engineer and sailed on dry cargo ships and tankers for many years. He was an advanced powerboat coxswain and experienced diver, as was Peter Goodhead, who was also a qualified and experienced marine engineer, aged forty. The deckhand and diver, Lewis Chale, aged thirty, had experience of sailing on tankers and working in the offshore oil industry. That's all the report says.'

'But?' Marvik prompted. He'd heard the query in Strathen's voice.

'The report doesn't give details of the crew's previous employers and, while we know that Timothy Landguard's next of kin was Meryl, we don't know the next of kin for the other crew members. Those details would have been on their employment records and those records would have been transferred to Almbridge on their acquisition of Helmsley. But there's no legal obligation to keep employment records longer than six years so they have probably been destroyed. There's a chance they were kept on computer and that the file has been archived, but I wouldn't bet on it. And I don't have access to Her Majesty's Revenue and Customs' database. I'm checking out the crew with the General Register Office to see if it throws up any relatives we can talk to. Gavin Yardly might have approached them.'

'Perhaps Meryl Landguard can give us their details. Now that Gavin's name's been released to the media she might be more forthcoming. I'll head back there.'

Marvik took a taxi. It was just after one o'clock when it pulled up outside the village hall. He walked the short distance to her house confident of finding her at home, if not immediately then at some stage, because she was looking after her grandchild. There was a chance that she had gone out for the day, in which case Marvik knew he would be in for a long wait but there were no other leads to follow up yet. If this drew a blank he'd ask Strathen to find out where Stephen and Karen Landguard lived and call on them later.

There was no car in the driveway and no answer when he rang the bell. He didn't think she was hiding from him. Perhaps she'd gone shopping. He settled down under the porch to wait. It had started raining lightly. While the minutes ticked into hours he thought back to the times he'd waited silently, sight unseen on missions, enduring extreme heat or freezing temperatures, sometimes wet, often hungry, physically uncomfortable and sometimes exhausted but mentally blocking all that out and focusing only on the task ahead. This was a picnic compared to what he and Strathen had experienced, even with the additional discomfit of the ache from the wound in his leg and in his shoulder, the latter as a result of a bullet last July while working as a private maritime security officer on board a luxury yacht. The drizzle turned into a long, slow, steady rain. Perhaps Meryl Landguard would return her grandson to Karen and arrive here early evening. He would wait no matter how long it took.

It was just after four thirty when her car swung into the driveway. Marvik ducked out of sight towards the side entrance where she wouldn't see him. He didn't want her turning round and taking off. He watched her take the child from the car. He was sleeping. As she reached the front door, Marvik stepped out. She gave a startled cry and stepped away from him but her fear swiftly turned to hostility.

'I'm calling the police,' she declared, trying to reach in her jacket for her mobile phone while shifting her grandson, who murmured but didn't wake.

'Fine. Then you can explain to them that Gavin Yardly visited you shortly before his death.' He had no proof of that, just a feeling and her initial reaction. Along with a belief that Gavin, researching into the *Mary Jo* and living so close to the widow of the master, would have been bound to have made contact. But she still denied it.

'I've told you, I have no idea who you're talking about.'

'He came to see you about his research into the loss of the *Mary Jo*. He was found dead yesterday morning at the foot of the cliffs not far from here, but then you know that.'

Her fair skin paled but there was still that air of coldness and determination about her. He sensed a resourceful, clever woman.

He pressed on: 'Gavin believed he'd found the location of the *Mary Jo*.' He saw her visibly start. Had Gavin kept that news from her or had he seen her *before* he'd found the *Mary Jo*? If so, it would have been before he posted that letter ten days ago.

Quickly recovering, in an icy tone, she said, '*If* the *Mary Jo* had been found then I would have been notified by the authorities, and unless you show me some identification to confirm who you are and what authority you have to talk to me then I *will* call the police. I know nothing about a man called Gavin Yardly and I am quite prepared to tell the police that. The *Mary Jo* was lost at sea years ago, my husband along with her. He's not coming back and I've got a grandchild to care for.' She made to insert the key in the lock but her hand was shaking slightly and she was finding it difficult. She was afraid, yes, but he didn't think it was of him.

'Have you kept in touch with the relatives of your husband's crew?' he asked as she succeeded in unlocking the door. Her hand stilled for a fraction of a second as she removed the key.

'No. Now leave me alone.'

Short of forcing his way in, there was nothing more he could do. At the entrance to the driveway, Marvik looked back at the house, half expecting to see Meryl Landguard at the window on the phone, probably to the police, but there was no sign of her.

He called the taxi firm who had brought him here and waited by the village hall for a car to arrive. He thought that if Medlowes were operating business as usual then perhaps Aquamarine were and Glenda, the office manager, could tell him more about Ian Bradshaw. But the Aquamarine offices were closed when he arrived, with a sign saying they would be shut indefinitely owing to a bereavement.

He returned to his boat, where he showered, changed and made himself something to eat. Strathen hadn't called which meant he had nothing new to report, and neither did he, Marvik thought with frustration. He hadn't got very far. There had to be others he could speak to about the *Mary Jo*. Had Bradshaw been killed solely to frame Gavin Yardly and cover up the real reason for his death and the manner of it — murder?

A movement on the pontoon caught his attention. It could be another boat owner but Marvik went on deck to make sure. A stooping, slender figure scurried down the pontoon. That was no boat owner. It turned on to the pontoon where Bradshaw's boat was moored. That didn't mean Bradshaw's boat was its destination but Marvik felt instinctively that it was.

He alighted and followed silently and carefully, and was in time to see the figure climb on to Bradshaw's boat. A few seconds later, a thin beam of light played around the cabin. Whoever it was had keys, unless they were expert at breaking in. It could be a thief who, hearing the news that Bradshaw was dead, was taking the opportunity to steal from the boat.

Marvik didn't think it was police or intelligence. The police had no need to act in so furtive a manner and the figure didn't have the demeanour of an intelligence agent.

Marvik's pulse quickened. He returned to his boat. He didn't board but crouched on the platform by his tender. He tensed in readiness, the adrenaline coursing through his veins. Could this be Bradshaw and Yardly's killer? Was the mission going to be resolved a hell of a lot quicker than he'd thought? There was only one way out of the marina aside from leaving by boat, and that was on foot. The intruder would have to walk right past him.

Within ten minutes, Marvik felt the pontoon move. As the stooping figure drew level Marvik leapt from the platform on to the pontoon, thrust his arm around the neck in a vice-like grip, forced the right hand high up the back and hissed, 'OK, so who are you and what the hell were you doing on Ian Bradshaw's boat? I'm waiting,' Marvik threatened, tightening his grip. 'I'll ask you one more time before I break your arm. Who are you?'

'Stephen Landguard,' he croaked.

Marvik hadn't expected that. He loosened his grip, but only slightly. 'Timothy Landguard's son?'

Landguard nodded.

'Let's see some ID.'

'Jacket pocket,' rasped Landguard.

Marvik removed his arm from Landguard's neck but kept a firm grip on the hand wrenched up his back. Although Landguard's other arm was free, Marvik didn't think he'd make any attempt to get out of the hold and, even if he did, Marvik was confident he could counter it. Landguard coughed as Marvik freed the grip on his neck. With his free hand, Marvik reached inside Landguard's jacket and pulled out a wallet. Flicking it open with one hand, he saw under the light on the pontoon that Stephen Landguard was telling the truth. Keeping a hold on the wallet and on Landguard, he thrust him forward towards the platform of his boat. 'Climb on board.'

Landguard tossed him a petrified look but obeyed. Only when they were on the lower deck did Marvik release him. Landguard rubbed his arm. His light brown, bloodshot eyes swivelled around the cabin, wide with fear. His angular face was ashen and pinched with worry and fatigue.

'Sit and put your hands on the table where I can see them and keep them there,' commanded Marvik.

Landguard quickly slid on to the bench seat behind the table and placed his long, slender fingers on the table as instructed. Marvik noted the nails were bitten. He took in the stubble on Landguard's chin and upper lip — the strain was etched on his cavernous face and he recognized before him a man driven to the end of his tether, frightened and desperate. Why? Perhaps his wife could answer that question. But perhaps there was another reason why Landguard was terrified. Could this be the man who had slit Bradshaw's throat in a jealous fit of rage? It was possible, except it didn't explain Gavin Yardly's death. Maybe that was suicide and had nothing to do with Bradshaw. But, even as he thought it, Marvik knew it wasn't so and, as he studied the petrified man in front of him, he also knew he wasn't looking at a killer.

'OK, so let's start with why were you searching Bradshaw's boat?'

# CHAPTER EIGHT

'I was looking for something.' Landguard's voice came out barely above a whisper. He swallowed hard. Marvik watched his large Adam's apple go up and down in his gaunt neck.

'That much is obvious,' he said scathingly, wondering whether to toss into the conversation the fact of his wife's affair. Was that the sole reason behind Landguard's visit — that he'd come to find and remove evidence of his wife's infidelity with her boss after learning of his murder? If it was then this had nothing to do with the mission and Marvik could let him go, but not before he found out more about his father and the *Mary Jo*. This was an unexpected bonus, particularly after a frustrating and fruitless day.

Hesitantly, Landguard said, 'Are you a friend of Ian Bradshaw's?' He studied Marvik with fear but there was a hint of defiance in his voice now that his initial shock was subsiding.

'No, but I'd like to know who killed him.'

'Not my mother, she knows nothing, if that's what you're thinking,' Landguard quickly replied.

It wasn't, but Marvik was very interested to discover why Stephen Landguard had so readily jumped to her defence. He hadn't known that Meryl Landguard had been acquainted with Bradshaw. He'd been asking her the wrong questions about the wrong man. 'Why should I think that?' he said evenly.

'Are you police?' But Landguard's gaze as he surveyed the boat was puzzled. 'No, you can't be,' he quickly added, his mind racing to the conclusion that a police officer wouldn't have a boat like this or be questioning him on board it. But again, the fear crept back. Marvik could see the thoughts running through Landguard's head: if he wasn't police then he could be in league with Bradshaw's killer or someone who wanted revenge for it and wouldn't care how he took it or on who he reaped it.

'My mother knows nothing about his death,' Landguard repeated.

'I never said she did.'

But it was as though Landguard hadn't heard him. 'His company, Medlowes, manage the lettings of my mother's properties. It's business,' he gabbled. 'It's all legal and above board.'

'Did I suggest it wasn't?'

'No, but . . .' He shifted.

'Why would I think there was anything other than business between Bradshaw and your mother?'

Landguard scrutinized his hands. He cleared his throat and, in a flat voice as though reciting something he'd learned a long time ago, said, 'My mother's known Ian Bradshaw for years. She worked for Antara Yacht Brokerage before Bradshaw bought them out. She was their accounts manager. She left a few months after my father was lost at sea. She moved from Newhaven to East Dean and started a property investment company. She's good with money.'

Landguard hadn't answered his question, or perhaps he had in a roundabout way. Marvik said, 'And your wife now works for one of Bradshaw's companies.'

Landguard flinched at the sneer in Marvik's voice. It was obvious he knew of his wife's affair. Marvik wondered when he had discovered that. Had Karen told him before he'd come here? Did she know her husband was here? Maybe Landguard thought his wife had killed her boss.

'Do you know why Ian Bradshaw was killed?' Landguard asked warily, studying Marvik.

'No. Do you?'

'No.' But he hesitated and fidgeted.

Marvik could see that Landguard was desperate to confide in someone. His thoughts were tormenting him. He said, 'But I do know that Gavin Yardly didn't kill Bradshaw and that he didn't kill himself.'

Landguard started. 'You know Yardly?'

'And clearly by your reaction, so do you.'

'But I don't.'

Marvik moved forward, causing Landguard to quickly add, 'I saw him, with my mother, and I heard her talking about him to Ian Bradshaw.'

'When?' Marvik rapped. At last, confirmation that Meryl Landguard had lied and more. In fact, much more than he could have hoped for. Meryl had felt the need to talk to Bradshaw about Gavin Yardly, so what did Bradshaw have to do with the *Mary Jo*? And why was this the source of Landguard's anxiety and not his wife's infidelity?

'It was nearly two weeks ago, the Friday before last.'

*Before he had posted that letter to GCHQ*. 'Go on,' Marvik said, not betraying his keenness.

Landguard took a breath. 'It was just after four o'clock. I'd left work early. I was feeling . . . well, I needed to get away.' He looked down at his hands and then back up. 'Charlie was at the nursery and Karen had arranged with my mother for her to pick him up from there. Karen had a late meeting.' He looked down again.

Marvik could see that Stephen Landguard had thought his wife was meeting Bradshaw. Maybe she was. And perhaps he'd left work early in an attempt to catch her with her boss.

'I parked at Birling Gap. I'd decided to take a long walk over the Downs to clear my head and think.'

About his marital problems, no doubt.

'When I turned into the car park I saw my mother's car. She's not one for walking and I thought she might be in the café having tea with a friend before I remembered they closed at four. I almost drove away. Then I caught sight of her at the top of the steps that lead down to the shore. She was talking to a man, about my age — early thirties, maybe younger. I could see by her expression and gestures that she was very cross but the man didn't seem to react to what she was saying. He just stared at her. He wasn't arguing back and he didn't look annoyed or upset. He just sort of looked blankly at her. I wondered who he could be and why my mother was so upset. I thought about interrupting but I knew she wouldn't thank me for it.'

Marvik noted the acidity in his voice.

'And if I had she'd only have demanded to know why I wasn't at work. I didn't want a scene.' He spoke wearily, as though there had been many scenes over the years. Marvik was getting the impression that the mother and son relationship was as strained as the one he'd witnessed that morning between mother and daughter-in-law. He wondered if Karen was the cause of the disharmony or had it always been that way?

'I thought that perhaps she'd caught him doing something foolish or illegal and was scolding him for it.'

'Like what?'

'I don't know. I was about to drive away when she marched to her car and drove off very fast. She wouldn't have registered I was there even if I'd been parked opposite her or close by.'

'And Yardly? What did he do?'

'He headed towards the Belle Tout Lighthouse.'

In the direction of Eastbourne. 'Did you see his expression?'

'He looked quite calm. He didn't seem upset or angry.'

'Did he show your mother anything? A map, mobile phone?'

'No. He was carrying a rucksack but I didn't see him take anything out of it or put anything inside it.' Landguard ran a hand through his lank, light-brown hair, and then, flicking his eyes to Marvik, quickly put his hand back on the table.

'Did anyone follow him on to the Downs?'

'Not that I remember. No, I don't think so. I wasn't really looking. I pushed it out of my mind and went for my walk.'

Marvik asked him to describe Yardly.

'Slim, short, light auburn hair.'

'What was he wearing?'

'Jeans and a navy-blue zip-up waterproof jacket.'

'So how did you know this man was Gavin Yardly?'

Landguard again swallowed hard. 'I walked for two hours.' He paused and took a breath. The wind was ripping through the marina and Marvik could hear the rain hitting the deck. He could see that Landguard was steeling himself to relay what had happened. It had disturbed him deeply enough to lead him to search Bradshaw's boat.

'I thought about going home as though I'd just come in from work. Karen wouldn't be there. She was fetching Charlie from Mum's after her meeting. Then I decided to fetch Charlie myself, go home and put him to bed so that Karen and I could discuss things.'

Marvik didn't need to ask what things.

'I parked on the driveway and was about to use my key to the front door when I saw the side gate was open, so I walked to the back of the house. There's a utility room that leads into the kitchen and the door was unlocked, so I went in and then I froze. Mum was on the phone. She was shouting and swearing. It was so totally out of character. My mother never has to shout to get what she wants.' The bitter tone was back in his voice. He blinked rapidly as though disturbed by the memory. 'She was talking to Bradshaw.'

'How do you know that?' Marvik sharply asked.

'Because she said the name Ian.'

'It could have been someone else called Ian.'

'It wasn't. She was talking about my father's ship, the *Mary Jo*, and Ian Bradshaw used to work for Helmsley Marine who owned it.'

Had he, indeed! This was getting even more interesting. Another connection. 'When?' Marvik asked, keenly interested.

'When the *Mary Jo* was lost at sea, in 2003.'

'What was his job?'

'I don't know, something to do with contracts and accounts, I think. It was him my mother was speaking to on the phone because I checked her call log when she left the room to fetch Charlie. It was Ian Bradshaw's mobile phone number.'

And Landguard would know that because he'd found it on his wife's mobile. 'And she mentioned Gavin Yardly?'

Landguard nodded. 'I heard her say, "Where the hell have you been, Ian, I've been trying to get hold of you for hours". Then she shouted, "I'll tell you what's wrong. Gavin fucking Yardly, that's what".' Landguard winced at the memory. Marvik knew it was because he was seeing a completely different side to his mother, one he'd never witnessed before. It had shocked him. 'She said that Yardly had called her on her mobile. She asked if Bradshaw had given the number to him. He must have said he hadn't because she asked how the hell he'd got it. She said that Yardly had asked her to meet him at the Birling Gap because he had something to tell her about the *Mary Jo*. She said, "He knows what happened. For Christ's sake, how can he?"'

'Were those her exact words?' Marvik sharply interjected.

'Yes. It puzzled me. No one knows what happened to that boat, only what's in the marine accident investigation report. She said that if Bradshaw didn't "sort it" they would "both be in the shit". She said she'd meet Bradshaw on his boat that night in an hour's time.'

'This was the Friday before last?' Marvik asked just to check because Landguard had already told him this.

'Yes.'

'And she asked Bradshaw for the security code to get into the marina?'

'Yes. She wrote it on the pad in the kitchen.'

'And you jotted it down. Why? Did you think of going to the boat to demand what it was all about?'

Landguard flushed. 'It crossed my mind but I knew I wouldn't be able to get Charlie home and get there in time.'

Yeah, and Marvik thought Landguard wanted the security code in case he wanted to catch his wife on board Bradshaw's boat at some stage. But hearing his mother agree to meet Bradshaw meant that his wife wouldn't be with him — not unless he ditched her first.

'My mother was about to come off the phone so I hurried outside and let myself in the front, calling out as I did. She met me in the hall. I told her I'd decided to leave work early and collect Charlie — he was upstairs asleep. I said I needed a drink of water. While she went to fetch him, I went into the kitchen. Her phone was lying on the work surface. That's when I checked the number she'd called, wrote the marina security code number down and stuffed the paper into my pocket.'

It explained how Landguard had entered the marina pontoons but not how he'd got inside Bradshaw's boat. Marvik asked him.

'It was open.'

Marvik eyed him disbelievingly. *He* certainly hadn't left it unlocked and he didn't think the police would have done.

'I didn't expect it to be,' Landguard hastily added. 'I thought I could force the lock but when I climbed on board and tried the door to the cabin it just opened.'

So who had been on board after him and Helen? Had Bradshaw's killer searched it in case he'd left some incriminating evidence there? But Marvik, not the killer, had the boat keys, unless the killer had a duplicate set, given to him by Bradshaw. Perhaps the plan had been to kill Bradshaw on his boat, only the killer hadn't expected him to follow Helen back to her flat.

'And you found what?' asked Marvik.

'Nothing.'

'What did you expect to find?'

Landguard again ran his hand through his hair. 'I don't know. Something. Anything that might tell me what's happening.'

Marvik left a short pause. 'Did you ask your mother about Gavin Yardly?'

He looked aghast at the suggestion. 'Of course not. She'd have been furious that I'd eavesdropped.'

'But it concerned your father.'

His mouth tightened. 'We don't talk about him or what happened.'

'Why not?'

His eye contact dropped. He muttered, 'She said it was too painful for her.'

*And what about you?* thought Marvik, studying Landguard, seeing the hurt in his eyes. Had his mother not considered it to be extremely painful for her son?

Landguard added in a slightly apologetic manner, 'She said we couldn't change what had happened so there was little point in discussing it and dragging it up all the time. It was the past and it doesn't pay to look back. You have to move on.'

His words struck a chord with Marvik. It was what he had told himself after his parents' deaths. He had blotted out his emotional feelings by mental and physical exertion, pushing himself to the limits so that he could obliterate the past, except the past was finally catching up with him through Sarah Redburn's death and that notebook. But, even now, he recognized that he was still pushing it away, waiting for the next incident, the next attempt on his life, the one thing that would force him to confront the past. For Meryl Landguard, that had been Gavin Yardly, and Yardly, along with Bradshaw, had been killed because of it. Was Meryl Landguard in danger? Possibly. Or was she their killer?

He said, 'Have you ever thought there was something suspicious concerning the loss of the *Mary Jo*?'

'No.'

But Marvik could see that was a lie.

Landguard quickly went on: 'When my mother was on the phone to Bradshaw I heard her say, "You know him?" meaning Gavin Yardly after she'd told him that Yardly had confronted her. I don't know what Bradshaw answered but my mother swore again and said something about Yardly living and working right under Bradshaw's nose. She asked if Yardly had said anything to Bradshaw about the *Mary Jo*. I don't know what his answer was. I thought that if he was living under Bradshaw's nose then he must be renting one of his flats. I couldn't ask Karen because she'd want to know why I was interested. The next day I called Medlowes. I didn't think anyone would recognize my voice because I don't phone Karen on the office line, only on her mobile, and then not very often. Danny answered. I pretended to be a friend of Gavin Yardly's and asked for his address. I said I'd mislaid it. He gave it to me.' Marvik could see where this was leading.

'You went to visit him?'

'Yes. But not until last Thursday. I've been, er, busy.'

Or ruminating over what to do and whether to follow it up, thought Marvik.

'I took the afternoon off work and waited outside the house in Harold Road. But he didn't show up.'

'What time was this?'

'I reached there at about four and stayed until eight. I usually get home between seven thirty and eight so I had to leave because Karen would have been suspicious if I'd got home too late. And I couldn't take any more time off work so I couldn't return on Friday. Karen was off over the weekend, which meant I didn't get the chance to get back there and we had an urgent project to complete on Monday and Tuesday. We worked well into Monday night and I stayed in London at a colleague's flat.'

That ruled him out of killing Bradshaw, if his alibi was genuine, but Marvik had already discounted Landguard as a killer.

Landguard was saying, 'I didn't know about Bradshaw being found dead until I was on my way home on the train yesterday and I was scrolling through the news and social media websites. Then Karen told me the police had been to the office and they'd been asking about Gavin Yardly. He was missing and I thought he might have got the better of Bradshaw in a fight or a struggle or something. I wondered if Gavin Yardly was related to one of the crew who had gone down with the ship. Maybe he'd discovered something that he thought put the blame on Ian Bradshaw for the loss at sea. Bradshaw could have been in charge of safety and he skimped on it and told my mother, only she forgot to tell my father or didn't think it was important. When I searched the Internet this morning at lunchtime I read that Gavin Yardly's body had been found at the bottom of the cliff close to where my mother had met him.'

'And not far from where she lives.'

He nodded miserably. Could Stephen Landguard really believe his mother capable of murder? Possibly. But it was also possible that he believed Bradshaw had 'sorted' Yardly by killing him. He wouldn't know the exact times of their deaths. He could be thinking that Yardly had died first at Bradshaw's hand or his mother's, or they'd both colluded in it, and then Meryl had killed Bradshaw because he threatened to blackmail her. And where did he think his wife fitted into all this? He was clearly tormented. Marvik could see he hadn't been sleeping properly and probably not eating either. He'd suspected his wife's affair for some time, and when he'd finally decided to face her about it, he'd witnessed the exchange between his mother and Yardly, followed by her uncharacteristic conversation with the man his wife was sleeping with and the connection to his father's death. He was mentally exhausted, and in his highly charged emotional state anything, no matter how irrational, seemed possible.

'How did your mother seem to you after Bradshaw's death?'

'I don't know. I haven't seen or spoken to her.'

Marvik was getting the impression that Landguard had rarely talked to his mother about anything other than routine and essential matters. But then he had hardly been in his own parents' confidence and he'd never had the opportunity to confide in them, not after he'd been sent away to school. In Landguard's case, clearly mother and son were not close. But he had once been close to his parents during the days spent on *Vasa*, their boat. Why had that changed so dramatically and suddenly? He pushed his personal thoughts and feelings aside.

Marvik wondered what Meryl Landguard had done when she'd heard the news of Bradshaw's death. How had she felt? Appalled? Upset? Not if she had killed him. When Marvik had first met her she'd been hostile and stunned by his mention of Gavin Yardly, but not fearful. From what he was learning about her from her son's description, Meryl Landguard was tough, resilient and resourceful, but Yardly's confrontation with her had rattled her enough to prompt her into rage and blasphemy which, according to Stephen, was uncharacteristic of his mother, but how did he know that? Perhaps that was the other side of Meryl Landguard which she'd kept well hidden from her son and his wife. He sensed that Landguard had more to tell but for now Marvik didn't press him. Instead, he asked if he had discussed any of this with his wife. Predictably, Landguard said he hadn't.

'But you have talked about Ian Bradshaw's death?'

Landguard flushed and looked away. That was a no, then. 'Did you tell Karen you were coming here?'

'No! We haven't spoken since this morning when I left for work.'

So Karen Landguard wouldn't have made any mention of seeing Marvik at her mother-in-law's house or the fact he'd visited her office.

'How did you get here?'

'My car's in the marina car park.'

'Give me your keys.'

Landguard reached into his pocket and handed them over.

'Get up.'

Landguard scrambled out of the seat.

'You want to know what was going on with *Mary Jo* and so do I, so let's go and ask your mother.'

# CHAPTER NINE

Marvik turned into the driveway. The house was in darkness but the car headlights picked out the front door, which was open. There was no sign of the Audi. It could be in the garage and Meryl Landguard could also be inside it, retrieving or checking up on something, but would she leave the front door open and the house in darkness? It seemed unlikely.

He glanced at the dashboard clock even though he knew the time. It was almost nine thirty. An unusual time to be poking about in the garage, or wandering around in the garden in the dark in this heavy rain and wind, unless she was trying to hide something that could expose whatever it was she and Bradshaw had been up to in 2003 which involved the *Mary Jo*. But she'd had well over a decade to do that. Perhaps she had forgotten to close the front door, or the wind had blown it open and she'd retired to bed. Perhaps Meryl Landguard had gone to visit friends and had left the door open by mistake. Again, unlikely. Or perhaps she'd been abducted and her kidnapper had left the door open behind him in a hurry, taking her car.

He stilled the engine and listened. Only the drumming of the rain on the car roof greeted him. He steeled himself for the fact that she could be dead inside the house, killed by the same person who had slit Bradshaw's throat and dumped Gavin Yardly's body on the beach.

Stephen Landguard voiced Marvik's question. 'Why is the door open?' he asked, bewildered.

'Do you have a key to the garage?'

'No, it's in the kitchen on a hook in the cupboard.'

'We'll try the doors first.' Marvik climbed out, leaving Landguard to follow. They were locked. Marvik peered through the side window. There was no car inside. Landguard was looking understandably mystified and worried. Marvik quickly scoured the outside of the house. If Meryl Landguard had been abducted, forced into her car and driven off there was the chance that someone was watching to see who showed up, although a better alternative was that they had placed a surveillance device. But if this killer had been in league with Meryl and Bradshaw over the loss of the *Mary Jo* and was the only one left who knew the truth of what had happened on that last voyage, he probably saw no need to mount any surveillance. He'd believe he was safe. Unless, said the small voice in the back of Marvik's mind, he'd seen him and Helen at her flat and was the person who had tipped off the police. He might be curious about him but he had no reason to suspect he knew anything about what happened to that vessel, not unless Meryl had gone blabbing to him after he'd shown up here twice today. And that meant the killer would know he'd been asking about Gavin Yardly and the *Mary Jo.* He'd come after him. That didn't worry Marvik. It was part of the deal but he needed to be alone. He didn't want to have to protect Stephen Landguard and neither did he wish to put him in danger.

His thoughts had taken him to the front of the house. He gestured at Landguard to keep quiet and stepped inside, into the darkness. Again, he stood absolutely still and listened. Only Stephen Landguard's laboured breathing greeted him. Marvik could tell there was no one here dead, which was a relief, but it was short-lived because Meryl's body could be in the garden, although he thought it more likely she'd be found slumped over the steering wheel of her car in a remote spot and her death made to look like suicide.

'Get the garage key,' Marvik commanded. Landguard made to switch on the hall light but Marvik quickly added, 'Use your torch and keep it low.'

'But—'

'Just do it.'

While Landguard went to the rear of the house, Marvik searched the two rooms in the front, keeping his torch low and screened with his hand, his ears attuned for any sounds from outside. There was no sign of any disturbance in either the living room or the dining room opposite it across the hall. And no sign of Meryl Landguard. There were also no photographs of her late husband, but then Marvik hadn't expected to see any — not after what Stephen and Karen had told him. There were a couple of pictures of the baby and one of Karen, Stephen and the baby.

Landguard returned with the keys. 'She's not in the kitchen,' he whispered anxiously.

'Are there any other rooms at the rear of the house?'

'No, the kitchen runs into the breakfast room and utility room and mum's not there or in the cloakroom. She must have gone outside and had an accident. We should—'

'Let's check upstairs first.'

He ordered Landguard to climb the stairs ahead of him. Marvik paused briefly to glance out of the landing window which gave on to the front of the property. There was still nobody in sight. All was quiet, apart from the weather.

'Take your mother's room. I'll do the others.'

It didn't take long to discover that Meryl Landguard wasn't in the house. None of the rooms had been disturbed. Meeting Landguard in the hall, Marvik asked if anything of his mother's was missing — clothes, toiletries.

'I didn't look.'

Marvik returned with him to her bedroom. It gave on to a bathroom and dressing room. There were two suitcases on a shelf in the dressing room, which indicated she hadn't taken anything, unless she'd packed just the bare essentials in an overnight bag, but it didn't look that way to him because there were toiletries and make-up in the shower room and jewellery in the bedroom. This had all the signs of an abduction. And that confirmed to him that she and Bradshaw must have been in league with someone else. Someone who knew exactly what had happened to the *Mary Jo* and who was involved in Bradshaw and Yardly's deaths.

'Where does she keep her passport?'

'In the safe in the dining room. I don't know the combination to it. Why would she want that?'

Marvik ignored the question. The dining room hadn't been disturbed but she could have been forced to open the safe and then close it. Not for her passport, though, but for any incriminating papers about the *Mary Jo* if she'd kept them.

Landguard's forehead was creased with concern. 'She must have gone outside and had a fall or a heart attack.'

Marvik shut the front door behind him after ensuring that Landguard had a key. Swiftly, he unlocked the garage. Meryl Landguard wasn't in it, unconscious or dead.

'Right, we check the garden.' Marvik didn't want to leave Landguard alone by his car, not because he thought he might drive off and abandon him but if anyone came they would easily get the better of him. With Landguard trotting at his heels, Marvik made a swift and thorough search of the garden. It didn't take long because there wasn't much of it. Most of the land was to the front of the house and Meryl Landguard wasn't there.

'She must have gone to a friend.'

'Do you know who that might be?'

'Not really,' Landguard said miserably. 'I could call her.'

He reached for his phone but Marvik stilled him. 'Not yet.' He'd already told Landguard to switch it off after allowing him to call his wife on their way here. Karen had left two messages and a text demanding to know where he was. He told her he was at his mother's and would be home soon, and had hastily rung off before she could ask more questions.

'What time would Karen have collected your son from here today?'

'Six o'clock.'

'And you haven't called or heard from your mother today?'

'No. Should I call the police?'

'In a moment.' Marvik wanted to be away from here when Stephen Landguard called them. He couldn't afford the time to hang around. And time was marching on. If the property was being watched then maybe they didn't have long before they were intercepted.

'Get in the car,' Marvik commanded, climbing into the driver's seat.

Landguard made to protest when a glance from Marvik stilled him. Marvik started up and pulled out of the driveway, scouring the road for any sign of a vehicle following. Instead of heading north he turned south towards the Birling Gap. He caught Landguard's nervous glance. Marvik wanted to make sure that Meryl wasn't there, dead in her car or possibly on the shore with her car parked close to the cliff edge. And he thought it was time he pressed Landguard for what he hadn't told him. Landguard sat in silence as Marvik drove the short distance. The car park was deserted. Wherever Meryl Landguard was, it wasn't here. Marvik pulled up but kept the engine running and his ears attuned for the sound of any approaching vehicles.

Watching Stephen Landguard closely, Marvik said, 'Tell me about your father.'

'But why? This is madness. How can what happened all those years ago matter now? The *Mary Jo* hit a freak wave and sank.'

'Fine. If that's what you want to believe and you don't want your mother found before she ends up like Bradshaw and Yardly, that's OK by me.' Marvik made to turn the car round.

'No. Wait,' Landguard said sharply.

Marvik stilled the engine.

Taking a deep breath, Landguard ran a hand over his face. In the dim light of the car, Marvik could see the strain etched on it. He exhaled heavily and said, 'My father was a very experienced sailor. He loved being at sea. He was a quiet man, thoughtful. He was also a very talented artist. He loved sketching. He did it all the time when he was at sea. He'd sketch the crew, the other ships he saw, the ports he'd put into. He always said it was where I got my artistic talent from.' A smile touched his tired eyes and vanished in a second. 'He didn't like a lot of company or socializing — the complete opposite to mum. She liked to go out and to entertain while he was content to stay around the house. It irritated my mother. I think my parents found it hard to adjust when he came home from sea.'

'They rowed.'

'Not in the shouting kind of way but there was always tension between them. Dad decided to leave working on car carriers and became a salvage master, first working on projects abroad and then at Helmsley. But being closer to home didn't seem to help them much. I could see that things were never going to be right. I think they were just waiting for me to leave home before splitting up. Then the accident happened. I was nineteen when Dad was lost at sea and about to go to university in the September of that year. I'd spent a gap year working with a design agency in Brighton and was keen to get away.'

'How did she take the news that your father was missing?' Marvik saw Landguard consider his answer.

'Stoically I think is how you would describe it. She didn't break down or act distraught but then that's not her way.' There was an edge of bitterness to his voice.

'And how did Ian Bradshaw react?'

Landguard said somewhat sourly, 'I don't know. I saw as little of him as possible.'

But Marvik was betting it had been the opposite for Meryl Landguard.

With a spark of spirit, Landguard said, 'The times when I did see him he was all sympathetic and supposedly cut up but everything was an act with him. He was loud, crass and a bullshitter. I'm not sorry he's dead.'

But was Stephen's wife? 'And how did *you* take the news of your father's disappearance?' Marvik asked.

'I couldn't quite believe that he would never come back. It wasn't really until the memorial service in November that it hit me.'

Of course, why hadn't Marvik thought of that? There had been a memorial service for his parents so why not for the lost crew of the *Mary Jo*? There were no bodies to bury or cremate, no ashes to scatter at sea, but the relatives, colleagues and friends would need to mourn and mark the deaths. He wondered if Strathen had found a reference to it on the Internet. The local media must have covered it and so too must the shipping press.

'Who was there aside from your mother and Bradshaw?'

'I don't really remember. I didn't take much notice. I just wanted it over and done with and to get away.'

Marvik could understand that. He'd hated every minute of his parents' memorial service, which had been held at the National Oceanographic Centre in Southampton. The room had been packed with their fellow professionals, colleagues and past crew members from all over the world. The memorial for the lost crew of the *Mary Jo* might throw up someone who could tell him more about Timothy Landguard and his crew. And some of those at his parents' memorial might be able to tell him where they had kept their back-up computer disks on their research.

'Where was the service held?' he asked.

'St Michael's Church in Newhaven.'

'Who organized it?'

'Duncan Helmslow and my mother, I guess. I don't really know.'

Helmslow was dead and Meryl missing but there would be others who had been there, perhaps who had also helped to arrange it, and those who would have given a reading or an address. He recalled who had done that at his parents' service. A lean man with eyes and a forehead that reminded him of an eagle; another smaller, stouter man with a voice like chocolate and the look of a badger about him; and a fierce-looking, slight woman with darting movements that reminded him of a bird pecking at the ground. He'd deliberately blanked out their names.

'Were there any relatives of the crew of the *Mary Jo*?' Marvik asked.

Landguard shrugged. 'If there were I didn't speak to them. What shall I do about mum missing?'

'Call the police when you arrive back at her house.' Marvik made to climb out.

'You're not coming with me?' Landguard asked, surprised.

'No.'

'But how will you get back to Eastbourne?'

'Try your mother's mobile first before you call the police. If she doesn't answer, leave a message to say you're at the house and you've found the door open, that you're worried and you're calling the police. Say if she picks up the message to ring you. Then call the police, tell them you came to see your mother and, after finding the door open, searched the house and gardens for her. Tell them there's no sign of her, her car's missing and she's not answering her mobile.'

'What will they do?'

'I don't know but don't mention me, don't say you were on Bradshaw's boat and don't mention Gavin Yardly. If you need to mention your father just imply that your mother could have been thinking of him and has become depressed. OK, so it doesn't sound like her to you but they don't know that and they'll put out a call for her. Give me your number.'

Marvik punched it into his mobile phone. He climbed out. Looking back into the car, he said, 'Just stick to what I say and you'll be OK.' At least, he sincerely hoped so and that whoever had come for Meryl wouldn't come for her son. But there was no reason for them to do that because Stephen Landguard hadn't known Gavin Yardly and he knew nothing about the *Mary Jo*. But some of those who had been at that memorial service might know. Now all Marvik had to do was find the people Gavin had traced and who he had spoken to.

## CHAPTER TEN

*Thursday*

As soon as Newhaven Library opened at nine thirty, Marvik was requesting access to the newspaper archives, which he was swiftly given. He'd moored up late last night on the visitors' pontoon in the small marina in the narrow, industrialized harbour of Newhaven opposite the giant scrap yard. His was the only boat on that pontoon, which wasn't surprising given it was early in the sailing season. He'd called Strathen while sailing to Newhaven after his walk back over the Downs in the rain, wind and dark. The weather hadn't bothered him. His thoughts of Meryl Landguard's possible fate had though, along with that of his parents' packed memorial service. He'd tried to conjure up a mental picture of it but, aside from some learned people wittering on, he remembered nothing and no names. His photographic recall failed him. He knew it was because he had been mentally determined to block it out in an effort to obliterate the pain, shock and bewilderment surrounding their deaths. With an effort, the vision of it might return. Perhaps if he sought out Hugh Freestone, his guardian of only two months before he had enlisted in the Marines, seeing and speaking to him might reconjure the long-forgotten memories. But Freestone could be dead. Marvik hadn't seen or spoken to him for almost twenty years. He supposed a hypnotist might be able to retrieve his memory but he wasn't certain he wanted to go down that route. Not yet, anyway. And just as he was searching for articles on the memorial service for the crew of the Mary Jo, he knew he could do the same for his parents' service. There would be photographs with names. And there would probably be details of the service in among his papers in the safe-deposit box in the bank vault in London.

He'd told Strathen that it looked as though Meryl Landguard had been abducted, adding, 'I suspect that she and Bradshaw knew something about the disappearance of the *Mary Jo* along with a third party and it wasn't only Bradshaw that Meryl telephoned for a meeting but this other person too. She could have plotted with him to kill both Gavin Yardly and Ian Bradshaw and now she's been taken out.' Maybe by the same men Helen had overheard using the phrase 'taken out' — Colbourne and Marwell.

Strathen had called him back earlier that morning to say that he could find no mention of the memorial service on the Internet and that records in the General Register Office for the crew members on the *Mary Jo*, with the exception of Landguard, didn't match the information Crowder had given them regarding the names and ages. Neither could he find any references to Simon Warrendale, Peter Goodhead or Lewis Chale on the Internet, which wasn't that surprising because their deaths had occurred over ten years ago. But Strathen had said the more he looked the less he found, which puzzled him. 'You'd have thought someone would have put something out there on the anniversary.' But then, neither Meryl nor Stephen Landguard had. They had succeeded in forgetting it, until now. Perhaps it was the same for the relatives of the rest of the crew, only Strathen couldn't find any.

Marvik turned his attention to the archive files but his thoughts kept flicking back to Stephen Landguard. He felt a little uneasy about him. How would he behave the longer his mother was missing? Would he tell the police about their encounter last night? Would Karen tell her husband that he had been at Meryl's house yesterday morning? Perhaps Stephen would come to believe that he was involved with Bradshaw's murder and his mother's disappearance. Maybe, Marvik thought, he'd played the wrong card in letting Stephen return to his wife and child. Perhaps he should have kept Landguard with him. But how could he progress the mission with him hanging around? He couldn't. But the more he thought of Stephen Landguard out there on the loose the more troubled he became. Worrying, though, wouldn't get him any closer to the truth. He concentrated on his search of the newspaper archives.

It didn't take him long to find what he was looking for — Stephen had given him the month and the year. There was almost a full-page article in the local newspaper, *The Argus*. The service had been held on 30 November 2003. Along with the article there was a photograph of Meryl Landguard and beside her a very gaunt man who was named as Duncan Helmslow. They were heading into the church. Helmslow looked bereft. Meryl Landguard looked dignified, smart and solemn. There was a group of people behind them. Marvik easily picked out Ian Bradshaw. Despite the intervening years, he hadn't changed a great deal. He had been bulky back then, with the same jowly features. Marvik couldn't see Stephen Landguard. He wasn't beside his mother. There were several other people, all men. Marvik didn't recognize any of them, but then he hadn't expected to. He took a photograph of the article using his mobile phone and sent it over to Strathen.

Swiftly, Marvik read the article. There was nothing new in it about the actual loss of the *Mary Jo* but there was a quote from the South Eastern Area Fundraising Director of one of the seafarers' charities, Seagoing, a Hugh Stapledon, who expressed his sorrow at the loss and said that by holding such a memorial service it not only honoured those who had died but also helped to raise awareness of the hazards for those working at sea, particularly those in the marine salvage industry like the crew of the *Mary Jo*.

Marvik called up the charity's website and saw that their main office was in Southampton. Strathen was closer to it than he was and could call on Stapledon if he still worked for the charity. He could have moved on by now or be dead. But Marvik quickly discovered from scrolling through the events page on the website that Stapledon was not only still employed by the charity but was a lot closer to where he was than to Strathen's location. He was, in fact, attending a cheque presentation ceremony at the Church of the Good Shepherd, Shoreham Beach, some twenty miles to the west of Newhaven, at eleven a.m. Marvik glanced at his watch. It was ten thirty. He could get the train but a taxi would get him there quicker. He didn't want to risk missing Stapledon.

He logged off, thanked the librarian and headed towards the taxi rank at the station in the blustery April day. He soon discouraged any idle chit-chat from the driver and let his thoughts roam as the taxi sped around the outskirts of Brighton and Hove. There was always the chance that this was a waste of his time and Stapledon hadn't known any of the crew. Maybe he should have tried to reach him by phone, but he was the only person quoted in that newspaper article other than Duncan Helmslow, and he was dead.

By the time the taxi pulled up outside the church, which was almost on the shingle beach of the seaside town and port in West Sussex, and he'd entered the adjoining hall, he was in time to catch the end of Stapledon's 'thank you' speech. Marvik slipped in at the back and earned himself a few smiles. The audience was predominately women in their sixties and seventies — a few were older, but there were some toddlers with their mothers and a handful of men also over seventy. About fifty people in total.

Stapledon's hair had thinned out considerably since the memorial photograph of 2003 and since the picture of him on the charity's website. What was left of it on a high-domed head was grey. He was still lean, though, and tall, but his face more lined and lantern-jawed than in the pictures. He sported dark-rimmed spectacles and a black suit with a maroon tie displaying the charity's logo. Marvik put him in his mid-sixties. He listened as Stapledon talked about the challenges and dangers of working at sea, the isolation and the exhilaration. His voice was strong and confident, his manner assured without being arrogant. It was a short and witty speech, one Marvik thought he must have delivered many times with slight variations, but he managed to make it sound fresh and the audience appreciated it. Applause was given, hands were shaken and photographs taken before cups of tea and coffee and cake were dispensed. The photographer, a woman in her mid-thirties whom Marvik guessed must be from the local newspaper, exchanged a few words with Stapledon. As she left, Marvik took the opportunity to quickly interject.

'I wonder if I could have a word, sir.'

Stapledon eyed Marvik as though trying to recall where he knew him from. Marvik could see two women heading towards them. Quickly, he said, 'I'd like to talk to you about the loss of the *Mary Jo*.'

Stapledon looked taken aback for a moment, then, quickly recovering, said, 'We'll talk outside.' He tossed a smile at the two ladies and said, 'I won't be long.'

Marvik wasn't sure if that was simply a polite way of indicating to him that he wasn't going to give him much time.

There was a wooden seat leaning against the church wall but Stapledon ignored it. Instead, he crossed the road to the shingle beach and Marvik fell into step beside him. Perhaps he needed time to compose himself because recalling the tragedy upset him. Perhaps he didn't want anyone to interrupt them. Or maybe, thought Marvik, Stapledon was rapidly thinking what to tell him and how much.

He stopped a short distance from the rolling waves of the water's edge. The clouds were building to the west, rapidly swallowing up the blue patches of sky that had intermittently appeared earlier in the day and were now casting shadows on the sea that in places made it appear almost black. The wind flipped at Stapledon's lank grey strands of hair. As he buttoned up his suit jacket to stop his tie flapping in the breeze, he addressed Marvik with a curious expression, as if he thought he should know him but his memory was failing him.

'I haven't been asked about the *Mary Jo* for years and now twice in the last fortnight,' he said, perplexed.

Marvik's heart beat a little faster. This news meant he was on Gavin's trail.

'I only wish I could have helped Stephen Landguard find some answers as to why his father's vessel vanished, but I couldn't tell him and I can't tell you either because I don't know. No one does.'

Marvik felt a stab of disappointment but it was only momentary. He knew it couldn't have been Stephen Landguard who had come here because he would have said. So either Stapledon was lying or Gavin had lied about his identity, perhaps in order to get more information from Stapledon. But surely Stapledon would have recognized Stephen Landguard from the memorial service. Maybe Stapledon thought Stephen had changed in the intervening years. Marvik would come to that later. First, he wanted to extract as much as he could from the slender man beside him.

Stapledon said, 'Can I ask why you're interested?' The question was asked casually but Marvik detected a hint of anxiety behind the words and in the pale grey eyes.

Marvik wasn't about to tell him the truth but he gave a very watered-down version of it. 'I'm researching lost ships and the circumstances surrounding the *Mary Jo* intrigues me. I didn't want to bother the family but saw from the press coverage in the local newspaper that you had been at the memorial service and, I believe, helped to arrange it.'

'I did. It was the least I could do, not only in my role as a fundraising director of the charity but because Tim was a former colleague.'

Marvik's interest quickened. He'd come to the right man. 'You worked for Helmsley's?'

'No. Tim and I worked on car carriers before he left to work in the marine salvage industry and before I joined the charity, Seagoing, in 2002.'

'What was he like?'

'Extremely competent and experienced,' came the quick reply that contained an edge of defensiveness, as though Marvik was about to accuse Timothy Landguard of negligence. Briskly, Stapledon continued, 'He'd had years at sea, rising from deck officer to senior navigation officer and then to captain on containers and car carriers before becoming a salvage master. He was a very good seaman, highly professional and respected. Whatever happened to the *Mary Jo*, you can take my word for it that it wouldn't have been an oversight or incompetence on the part of Tim Landguard.'

'Of course. I never suggested it was,' Marvik mollified him. 'I was just curious to gain some background about the proposed salvage operation and learn more about the crew.'

Stapledon took a breath and stared out to sea as though trying to calm himself. The wind was picking up, buffeting against them, determined to push them back. The waves were getting deeper, crashing on to the stones. They had the beach to themselves — even the dog walkers had deserted it. And there was no sign of a boat out at sea.

After a moment, he turned back to face Marvik and seemed to have got his emotions under control. 'Tim had worked with Duncan Helmslow at sea, as had I. Duncan was an engineering officer like me. Martin Elmsley, Duncan's business partner, was a senior deck officer but he preferred the more convivial atmosphere of the cruise liners to the solitary life on car carriers and containers so he didn't work with us for very long. But he and Duncan joined forces again in 1999 when they started up the company, initially supplying workboats for marine-based construction projects along the coast. They soon expanded into vessel salvage and wreck recovery when Tim joined them in 2000.

Then, tragically, Martin was killed in March 2001 while trying to fix a line to a stricken fishing boat to the west of Newhaven. His body was swept out to sea. The death hit Duncan very hard. Martin was the business brains behind the company and the ambitious one. Duncan was always happiest when he was fiddling about with engines or at sea. The loss of the *Mary Jo* and its crew finished that for Duncan who had, by then, been diagnosed with pancreatic cancer. When Almbridge came along with an offer, Duncan jumped at it.'

'And Almbridge was one of their competitors.'

'In one sense, yes; in another, no. Almbridge were far more successful. A much more substantial operation. They took over the contract to salvage the SS *Celeste* and towed her to India, where she was broken up.'

'Why to India?'

'It's a major ship recycling centre and it was thought best not to bring her back to Britain because there was some controversy at the time over ship recycling.'

Which Crowder had mentioned. The toxic American warships due to be dismantled at Hartlepool.

'Is there anyone who worked for Helmsley at that time that I could speak to? I don't want to disturb the family.'

Stapledon paused to reflect. 'You could talk to Ian Bradshaw. He was in charge of tenders and contracts.'

So he hadn't heard the news of Bradshaw's death. It had been covered in the Eastbourne media, which was thirty-two miles to the east, not that far away, but it was in a different county, this being West Sussex and Eastbourne being situated in East Sussex. And Stapledon might live further away in the neighbouring counties of Kent to the east or Hampshire to the west. The news had been on the Internet, but perhaps Stapledon didn't bother with that.

Stapledon looked pointedly at his watch. 'I'm sorry but I have to go. They'll think I'm being rude.' He turned and Marvik fell into step beside him as they made their way back towards the church.

'What do you think happened to the *Mary Jo*?' Marvik asked.

'You've read the marine accident investigation report?'

'Yes.'

'Then you know as much as I do. Whatever it was it happened very quickly without any chance of a distress signal being put out. It must have been a freak wave rather than an explosion because the boat had been surveyed not long before it sailed and it was passed as seaworthy. The crew might have got clear or been knocked overboard but they wouldn't have survived in that sea. Do you have a seafaring background, Mr . . . ? I'm sorry, I didn't catch your name.'

*That's because I didn't give it.*

Stapledon's eyes flicked apprehensively to Marvik's scarred face.

*Perhaps he thinks I was a pirate.* 'I know that Timothy Landguard left a widow, Meryl, and a son, Stephen. Do you know of any relatives of the other crew members?'

'As far as I'm aware there weren't any, but you could ask Stuart Moorcott. He was Helmsley Marine's accountant. A fund was set up to help the relatives of the bereaved, which was administered independently by Moorcott. His offices are based in Newhaven.' Stapledon looked about to say more, perhaps to again ask Marvik's name, but his phone rang. With irritation, he glanced at it. His frown deepened. He didn't answer. 'It's my ex-wife fussing over my son's wedding tomorrow. Anyone would think it was being held in Buckingham Palace instead of The Royal Victoria, Hastings.' He smiled. Marvik returned it but thought Stapledon looked more unsettled than when they had first started the conversation. Perhaps that was due to the phone call and the forthcoming nuptials. The sound of chatter coming from the hall reached them as they crossed to the church.

Marvik said, 'Did you tell Stephen Landguard about Mr Moorcott and the fund?'

'No need. He'd already know about it, his family being one of the beneficiaries.'

'But Stephen did mention it?' pressed Marvik, seeing the small flicker of concern in Stapledon's expression and the beads of perspiration on his forehead.

'Well, yes, we did talk about it but only because, like you, he wondered if the accountant had details of the relatives of the crew who had benefited from the fund. I told him the same as I've told you — that he'd have to check with Moorcott.'

'When did Stephen visit you?'

'As I said — a fortnight ago, Thursday.'

Before he had sent the letter to GCHQ, which he had posted on the Sunday after his visit to Stapledon.

Stapledon made to enter the church but Marvik had one more question to ask.

'I haven't seen any photographs of Timothy Landguard. What was he like?'

'Stocky, dark hair and brown eyes,' Stapledon answered quickly, now seemingly very impatient to get away.

'Is his son like him?'

'No. He's fair like Meryl, or rather light auburn. Now, I must—'

'Of course.' Marvik thanked him for his help, taking his hand and finding the grip dry and strong, but the eyes behind the glasses were very troubled.

Marvik headed back towards the centre of the small town. Had Stapledon really failed to recognize Stephen Landguard? Could he genuinely have believed Stephen to have changed that much in the last eleven years? Stephen was dark-haired, and by no stretch of the imagination, even including hair dye, could he have looked light auburn and fair-skinned when he was nineteen. Maybe Stapledon just wasn't very observant or had forgotten what Stephen had looked like. True, Meryl Landguard was fair. So perhaps it was natural for Stapledon to have assumed when Gavin introduced himself that he really was Stephen. But Marvik wasn't sure that Stapledon was on the level. On the surface he seemed helpful and cooperative but he was disturbed by having to talk about the *Mary Jo* — not, Marvik thought, because the tragedy haunted him or that he'd lost a former colleague in the disaster, but because there was something he knew about it that he'd kept silent about for years. He'd managed to push it to the back of his mind but now two people enquiring about the *Mary Jo* was making him edgy.

Perhaps, Marvik thought, he was just being overly suspicious, but something about Stapledon didn't feel right. And he was no nearer to discovering why Gavin Yardly had been killed or what had happened to the *Mary Jo.* But there was one thing he knew for certain: he was on the right trail because it hadn't been Stephen Landguard who had approached Hugh Stapledon but Gavin Yardly and, considering what Yardly would have done next, Marvik did the same. He caught the train to Newhaven.

# CHAPTER ELEVEN

Another trip to the library gave him Moorcott's office address, which was close to the marina. Marvik hadn't wanted to use his mobile phone to check the address on the Internet in case he could be tracked. He didn't think the killer would have got that far yet but it paid to be cautious. He didn't have any worries about confronting the killer but he would be failing in his mission if that happened now without him discovering the truth behind the loss of the *Mary Jo* and subsequently Bradshaw's and Yardly's deaths. His interest in Stuart Moorcott sharpened when he recognized that the address of his office was the same Strathen had given him for Bradshaw's registered company.

Marvik studied the building in front of him, pictures of which he'd already seen on Moorcott's website, along with photographs of the self-assured, prosperous-looking, sleek accountant. The office's position and design suggested it had started life as a small waterfront warehouse. Once it had probably been surrounded by others; now it was dwarfed by waterside apartments. It had been tastefully and expensively renovated. Behind double glass doors emblazoned with the firm's name, Marvik could see a pretty blonde receptionist, but it was the Aston Martin parked in front of the building that drew his attention, along with the personalized number plate which told him that the owner, Stuart Moorcott, was doing very well indeed. There was no reason why he shouldn't be but Marvik smelt the stench of something and it wasn't the harbour.

He was about to make for the entrance when the doors opened and a square-set man of average height, dark hair flecked with grey, wearing a black suit of immaculate cut, a crisp white shirt and pale yellow tie strode out. He was carrying a computer case. It was Moorcott. An expression of distaste and aloofness crossed the accountant's features as he took in Marvik's casual clothes, muscular frame and scarred face. But there was no surprise in the dark eyes. Was that because Hugh Stapledon had called to warn him that a scarred man might come asking questions? Or had he dismissed Marvik as being of no value to him and therefore of no consequence? Marvik didn't budge from the driver's side of the Aston Martin.

'I'd like to talk to you about the *Mary Jo*, Mr Moorcott.'

'Who? Never heard of her,' Moorcott crisply replied. 'Now, if you'd get out of the way, I have a business appointment.' Moorcott made to zap open the car but Marvik held his ground. If Moorcott had given him an honest and civil response he might have got away with it but his reply caused Marvik's already underlining suspicions to deepen. Now he smelled not just one rat but a whole sewer full of them. He held Moorcott's disdainful and cocky stare until the sleek bastard shifted. Sniffing and with a twitch of a sycophantic smile, Moorcott said, 'Oh, you mean the salvage vessel. That was so long ago I'd forgotten about it. You'll find the details in the marine accident investigation report.'

Marvik sidestepped towards the bonnet of the car as Moorcott zapped it open and put the computer case on the back seat. Marvik said, 'It says nothing in it about the fund you administered on behalf of Meryl Landguard and the other relatives of the crew.'

Moorcott almost banged his head on the top of the door as he straightened up. 'I don't know anything about a fund,' he said, emerging and scowling at Marvik. So maybe Stapledon hadn't forewarned him, because his alarm had been genuine.

'Wrong answer, Mr Moorcott. I *know* you administered it.'

Moorcott eyed him warily. 'I don't see what business it is of yours.' Then he faltered and looked vexed. 'Are you related to one of the crew?'

Marvik didn't reply.

'If you are, I will need proper identification and proof of it.'

'Why? Is there money to pay out?'

Moorcott's nose twitched. 'I'm late. Make an appointment with my secretary.'

'Of course.' Marvik made as if to head for the entrance but, as Moorcott climbed into the driver's seat, Marvik darted around to the passenger side and got in.

'What the hell do you think you're doing?' Moorcott exclaimed, flushing with anger.

'Start the car.'

'I'll do no such thing. Get out now or I'll call the police.'

'Suits me. Or, better still, drive to the police station and then you can make a complaint against me, and in my defence I can tell them all about the *Mary Jo*, its fund and where I think the money is.'

Moorcott's mouth tightened but his eyes at last registered fear.

Marvik continued, 'Or shall we just take a drive and you can tell me how you've spent it. Nice car. Expensive, too.'

'I don't know what you're—'

'Drive,' Marvik sharply commanded. 'Unless you want your staff to wonder what you're doing in the car talking to me.' Marvik jerked his head to where two men were leaving the office. Moorcott quickly started up and pulled away. 'Head for the fort,' Marvik ordered. 'We'll talk there.'

It was only a short distance. A mid-nineteenth-century ruin perched on the hill overlooking the sea. It had been restored and was open to the public, but touring it was the last thing Marvik had in mind. He said nothing as Moorcott drove there, tight-lipped and frowning, probably as he tried to think of a way to extricate himself from this situation. He pulled into the deserted gravel car park, surrounded by bushes and trees, not all in bud. He silenced the engine. Marvik ordered him out of the car.

Moorcott squinted at the rain-spattered windscreen and hesitated.

'Do you really want me to go to the police and the Inland Revenue and tell them my concerns about that fund?'

Moorcott hastily obeyed. But Marvik could see him thinking that he might be able to dart back into the car, start it up and drive away before Marvik could reach him. To counter that, Marvik slid across to the driver's seat, snatching the car keys from the ignition before climbing out.

'Let's take a walk.'

Moorcott looked panic-stricken.

Marvik jerked his head at the footpath that led up through the trees and shrubs to the top of the hill and the fort. The wind and rain ensured they would be alone.

'I don't know what you want but this is ridiculous,' Moorcott said fearfully.

Marvik ignored his protest. 'Walk, or do I have to make you?'

Moorcott walked. Marvik would have approached this differently if Moorcott had been cooperative, but he had seen almost from the moment he'd set eyes on him that threats would be the only thing to make this slime ball tell the truth. What that was Marvik had yet to discover but he suspected fraud. And murder? Maybe.

They came out into a clearing. Marvik told him to stop.

'What are you going to do?' Moorcott asked, his hands twitching. Marvik wondered if the accountant was thinking he could reach for his phone and somehow summon help before Marvik could reach him. He'd be a fool to try.

'*You're* going to tell me exactly what you've done with the memorial fund money.'

'I could have told you that in the car.'

'Much better to get it out in the open with no one listening or around to see us,' Marvik smirked.

Moorcott gulped. He wasn't stupid but it had taken the implied threat to make him realize that he was alone and there was no one to witness any harm that the scarred stranger might do to him.

'Whose idea was it to set up the fund?'

'Ian Bradshaw's,' Moorcott hastily replied. 'And Duncan Helmslow was keen to go along with it. Meryl too.'

'And the other relatives of the crew: Warrendale, Chale and Goodhead? Were they keen?'

Moorcott's mouth twitched nervously. 'We couldn't trace them.'

'How hard did you try?'

'*I* didn't. That was Bradshaw's job. He recruited them.'

*Did he indeed.* His job description seemed pretty expansive — contracts, tenders, accounts and now recruitment. 'How?' asked Marvik.

'I don't understand.'

'How did he recruit them?'

'I don't know. I guess he must have advertised somewhere.' Moorcott wiped the rain from his face. 'I never asked him and he didn't say,' he quickly added as Marvik watched him closely.

'He must have held records giving the name of the next of kin or a contact number in case of emergency.'

'I suppose so.' Moorcott looked miserable. 'I took him at his word when he said there was no one he could find related to them.'

'I bet you did. So how much did the three, or was it four of you including Duncan Helmslow, split between you?'

Moorcott said nothing. Marvik stepped forward menacingly.

'Not Duncan, he was dead by then,' Moorcott gabbled, then mumbled. 'Three hundred thousand pounds.'

Marvik was taken aback. He'd expected maybe fifty grand at the most. 'How come it was that much?'

'The public always like to donate. There were also a few large corporate donations from ship owners and others in the industry.' Moorcott ran a hand over his hair, which was now as wet as his suit.

'And did you tell them how the money had been distributed? No, I bet you didn't, and no one asked until now. So you split it three ways, which made a very tidy sum for each of you.' And was that why Meryl Landguard had been so twitchy when Gavin had come calling? She believed he'd discover the scam. Was that what her son had overheard when she'd called Bradshaw, when she'd said that he knows about the *Mary Jo*? Marvik could be looking at Bradshaw's killer — Gavin's too — and Meryl Landguard's abductor, but he could swear that Moorcott didn't have it in him except he had a very expensive lifestyle to protect.

Moorcott mistook Marvik's silence. 'Look, if you're related to one of the crew we can do a deal.'

Marvik thrust his hand on Moorcott's chest and pushed him back with such force that he crashed against the trunk of a tree. Marvik thrust his face close to the trembling accountant. 'So what other scams were the three of you operating?'

'We weren't.'

'Another wrong answer.' Marvik grabbed him by his expensive suit and balled his fist.

'All right, I'll tell you. Don't hurt me, please,' Moorcott pleaded, putting his hands up.

Marvik could see that Moorcott wasn't faking his fear. He didn't believe he had killed but he could have hired a killer. If so, Marvik didn't hold out much hope for Moorcott living a long and healthy life. With disgust, he released his hold.

Moorcott couldn't talk quickly enough. 'Ian Bradshaw was in charge of invoicing. In fact, he had a say in nearly all aspects of the running of Helmsley's. Duncan was ill and he didn't have a business brain. He was a plodder, a hands-on man. He'd have been happy enough to provide tugs and workboats around the harbour but Martin Elmsley, his business partner, was keen to expand into marine salvage, and when Tim joined them in September 2000, they did. Six months later, Martin was dead. It hit Duncan hard.'

'And he was ripe for the plucking by scumbags like you and Bradshaw. You were Helmsley's accountant — you prepared the company accounts and carried out the audit. You assisted Bradshaw in fraud. He created false invoices and creamed off money from contracts, paying you a percentage.'

Moorcott was looking very bedraggled and dispirited. Perhaps he could see his precious Aston Martin being driven into the sunset. 'It wasn't just us. Meryl also took advantage of the situation.'

'Oh, and that makes it OK,' Marvik hissed scornfully.

Moorcott winced. 'She was having an affair with Bradshaw, had been for some time. She and Bradshaw were in it together. She's clever, knows her way round figures. She was accounts manager for Antara Yacht Brokerage.'

'The company Bradshaw bought,' Marvik said, recalling what Stephen Landguard and Strathen had told him.

Moorcott nodded miserably.

Marvik continued. 'She manipulated Antara's accounts and extracted money from the company so that, when it was on the verge of collapse, Bradshaw stepped in and bought it for a knockdown price.'

Moorcott's eyes flicked down to his muddy, sodden shoes.

'And I bet your firm also handled the accounts for Antara,' Marvik sneered. 'And you, Bradshaw and Meryl Landguard repeated the process at Helmsley, running it down after taking what you could from a dying man before selling it to Almbridge on the cheap.'

His head came up. 'Alec Royden paid a fair price for it.'

Marvik looked doubtful. 'In whose eyes?' he scoffed. 'He probably paid bugger all. Was he in on your nice little scam?'

Moorcott's expression was simultaneously sly and frightened. 'I prepared the accounts for the sale to Almbridge and their accountants went over the books.'

'Which, of course, were all in order,' Marvik sneered.

In a defensive tone, Moorcott said, 'Duncan was only too relieved to get the business off his hands for a nominal fee before—'

'He died, yes, three months later, and who inherited his estate?'

'There wasn't much.'

'Who got it?' Marvik repeated sharply.

Moorcott started. 'There were a couple of bequests to the coastguard and the Royal National Lifeboat Institution. Duncan was widowed years ago — no kids. The house was sold. The majority of the estate was split between Meryl Landguard and the charity, Seagoing.'

Hugh Stapledon's charity. And, once again, Meryl had benefited. Had she made sure that Duncan named her in his will? Had she used her charm on him? If he could believe Moorcott, and he did, then Meryl Landguard was a scheming woman and a fraudster, in league with Bradshaw. Marvik felt sorry for Stephen Landguard because Marvik was convinced Stephen didn't know the depths of his mother's criminality. He knew about the affair, though, and it wasn't surprising that he had been so emotionally drained knowing that both his mother and his wife had slept with a man he despised. And Marvik was betting that the fraud he was hearing about wasn't the only one. Bradshaw had recruited that crew. Had he made sure they were insured? Timothy Landguard would have been, and the *Mary Jo.*

'Whose idea was it to sabotage the *Mary Jo* and murder that crew?'

'Murder! It was an accident.'

'But Meryl Landguard collected the insurance on her husband's life.'

'I suppose she must have done but I don't know the terms of the policy.'

'And the insurance on the *Mary Jo* went into the company, which the three of you then helped yourselves to.' Marvik didn't need Moorcott to reply — he saw the answer in his shifting eye contact.

'Were the crew insured? Was Bradshaw named as the beneficiary?' Moorcott shook his head.

'Who got the crew's wages?'

Moorcott looked blankly at him.

'Come on, you know what I'm talking about, but let me explain,' Marvik said menacingly. 'All the crew were working for Helmsley, and in the case of a workplace death they'd have been entitled to their salary up until the day they were declared dead. So who got their paycheques?'

'I don't know.'

Marvik stepped forward.

'They were casual staff, taken on for that one job on a pay-on completion basis.'

'Did Duncan Helmslow know that?'

'I guess so. There was nothing unusual about taking on crew for a specific job.'

Bradshaw had chosen his casual staff very carefully. The whole set-up was rife with corruption. Had the crew been killed for money?

'So the three of you were doing very nicely, thank you, until Gavin Yardly came along and started asking questions. He discovered the fraud. You, Bradshaw and Meryl Landguard decided to kill him but, unbeknown to Bradshaw, you were having an affair with Meryl and the two of you decided to kill Bradshaw and frame Gavin Yardly for Bradshaw's murder.' Moorcott was studying him in horrified bewilderment. 'Did you then decide that Meryl had too much over you so she also had to die?'

'I haven't killed anyone,' Moorcott protested, rubbing a shaking hand over his sodden face.

'If you haven't then I'd start to get very worried, because it means there is a killer out there and you could be next on the list.'

Moorcott's eyes widened, petrified as it dawned on him that Marvik could be the killer.

'I swear to you, I know nothing about what else was going on at Helmsley or about the disappearance of the *Mary Jo*,' he gabbled. 'I don't know who killed Ian or that man Gavin Yardly and I haven't seen Meryl for weeks.'

'But she phoned you to warn you about Gavin Yardly?'

Moorcott looked about to deny it but changed his mind.

'She called me the Saturday before last.'

The day after Stephen Landguard said he'd seen Gavin Yardly talking to his mother and after her meeting with Bradshaw that night on his boat.

'And?'

'She said that someone had come asking her about the *Mary Jo* and to keep quiet about the fund. She said that Ian had agreed to get rid of Yardly. By that I thought she meant evict him and sack him because Yardly was working for Ian and renting one of his flats. I had no idea they intended to kill him.'

'So who killed Bradshaw?'

'Not me. Maybe Meryl did. You said she's been abducted but perhaps she's gone on the run.'

Without her clothes or her belongings? It was possible and, even if her passport was in the safe, she might have another one with a false identity. But there was a flaw in that theory.

'Why would she leave you behind to blab to the first person who comes along?'

'Maybe she got scared and isn't thinking right.'

'Or perhaps she had nothing to do with killing Bradshaw and Bradshaw didn't kill Yardly, and if you're as innocent of that as you claim then I'd be very careful crossing the road and driving your expensive car. Accidents do happen.'

Moorcott went so pale that even his lips went white.

'Did Gavin Yardly come to see you?'

'No. I swear he didn't. No one's been to see me about the *Mary Jo* except you.'

And if Gavin hadn't then that meant he hadn't followed the lead about the fund. Did it mean he was unaware of it or had he thought it irrelevant? Marvik swiftly recalled his conversation with Stapledon. He'd said that the man who had come to see him, posing as Landguard, hadn't been interested in the fund. It was the crew that Yardly had been primarily interested in.

'You handle the financial accounts of Meryl Landguard and of Bradshaw's company.'

Moorcott nodded.

'Let's go and get a copy of them.'

'I can't—'

Marvik balled his fist.

'OK.'

'And while you're at it, I want a list of all the donors to that memorial fund.'

Marvik wasn't sure what the accounts would tell him because Moorcott was bound to have hidden the extent of his and his clients' fraud, but a forensic accountant would have fun picking through them and Marvik would be happy to hand them over to Crowder. Marvik didn't think it was the result Crowder was looking for — not unless the fraud went deeper and to the top of the political tree or led them to someone in a position of power and social influence, someone who had benefited either financially, politically or internationally or all three from the disappearance of the *Mary Jo* and its crew. Did Moorcott know who that person was? Marvik wondered as they headed back to his office. If so, then he would end up the same way as Bradshaw and Gavin Yardly and probably Meryl Landguard.

Had Stephen Landguard heard from his mother? Stephen hadn't called him to say he had but then maybe he wouldn't. Landguard probably believed he was mixed up in the murders. What did Karen Landguard think of her mother-in-law's vanishing act? Had Stephen confronted his wife over her affair with Bradshaw? He recalled Karen Landguard saying that the accountant had told her to continue trading and that accountant was sitting next to him in the driving seat. Marvik wondered if Moorcott was also a director of Bradshaw's company as well as accountant to it. Strathen hadn't said, so he probably wasn't. The accounts might not tell him much about Bradshaw, his contacts and his past, but Karen might be able to, and she might also be able to tell him more about Gavin Yardly. Marvik decided that, after getting the accounts and donor list from Moorcott, he'd return to Eastbourne and ask her.

## CHAPTER TWELVE

The rain had stopped but the sky was still grey and turbulent with the threat of more to come when Marvik pushed open the door of Medlowes in Eastbourne.

Moorcott had given Marvik what he had asked for on a USB stick. His bedraggled appearance and that of his companion had drawn shocked expressions from the staff. Marvik had expected one of them to call the police, but Moorcott had given implicit instructions to his manager that he was not to be disturbed and had closed the door and the blinds to his office while he backed up the information. Marvik had watched him carefully but he couldn't be certain that Moorcott wasn't skipping vital information. A forensic accountant would discover if he had.

He'd glanced at the photographs on the wall while he had waited and one in particular had caught his attention. It was a large, expensive motor cruiser, although not of the same make as either Colbourne's or Marwell's. Moorcott told him he kept it in Newhaven Marina. Maybe Moorcott would take off on it, afraid he was going to be the next target of the killer or to escape being investigated for fraud.

Karen Landguard looked up from her desk as Marvik entered. Her eyes held their usual hostility but there was also anxiety and she looked even more tired than on the previous occasion he'd seen her, which wasn't surprising given that her life was in turmoil. He wondered if Stephen had finally confronted her last night on his late return home.

'I've got nothing to say to you,' she snapped, darting a nervous glance at Danny.

'How's Stephen?'

'Are you threatening me?'

'With what? I just asked how your husband was, especially given the fact his mother seems to have vanished.'

Her startled reaction told him that Stephen had omitted to mention being with him last night. 'What do you know about that?' she asked suspiciously.

'I know a great deal. For example, Meryl Landguard had an affair with Ian Bradshaw some years ago and was probably still having an on-off relationship with him while you were also—'

'We can't talk here. Danny, I'll be five minutes.' She leapt up and stormed out, expecting Marvik to follow. He did. Outside, she rounded on him. 'I don't know what you want but can't you leave me alone?'

'I will after we've had a chat.'

Her lips tightened and her eyes narrowed. Then she spun round and headed towards the promenade, saying, 'OK, let's get this over with as quickly as possible. What do you want to know?'

'How long have you worked for Ian Bradshaw?'

'Why should I tell you that?'

Wearily, Marvik said, 'Karen, we can get this over much quicker if you just answer me. I'm not trying to cause you trouble; in fact, I'm trying to make sure both you and Stephen stay out of it. Your mother-in-law is missing. Ian Bradshaw and Gavin Yardly are dead. I'm trying to discover why they were killed in order to prevent any more deaths.'

'Gavin Yardly committed suicide after killing Ian,' she snapped, her long legs striding out.

'Did he?' Marvik stared at her quizzically.

'That's what the media are saying.'

'And you believe everything they say!'

'The police wouldn't have said it if they didn't believe it. Why are *you* so interested? Just who are you?' she cried, tossing him an exasperated glance.

He didn't answer. She gave an irritable sigh and, pointing to a bench on the promenade, said, 'We'll talk over there.' Only when seated with her jacket pulled around her did she answer his question. 'I started working for Ian last July. Charlie, my son, was four months old. I was keen to get back to work. I thought I'd enjoy being a stay-at-home-mum but I was bored rigid and lonely. Stephen works long hours. He's a graphic designer for a marketing agency in London.'

She looked out to sea. Marvik followed her gaze. There were only the seagulls on the shore and a few people hurrying along the promenade as though to get ahead of the rain, which he could see was already falling on the Downs to their right back towards Newhaven from where he had come.

She continued, 'I asked Meryl if she would mind looking after Charlie if I found myself a job. She said she'd do so but only one day a week, Thursdays, and I'd have to make arrangements for the other days. My parents live too far away to look after Charlie and they both work full-time so that was out of the question, but I found a good nursery that would take him and I began to look around for a job. I'd worked for an estate agent before I had Charlie but they'd closed down. Then I thought about Medlowes. I knew they managed the letting of Meryl's properties. She owns five terraced houses in Eastbourne and three in Newhaven. I used her name to approach Ian and he snapped me up. He soon made me up to manager. I'm bloody good at my job,' she declared defensively, as though he was about to accuse her of sleeping her way into the position. He didn't care if she had. 'Charlie goes to the nursery Tuesdays, Wednesdays and Fridays and Stephen looks after him on Saturdays. I have Sunday and Monday off.' She pushed her fair hair off her face.

'And the affair? When did that start?'

'Why should I tell you that? It has nothing to do with Ian's death.'

He shrugged as though to say *please yourself.* Besides, she was right. He wasn't interested in the affair itself, although he did have some questions to ask her regarding it, but he'd come to that later.

'Did you break the news to Meryl that Ian was dead?'

She took a breath. 'Yes. I phoned her on Tuesday after the police had been to see me. I first heard about it on the radio on Tuesday morning as I was coming to work. I didn't dream it would be Ian. I didn't even think it would be in one of our properties. The news just said that a man had been found dead in a property in Harold Road. When I got to work the police were waiting for me. It was terrible. I couldn't believe it. Still can't in a way. It just seems so incredible.'

Marvik left a short pause. 'How did Meryl take the news?'

'She went silent. I thought we'd been cut off. Then she asked me how and where he'd died. I told her what the police had told me — that Ian had been found in the flat of a tenant, Helen Shannon, but they hadn't said how he had died. The police asked me about Helen Shannon and so did Meryl, but I couldn't tell either of them anything about her except that she was a Goth and had weird purple hair. The police also asked me about Gavin Yardly, another tenant who worked with Helen Shannon for Ian's boat-cleaning company. They asked me if I knew where they were and if I had any contact details for them. I said I had no idea where either of them were but I gave them the mobile telephone numbers we had on record and said that was all we had.'

The police must have tried Helen after she had rung him and after she had switched off her mobile phone, which had remained disabled ever since. They'd be getting no answer, just as the killer had disabled and ditched Gavin's phone.

'What did Meryl say after that?'

'Nothing. She rang off, but then she can be abrupt to the point of rudeness. You saw me at her house yesterday — you could see what she was like. I didn't have time to talk to her because I was late for work and Charlie had kept me up half the night. When I collected him she asked me if the police had spoken to me again about Ian. They hadn't but I said that I'd heard that Gavin Yardly's body had been found at the bottom of the cliffs not far from where she lived, close to the Birling Gap. She said she already knew that. She was very short with me but then that's not unusual. She seemed keen to get rid of me as quickly as possible, which suited me fine. Then, last night, Stephen said he found the house empty and the door open. He told me he'd reported it to the police and given them details of her car and a description of her but that they hadn't seemed very interested. They said it was too early to worry and that she'd probably gone to stay with friends, which is what I told him. The door probably blew open because she didn't close it properly. She wouldn't give a toss about Stephen being worried. She wouldn't have expected him to call round anyway. I don't know why he did. He only visits her out of duty. That's not his fault but hers. She's made it that way.'

'You don't like her, do you?'

'No, I don't,' she vehemently declared. 'And she doesn't like me either. That's no skin off my nose. The less I have to do with her the better. And that's not jealousy talking. I broke off my affair with Ian in December. OK, so I was an idiot. I was flattered by his attention. I felt frumpy and neglected. I needed to know if I was still . . . well, you know.' She sniffed and looked down at her high-heeled shoes.

Marvik thought he did.

'I wouldn't even bother with her if it wasn't for Charlie. She doesn't give a shit about Stephen. She never misses an opportunity to tell him how weak and pathetic he is. I've told him to tell her to go to hell but he won't. I've lost count of the times we've argued about her.'

And Stephen discovering his wife had been having an affair with the same man his mother had been shagging while his father was alive wouldn't have done Stephen's self-esteem much good either.

'Has she helped you financially?'

Karen shifted. 'Well, yes. She gave us the deposit to buy the house, but that was only fair,' she added, again defensively. 'Part of it was Stephen's money anyway from the memorial fund set up after his father died. We've had nothing more from her since.'

'What about the life insurance money?'

'I don't know anything about that. She said she'd put Stephen through university and as far as she was concerned he now had to make his own future. She had to look after hers. I said what about your grandson's future? She told me that was down to me and Stephen.'

Marvik left a short pause as he swiftly considered this. Perhaps Meryl was just trying to make them forge their own way in life rather than being mean and, when the time came, as Charlie grew older, she would have helped out. But she was under no obligation to do so and if Karen could be believed then Meryl wasn't close to her son or his family.

'What did the police ask you about Gavin Yardly?' he asked.

'Just the usual. How long had he been living in the flat? What was he like? Who gave him his references?'

'And you told them what?'

'He took the flat eight weeks ago, and his references from his bank and from two former employers were excellent.'

'You checked them?'

'Well, no. They seemed in order.' As though justifying her decision, she briskly added, 'He paid the deposit in cash. He was quietly spoken, polite and clean, which is more than some of our tenants are — something of a rarity when letting certain properties. And he was very keen to take the flat even though I thought it would be too big for him. We had others on our books that I thought would suit him better but he was very insistent on having something in Harold Road.'

Marvik's ears pricked up at that. 'He specifically asked for that road?'

'Yes.'

'And is that the only property you manage for Ian Bradshaw in that road?'

'Yes.'

Marvik felt sure this piece of information was significant. But why would Gavin specify that road? Because it was convenient? For what, though? It wasn't close to the marina where he had worked. Was Ian Bradshaw the reason? He owned other properties in the town though so why hadn't Gavin specified any one of those?

'Did you tell the police this?'

'No, because I've only just remembered it and it's not important.'

Marvik watched her brush her hair off her face as she looked out to sea. 'Have any other tenants insisted on being in that property or that road?'

'No.'

'Did you let any of the other flats in that building shortly before or after Gavin took it?' Marvik asked, wondering if Gavin's killer had quickly installed himself there.

'Only the one to that woman, Helen Shannon. I suppose she and Gavin Yardly could have known one another beforehand. She never said and her references seemed in order.'

'What did the police ask you about Ian?'

'When had I seen or heard from him. I told them that I spoke to Ian on Monday when he came into the office but it was only briefly. I had to go out to meet a prospective tenant at a property.'

'Was it usual for him to come into the office?'

'He'd visit occasionally.'

'What did he want on Monday?'

'I don't know but he returned later that afternoon and went into the safe. I asked if he wanted the keys to any of the properties but he said he was just checking something.'

Marvik quickly considered this. 'Are any of the keys missing?'

'No.'

'Were they after Ian's death?'

'No.'

And none of Bradshaw's keys on the key ring Marvik had taken from the body had been to Helen's flat. Karen Landguard's information meant that Bradshaw could have collected a set of keys for both Helen and Gavin's flats on Monday morning, had them copied, given a set to his killer and then returned the keys to his office in the afternoon, when Karen had seen him. He could also have given a duplicate key to his boat to the killer because perhaps the plan had been to lure Gavin there or to kill Bradshaw after Helen had left. The killer had returned to Bradshaw's boat after Marvik had searched it to make sure nothing incriminating had been left on board and had carelessly omitted to relock it. It didn't sound like the act of this killer, who surely wouldn't have been so sloppy, but perhaps he had an operative working for him who had been careless or had been disturbed and distracted while on board so that, when Stephen Landguard showed up, the cabin door was unlocked.

Karen Landguard looked pointedly at her watch. 'There's nothing more I can tell you. I must get back.' She rose.

They turned back towards the office. Marvik thought it was time to ask her questions regarding her affair. 'Did Ian mention to you at any time any business associates or friends?'

'No.'

'Did you see him with anyone at his apartment?'

'I never went there.' She set her lips firmly and glared at him, but a faint flush flooded her face.

'On the boat, then?'

'No.'

'It was always just the two of you on the boat?' She nodded.

'Did he ever talk about his days at sea or any of the men or women he worked with?'

'Only that it bored him to death being stuck out on the ocean for days on end. He didn't mind it so much when he transferred to the cruise liners; he said it was livelier.'

And more women to pick and choose from, Marvik thought, both passengers and crew.

She added, 'Ian was very lively, good fun. He was also a very good salesman, which is why we have so many landlords on our books and why his other businesses, the yacht brokerage and the boat-cleaning company are doing so well. Ian knows . . . knew . . .' she corrected herself, '. . . a lot of people and he could spin a yarn.'

Which he had to her and which she'd fallen for. Judging by her slightly sour expression he'd say she was recalling their affair with self-disgust.

'Have you heard of a man called Hugh Stapledon?' He could see she hadn't by her blank look. She shook her head. 'Was Ian flash with his money?' he asked.

'Not really. He had plenty. He liked to gamble.' Marvik recalled seeing the card in his wallet.

'And he liked going out on his boat, to Jersey, France and along the coast. He'd go up to London quite often but I don't know why.'

'And his property portfolio is quite large?'

'Yes. He owns several properties in Eastbourne and along the coast. He used to buy up large houses that needed renovating, get in a team of builders, do them up as cheaply and as quickly as possible and then let them.'

He hadn't bothered doing much renovation on the Harold Road property, thought Marvik, recalling its shabby state. And he was betting the builders had probably been Polish or of Eastern European extraction and therefore employed on the cheap. With Moorcott as Bradshaw's accountant, Marvik was beginning to wonder if property investment was another of their fraudulent schemes.

'Did Gavin Yardly ask you about Ian Bradshaw or your late father-in-law?'

She looked bemused at the question. 'No. Why should he?'

'Did Ian ask you about Gavin or did your mother-in-law mention him before Ian was killed?'

She halted outside the office, looking perplexed. 'No.' Again, she dashed a glance at her watch and at Danny inside the office on the phone.

Marvik had a couple more questions for her yet. 'Has Stephen talked about his father either in the past or last night?'

'No. Like I said to you before, the *Mary Jo*, and Stephen's father, have always been no-go areas and I've no idea why. Now, I must—'

'What's Stephen's doing today?'

'Looking after Charlie. He couldn't go into work. He's too uptight about Meryl missing. Why? You're not going to talk to him, are you?' Her face went rigid with alarm.

'No.' *Not yet,* he added silently.

Marvik let her go and made for Harold Road, curious as to why Gavin had specified he wanted a flat there. He knew the reason that Gavin had been keen to rent a property belonging to Bradshaw and had managed to get a job with him was because Bradshaw was integral to the mystery surrounding the *Mary Jo*, but why Harold Road specifically?

He took his time walking the length of the shabby street, studying the properties, not really sure what it would achieve. He saw nothing different from his first visit when he had walked along the length of the street with Helen in the early hours of Tuesday morning. There were some terraced houses interspersed with large decaying Edwardian houses, some shut-up shops with 'to let' boards in the grimy windows and junk mail gathering behind the filthy doors, a launderette, a cycle shop, a Chinese takeaway and the modern convenience store with a small car park and the café on the corner of the road.

The crime-scene police tape had gone, along with the police officers. Marvik glanced up at the window of Helen's flat. The curtains were drawn. It would probably still be sealed, as would Gavin's flat on the ground floor, the curtains of which were also drawn across the window. Something nagged at him as he stood there. He couldn't put his finger on it, though.

It was clear from what Karen had told him that Bradshaw had been detailed to get a set of keys for the killer and to make sure that Helen was lured to his boat. She wasn't Bradshaw's usual type so he was under orders to get her out of the way for a short time. Had Meryl been giving the orders? Had Bradshaw and Meryl hatched the plan with the third person who had made plans of his own, plans that involved Bradshaw's death and Gavin as the fall guy for it?

Bradshaw had embellished his part in the scheme by actually making a pass at Helen, probably thinking he might as well satisfy his sexual urges while he was at it and not expecting her to storm off, so his plans had to be changed. He called in and told the killer what had happened. The killer, who all along had intended Bradshaw to be the victim, simply brought his plans forward. Bradshaw had probably been instructed to take Helen back to her flat. And, if he had, Marvik would have read the news that Helen, too, had been found beside Bradshaw with her throat cut. He stiffened at the thought.

Bradshaw had let himself into the house with his own set of keys after Helen had taken off. The killer, who could have been waiting in Gavin's flat, followed him upstairs, shut the door behind him and slit Bradshaw's throat. He planted the bloodstained clothes in Gavin's flat, then cleared out. The motive for Gavin's suicide was intact. Only one other person aside from the killer knew it was phoney and that was Meryl Landguard. So she, too, had to be dealt with. But who had she and Bradshaw been in league with? Moorcott? Maybe. Marvik made his way to the railway station and caught a train back to Newhaven and his boat.

# CHAPTER THIRTEEN

He marked out Moorcott's boat in the marina, not far from the visitors' pontoon where his own boat was still the sole occupant. Studying it, he wondered if Gavin Yardly had been held prisoner on it before Moorcott had taken the body by boat to the shore under Bailey's Hill. Moorcott would have had a lot to lose if Gavin's findings had come out. But again, Marvik didn't think Moorcott had the stomach for killing. Meryl Landguard might have, though, and could easily have lured Gavin here with promises of telling him more about the *Mary Jo* and then drugged his drink. Did Crowder have the results of the autopsy? Marvik was guessing a drug overdose. But he didn't think Meryl could have slit Bradshaw's throat and neither could Moorcott. That didn't mean he wasn't involved, though. Perhaps there had been four of them in the secret behind the *Mary Jo*'s disappearance and now only two of them were left, Moorcott and this other unknown person — a killer.

The royal-blue canvas cover was stretched over the cockpit. Marvik unzipped it and climbed on board. Wherever Meryl Landguard was, Marvik didn't think she lay dead inside but he'd make sure anyway. He'd also see if there was any evidence to suggest that Gavin Yardly had been here.

There was no alarm on the boat. At the helm he noted the standard electronic equipment: plotter, radar and so forth. The deck was clean and the cream vinyl upholstery spotless. The door leading down to the main cabin and berths was locked but that didn't pose a problem. Taking a key ring from the pocket of his jacket, he selected a slim metal device and inserted it between the doorjamb and the lock and, without much exertion, clicked it open. Descending, he noted that the cabin was also well kept.

Swiftly, he searched the cabins and found only what he expected to find: some clothes and toiletries, all male, an empty bottle of wine, a half-full bottle of gin and the basic supplies of coffee, tea and sugar. That was it. There was no body on this boat, no blood and it didn't appear as though Gavin had been held here. There were no auburn hairs that Marvik could find, but then he wasn't a crime-scene expert. The boat could have been thoroughly cleaned, which made him think of Helen. He wondered how Strathen was getting on with working so closely with her. And whether Helen was getting restless or increasingly disturbed about being wanted by the police.

Climbing off and zipping up the canvas cover, Marvik knew that Moorcott would see the lock had been forced and, equally, he knew that Moorcott wouldn't report it to the police or the marina staff and so draw attention to himself. Whether he would tell someone he was in league with, Marvik didn't know, and he wasn't worried if he did, or if he told the killer about his visit to him that afternoon. If the killer came looking for him, fine, but he needed more. He wasn't convinced the *Mary Jo* had been sabotaged for financial fraud, a thought he was keen to share with Strathen. He sent Strathen two photographs of Moorcott's boat. Strathen sent him a text to say he'd call him in five minutes.

Marvik swiftly checked over his own boat. Everything was exactly where he had left it. No one had boarded it. And no one had planted anything under it, according to the sonar equipment Strathen had given him. Marvik wasn't expecting

Bradshaw's killer to have done so but there was still the person who had murdered Sarah who, according to Crowder, was keen to make sure he didn't delve too deeply into his parents' deaths. If Crowder was so convinced that it wasn't an accident then Marvik again wondered why he didn't treat it as a mission and ask him to investigate it.

Marvik put that aside and waited for Strathen's call. He guessed Shaun wanted to be away from Helen in order to talk to him more freely. He didn't have long to wait. Strathen confirmed he was in the hall by the door that led to the basement and the gym. Strathen said he'd told Helen he needed to take some time out and exercise. He wasn't sure Helen believed him. From Marvik's knowledge of Strathen's house, he knew he'd have a good view of the front door and the door to his apartment. He would be able to see anyone entering or Helen leaving if she decided to take off. Strathen also had alerts on his apartment windows and front door which sounded on his mobile phone and computers the moment someone entered, as well as surveillance devices fitted on the entrance gates, the main door and around vulnerable points in the grounds. Strathen's need for secrecy for his call was to protect Helen, not because he didn't trust her.

Marvik swiftly told Strathen about his interviews with Stapledon and Moorcott. Strathen agreed that fraud alone, although a powerful enough motive for murder, especially if vast sums of money were involved and there was a reputation to protect, might not be enough for Crowder's unit to become involved but added, 'Not unless the National Intelligence Marine Squad is working in conjunction with the National Intelligence Fraud Bureau, which is possible. But perhaps there was even more money at stake than that creamed off through false insurance policies and false accounting, not to mention the theft of the memorial fund.'

'Such as?'

'Drugs, arms, stolen art, artefacts, diamond smuggling . . . take your pick. The *Mary Jo* could have been involved in smuggling and Helmsley's operation, courtesy of Ian

Bradshaw, was also being used as a front for cleaning dirty money. Bradshaw was in charge of tenders and contracts. What's the betting that half or even more of those contracts Helmsley won were phoney and the money paid to Helmsley came from companies that either didn't exist or were shell companies, set up with a name, a registered address and bugger all else using money gained through smuggling. It's handed over to Bradshaw and he filters it through Helmsley.'

'With Moorcott as the accountant,' Marvik added. And both he and Strathen knew what that meant: Moorcott was living on borrowed time.

Strathen said, 'Moorcott told you that Bradshaw was also involved in recruitment at Helmsley's. The fact that the crew were specially selected because they had no dependents or living relatives, and they have no visible employment record that I can find, throws up two possibilities. One, they were using false identities and were crooks detailed to meet the dealers and bring back the haul or offload it at a pre-arranged meet; or two, they were working undercover for one of the intelligence or crime agencies in order to expose whoever was behind the smuggling. And because it was a seagoing mission needing specialist expertise, it means they could have been in the same outfit as we once were, Art, the Royal Marines, Special Boat Services.'

Marvik rapidly caught on. 'They were selected because of their lack of relatives.' Just as he had been for some potentially deadly missions. And that could explain why Gavin had written to GCHQ, because he'd discovered or suspected the crew had been working on behalf of the intelligence agencies. 'They were given fake IDs, only there was a leak and the crew — Warrendale, Goodhead and Chale, along with Timothy Landguard — were taken out. Landguard must have been involved in the smuggling.'

Strathen took it up. 'Perhaps his wife persuaded him, or perhaps he was the brains behind it. He set it up after meeting a supplier abroad and got himself a job with his old pal Duncan Helmslow so that he could use marine salvage trips as an excuse to pick up the consignments. We don't know when Bradshaw started working there but I wouldn't mind betting it was shortly after Landguard joined the company, unless Bradshaw set it up and enlisted Landguard.'

'I could ask Stephen if he knows when Bradshaw started there.' Marvik climbed on deck and scoured the marina. All was quiet.

Strathen said, 'The salvage of the SS *Celeste* was a genuine contract but it's possible it was used to make sure that the *Mary Jo* was detailed to rendezvous at sea with a narco-submarine, or rather a narco-torpedo given this was 2003, and we both know that narco-submarines have been perfected since then.'

Marvik did. Both he and Strathen had come across them in the course of their service. They were submersibles carrying narcotics, hence the name. They were difficult to detect by radar, sonar and infrared systems, and used by Colombian drug gangs to export cocaine from Colombia to Mexico, which was then transported overland to the States. Early versions of narco-submarines were towed out of port by a fishing vessel and then released. They contained a ballast tank to keep below the water while being towed. If spotted by a patrol vessel the narco-submarine would be released, and while submerged was designed to automatically release a buoy equipped with a location transmitter system so that it could be retrieved later by another boat. There was always the chance that the authorities would pick up the transmitter but perhaps the one the *Mary Jo* was destined to retrieve didn't have one.

Strathen continued, 'The *Mary Jo*'s mission was to pick up the drugs from the narco-torpedo, not to bring them back to Britain but to offload them somewhere off Newfoundland before heading for the SS *Celeste*. But either the *Mary Jo* never reached its rendezvous with the fishing vessel towing the narco-torpedo or it did and something went wrong after it collected the consignment. Or the crew of the fishing boat towing the narco-torpedo suspected something was wrong, or received information the operation had been infiltrated. They killed the *Mary Jo* crew, dumped their bodies at sea and let the vessel drift.'

'It would explain both Crowder's involvement and Gavin's letter to GCHQ,' Marvik said. 'Hugh Stapledon believes Gavin was Stephen, which I find hard to stomach. Stapledon hadn't heard that Bradshaw's dead and I didn't enlighten him. He said he hadn't known any of the *Mary Jo*'s crew except Timothy Landguard. Stapledon, Duncan Helmslow, Martin Elmsley, his business partner, and Timothy Landguard all worked together on car carriers. Moorcott told me that Stapledon's charity was a benefactor in Duncan Helmslow's will. I'd like to know if the charity got all the money or if Stapledon creamed some off. Maybe he's our fourth man.'

'I can get on to the probate office and find out how much was left. And the charity's accounts should be transparent because they have to declare where their money comes from and how much, but if Stapledon was manipulating the figures then it might be hard to find, and it means delving back some years, which could take time.'

And they both knew that was one thing they didn't have.

Marvik said, 'I've got copies of the accounts for Bradshaw's company and for Meryl Landguard's property business, along with a list of donors for the *Mary Jo* memorial fund. I'll load it on to my laptop computer and then email it over to you. There is another thing: Karen Landguard said that Gavin specifically asked for a property in Harold Road. Why?'

'Don't know, but we'll poke about to see if we can come up with anything.'

Marvik noted the 'we' and wondered how deeply Strathen was getting involved with Helen.

As though reading Marvik's thoughts, Strathen said, 'Helen's still monitoring social media but there's been nothing posted from anyone claiming to know Gavin Yardly or having been best buddies with him. He seems to have been very much a loner.'

'Crowder's words exactly. I'll stick around here to see if anyone shows or if Moorcott decides to take off on his boat. I'll also call Crowder to see if there's more on Gavin's death.'

Using the mobile phone issued to him by Crowder, Marvik didn't have long to wait before he answered. Marvik asked if he knew the results of the autopsy on Gavin.

'No multiple fractures consistent with a fall,' was Crowder's reply.

'So he didn't jump and neither was he thrown or pushed off that cliff?' Which Marvik had known to be the case anyway.

'The East Sussex police are awaiting the toxicology tests to determine whether he'd taken drugs. But there wasn't any alcohol in his blood.'

'Time of death?'

'Tuesday, sometime between two and six in the morning, which fits with it taking place after Ian Bradshaw's death.'

'Is there evidence that he was held captive anywhere or restrained?'

'No. There's nothing to say that he didn't walk into the sea with those weights in his clothes.'

'And if drugs are found in his system the coroner could still find that he took them voluntarily to aid his suicide. Any sign of the *Mary Jo*?'

'Not yet.'

Marvik wasn't sure he believed that but for now he made no comment.

Crowder said, 'The blood spatter on the jacket found in his flat matches Ian Bradshaw's. So too does that on the trainers. But, as we have already discussed, that doesn't mean Gavin was there or is the killer. So far none of Gavin Yardly's relatives have been traced or come forward, and neither have any friends of his.'

'Strathen's still looking for the latter. He's also drawn a blank on relatives. But we've now got a missing woman, Meryl Landguard,' and Marvik swiftly relayed what had happened and his conversation with Strathen. Crowder made no comment about the possible smuggling.

Marvik rang off saying he would keep Crowder briefed when he could. Was it drugs, arms or some other commodity that the *Mary Jo* had been involved with smuggling? How many other trips had she made and to where? Or was it nothing to do with the vessel but everything to do with Helmsley Marine and Bradshaw's role there cleaning dirty money?

He fired up his laptop while being attuned to any unusual movement or sound on the pontoon or approach from the water. The wind was howling through the masts and the boat was rocking gently as he loaded the files. Soon he was scrolling through the list of donors and the size of donations. Moorcott had been right — there were some sizeable ones from the industry, including a very generous one from Almbridge. Guilt money because Almbridge had acquired Helmsley Marine for a song?

He called up the Almbridge website and read how Alec Royden, its managing director, after working on container ships and passenger liners had founded the company in October 2000, a year after Martin Elmsley and Duncan Helmslow had founded Helmsley Marine. Almbridge, according to the website, had begun operating very much in the same way as Helmsley Marine with one tug on localized salvage contracts. The two companies would have been competing for tenders.

Then Almbridge had got a breakthrough that put them ahead of Helmsley if the website information could be believed. In June 2001, they were hired to assist a Dutch firm on a salvage and wreck removal operation in the Caribbean. When the Dutch company went bust in the middle of it, Almbridge took sole charge of the project and successfully completed it. After that they won several projects and expanded their operations, leaving Helmsley behind in terms of successful growth. Instead of buying more tugs, barges and cranes, though, Alec Royden took the decision to fly his highly trained and experienced project teams out to marine casualties, wreck recoveries and salvage disposal projects by helicopter and private plane to wherever the project was in the world and charter vessels and equipment near the site of the casualty. It had paid off. Now, in addition to their base in Newhaven they had offices in Singapore and Canada.

Marvik sat back and contemplated the facts of what he'd read. He wondered why Royden, or rather Almbridge, had bothered acquiring Helmsley even for a knockdown price. Almbridge wouldn't have wanted the equipment owned by Helmsley, which, without the *Mary Jo*, didn't amount to much anyway. Perhaps they were keen to acquire the staff or the client list and Helmsley's outstanding contracts, which included the SS *Celeste*.

He sent the files over to Strathen and made himself something to eat. It was dark and the wind was rising with a fretful and sporadic rain in it. Marvik couldn't see Moorcott's boat from where he was but he had a good view of anything leaving and entering the port. Only a fishing vessel and the eleven p.m. ferry to Dieppe had sailed; nothing had come into or left the marina.

He climbed to the exposed upper helm. The few petulant raindrops had ceased for a moment, and as he drank his coffee he let his thoughts mull over the events of the past few days. Strathen's comments about the *Mary Jo* and Helmsley being used for smuggling conjured up thoughts of Sarah Redburn's death in connection with that of his parents.

The underwater tremor that had killed them could have been triggered by an explosive device planted on an undersea obstruction, except none was found. Marvik didn't know how hard anyone had looked for one. A diver could have removed any evidence of the remains of one. If an explosive device had been used then it had been planted by an expert — someone who knew where to place it so it would cause a ripple effect at the right time, when they were diving.

He looked up as a man walked down the far pontoon and climbed on to his boat. It wasn't Moorcott. The boat's engine throbbed into life. He wondered about the evidence given at the inquiry into his parents' deaths. How certain was he that it hadn't been fabricated as a cover up? For what, though? And was it the same for the *Mary Jo*? The marine accident investigation report relied on the testimony of others. How could the inquiry know if they were being told the truth? There were so many questions about that last and fatal voyage of the *Mary Jo* and about Helmsley Marine. And how certain was he that the handwriting in the notebook he'd found in Sarah's possession was actually his father's? It looked like it but it could have been faked, just as Timothy Landguard's crew had fake IDs and possibly phoney CVs. Who had seen that crew, spoken to them and waved them off on the harbour side? Maybe they had never existed and, if that was the case, then someone had done a very thorough job on choosing those names and creating their CVs with enough background experience to make it sound genuine. Had they actually ever been on the *Mary Jo*? Did Stapledon know them? He had a lifetime's experience of being at sea. He must have known the companies mentioned on their CVs. Had any of their former colleagues and friends come forward at the memorial? Had Stapledon spoken to them? He should ask him. Marvik didn't know where Stapledon lived but he knew where he would find him tomorrow.

It was time he gate-crashed a wedding.

# CHAPTER FOURTEEN

*Friday*

Marvik's phone call to the Royal Victoria Hotel in Hastings earlier that morning told him that Darren Stapledon's wedding was at eleven a.m. That gave Marvik plenty of time to reach the coastal town once famous for smuggling, shipbuilding and rope-making before becoming a popular seaside resort in the late eighteenth century. Its popularity had declined somewhat since then and, from what Marvik could remember of it from his last visit here to talk to the relatives of a former Marine comrade who had died in action, it had been just before the pier had burned down in October 2010.

He'd spent an undisturbed night at Newhaven Marina. Moorcott had made no attempt to leave by boat, although he might try to do so today, and no one had come asking who the hell he was and why he was nosing around about the *Mary Jo*.

He'd reflected on what Karen Landguard had told him about Gavin Yardly and wondered if Bradshaw had owned that property in Harold Road in 2003, perhaps bought with the proceeds of his financial frauds and other illegal activity. Or had there been or was there a tenant in that building who Gavin believed had a connection with the *Mary Jo*'s disappearance? The latter seemed unlikely given the timeframe — surely they would have moved on by now? But, by being a resident there, perhaps Gavin hoped to get a list of tenants from 2003 from Karen Landguard or her colleague, Danny. Marvik decided he'd head for Eastbourne once he'd spoken to Stapledon.

It was just turning eleven fifty when Marvik arrived at the hotel on the seafront. The ceremony would be over by now and he'd catch Hugh Stapledon in between the photographs and the wedding breakfast. He looked down at his combats, boots and waterproof jacket. Maybe it's informal dress, he thought with a wry smile as he stepped into the hotel, but even if it were top hat and tails Marvik would still make sure Stapledon spoke to him.

The wedding party had spilled out into the immaculately kept and resplendent grounds of the large hotel built in the reign of Queen Victoria and refurbished many times since. No one stopped him as he headed through the hotel to the gardens. Marvik noted that the bride and groom were being fussed over by the photographer. Beside them were five bridesmaids in turquoise dresses. The large wedding crowd, with drinks in their hands, milled around them, laughing and chatting. It wasn't quite a top hat and tails wedding but it was formal.

He spotted the lean figure of Stapledon some distance from the guests, standing by the edge of a lake, listening to an elderly couple who looked to be in their nineties. Marvik could sense his boredom even through the polite expression on his narrow features, which turned to something akin to horror as he recognized Marvik making a beeline for him. Hastily he broke off his conversation, leaving the old couple momentarily stunned, and hurried towards Marvik, his expression turning to one of annoyance. Behind it Marvik detected anxiety.

Stapledon made as though to take Marvik's arm to steer him away but something in Marvik's expression or manner prevented him at the last moment. He jerked his head and

Marvik walked with him farther away from the wedding group and around the edge of the lake.

'This is a private occasion. What are you doing here?' Stapledon asked tersely.

'The man you believe was Stephen Landguard who came to see you was in fact Gavin Yardly and he's dead.'

Marvik watched Stapledon's reaction carefully. He looked nonplussed.

'He *told* me he was Tim's son.'

But Marvik wasn't sure that was the truth. Stapledon's voice held conviction and astonishment but his eyes said something else.

'Yardly's death is linked to the murder of Ian Bradshaw and to the loss of the *Mary Jo*.'

Stapledon looked genuinely confused. 'But how? That's ridiculous.'

'You know about Bradshaw's death, then?'

'I read about it last night.' His eyes darted away from Marvik. 'It can't have any connection with the *Mary Jo*. That was years ago.'

'But Bradshaw worked for Helmsley Marine.'

'Yes. But only for a couple of years. He joined them in January 2002. Helmsley Marine was sold to Almbridge in 2004.'

'And Bradshaw negotiated the purchase of the *Celeste* and recruited the crew for the *Mary Jo*. A crew that doesn't seem to exist.'

A loud burst of laughter came from the wedding group. Stapledon scowled across at it, then snapped, 'We can't talk here.' He made for the hotel entrance. Marvik followed him.

Their progress was impeded by a stout woman in a lilac outfit too small for her. She threw Marvik a curious and nervous glance and addressed Stapledon, saying he was needed for the photographs. Stapledon curtly replied that he'd be back shortly.

'What do you mean the crew didn't exist — of course they did,' Stapledon said curtly as they walked along the thickly carpeted corridor towards the reception.

'You met them?'

'No.'

'Then you met their relatives and friends at the memorial service?'

'Well, no, I can't seem to remember—'

'You know the shipping companies they worked for?'

'Probably. But I didn't see their CVs.'

'But you know their names — Simon Warrendale, Peter Goodhead and Lewis Chale.'

'I can't remember.'

'Three men who died on board a salvage vessel that you helped to arrange a memorial for and you can't remember their names! Suffering from some sort of amnesia, are you?' Marvik quipped.

'What I mean is I know nothing about them.'

'Then who gave the address at the memorial service?'

Stapledon took a handkerchief from his trouser pocket and wiped his forehead. 'Duncan said a few words.'

'About the crew?'

'Well, of course, and about Tim. The port chaplain conducted the service.'

They came out into the resplendent reception, an impressive display of amber marble and gilt. Stapledon halted.

Marvik said, 'Someone must have given the chaplain background information on the crew.'

'I guess so. I didn't.' He twisted the handkerchief in his hands. More beads of perspiration had broken out on his forehead.

'You are the area fundraising director for a seafarers' charity, aren't you?' Marvik said disdainfully. 'So how come you don't give a shit about that crew?' Before Stapledon could stammer an answer, Marvik stepped closer and, keeping his voice low and menacing, said, 'I'll tell you why. Because you, Bradshaw, Moorcott and Meryl Landguard shared out the proceeds of that memorial fund.'

Stapledon's skin paled. 'That's a lie.'

'Was there ever a crew? Perhaps Tim Landguard set sail on the *Mary Jo* alone. Perhaps he was in on the scam along with you, Bradshaw, Moorcott, Meryl and Duncan Helmslow. Perhaps Tim Landguard was meant to return only something went wrong. He died, the *Mary Jo* was lost and you all shared out the insurance money as well as the memorial fund.'

'I don't know what you're talking about. Duncan was bereft when the *Mary Jo* and its crew were lost.'

'Not Meryl Landguard, though.'

Stapledon squirmed. 'Well, of course she was upset.'

'So upset that Bradshaw continued to comfort her,' sneered Marvik. 'She and Bradshaw were involved in fraudulent accounting.'

'This is madness.'

'He might also have been involved in smuggling and money laundering.'

Stapledon mopped his forehead. 'I won't listen to these scandalous and ridiculous accusations a moment longer and if you persist I'll—'

'What? Call the police? I doubt it. So isn't it about time you told the truth about what really happened to the *Mary Jo*?'

'I don't know the truth, as you call it. All I know is what I was told: Tim Landguard and his crew were on their way to Newfoundland to the *Celeste* when they were lost at sea. No one knows why.'

'Someone does, which is why Bradshaw and Yardly are dead and Meryl Landguard is missing. Moorcott could be next, and then you.'

Stapledon swallowed hard. 'I have nothing to do with any of this. I didn't work for Helmsley. I didn't know the crew. I didn't recruit them and I wasn't involved in the contract to bring the *Celeste* back to Britain for scrapping. I didn't benefit in any way from the tragedy.'

'Almbridge did, though. Alec Royden bought Helmsley Marine on the cheap and took the *Celeste* contract off them.

And Royden gave a very generous donation to the memorial fund.'

'Why shouldn't he?' Stapledon was stung to retort. 'He was upset by the tragedy. He was good friends with Tim Landguard. We all were — me, Duncan and Martin.'

Stapledon was sweating profusely and his eyes barely rested anywhere for a few seconds. Was he the fourth man involved in this? Had he slit Bradshaw's throat and abducted Meryl Landguard? He looked pretty ineffectual to Marvik, but he knew you couldn't judge by appearances and he could have given the orders to kill. Marvik watched him keenly. The man was afraid, that much was clear, but of him or of what had happened in 2003? Had he really never bothered to find out about the crew? Had he assumed everything he was told was correct?

Stapledon gained a little more confidence in Marvik's silence. 'Alec Royden is a hardworking very astute business-man. He's taken risks and they've paid off.'

'Such as sabotaging the *Mary Jo*?'

Stapledon looked horrified that his remarks had been misinterpreted. 'Of course not. I didn't mean that. Alec is above reproach and if you're implying—'

'*I'm* implying nothing. I'm sure he'll be very helpful when I speak to him.'

A horrified expression flitted across Stapledon's face. 'You can't bother him now. He's in the middle of some very delicate negotiations. His company is about to be acquired by Drakes Marine, a multinational marine salvage and shipping company.'

'So he's in line to make a lot of money,' Marvik said, rapidly considering this.

'What if he is? There's no law against that.'

'But there is about gaining it by illegal means.'

'I've heard enough of this slanderous rubbish. If you don't stop making accusations I'll—'

'What? Silence me?' Marvik scoffed. With menace, he added, 'I've only just begun to make accusations and I'll carry on making them until I know exactly why the *Mary Jo* was lost at sea, so tell Alec Royden that. He'll find me at Newhaven Marina.'

Marvik stepped outside into a blustery, fresh April day. Almbridge's offices, he had read on the website last night, were the other side of Newhaven Harbour, just a stone's throw from where he was moored. It would be interesting and perhaps telling if Royden responded to Stapledon's message, especially as he was up to his neck in negotiations for a lucrative acquisition of his business. Marvik knew the message would be delivered. Now all he had to do was wait for Royden to show up. Maybe Stapledon was on the level and didn't know anything about the phoney crew, the financial fraud and smuggling. Perhaps it was Royden who had colluded with Ian Bradshaw to ensure the *Mary Jo* never reached Newfoundland. His company had profited by it. Had he been involved in killing a man he had worked with at sea, Timothy Landguard, and ruining another, Duncan Helmslow? Yes, if he was ruthless. Or perhaps he hadn't realized how far Bradshaw would go for money and how deeply he was in league with smugglers. And, having once committed himself, he couldn't get out. Gavin had shown up at a very delicate time in Royden's career if Stapledon was correct, an acquisition that would see Royden make a fortune. Meryl Landguard had warned Ian Bradshaw about Gavin's questions and Bradshaw had told Royden. Royden had devised a scheme to get rid of both of them and of Meryl and protect his back, his deal with Drakes and his fortune.

Marvik headed for the railway station and the train to Eastbourne. There was still the fact that Gavin Yardly had specifically requested a flat in Harold Road.

It was just after two p.m. when he pushed open the door of Medlowes. There was no sign of Karen and he hadn't seen her Mini parked nearby but Danny was there.

Marvik said, 'Karen was going to give me a list of the tenants in the Harold Road property.'

Danny rose and crossed to her desk. 'It's not here.'

'She must have forgotten. Could you print it off for me?'

'Of course.' He returned to his seat and his computer, and within a couple of minutes Marvik saw the paper slide out of the printer. He expected Danny to tell Karen he'd given him a list of tenants but Marvik knew she wouldn't reveal that to the police for fear of them probing her about her affair with Bradshaw. Danny handed it to Marvik, who glanced at it before folding it and thrusting it in his jacket pocket.

'Did Mr Bradshaw own that property in 2003?'

'No. He bought it a couple of years ago.'

So that ruled out one of his ideas. 'When will Karen be back?' he asked, in order to make his request seem more natural.

'She won't. Not today, anyway. She had to rush off — had a call from her husband.'

Marvik felt an uneasy pricking between his shoulder blades.

'When?'

'About twenty minutes ago.'

'She went home?'

'No. It was something to do with her mother-in-law. I heard her say that she'd meet him at her mother-in-law's house. She was pretty cross but—'

Marvik didn't stop to hear any more. This didn't smell right. He grabbed the first taxi he could find and gave instructions for the driver to head for East Dean as quickly as he could. Had Meryl Landguard returned home and summoned her son and daughter-in-law? Maybe they were all safe and well, drinking tea, but as the taxi went as quickly as the traffic permitted, Marvik didn't think so. His gut told him that Stephen could have been lured there by the killer, who had sent him a text from Meryl's mobile phone, much in the same way as Sarah Redburn had received a text from her killer to lure her to the beach at Ballards Point in Dorset, sent by someone she either knew or who purported to be a friend. Once at Meryl's house, had Stephen been forced to call Karen and summon her there? Or had the text Stephen thought had been sent by his mother also requested Karen's presence? And what of Charlie? Had Stephen taken his little boy with him or left him with a neighbour or a friend? Maybe Charlie was at the nursery as usual.

He had Stephen Landguard's mobile number but the phone might well be in the hands of the killer. He could chance trying it in the hope that the killer would respond and think he could lure him to his death. Or perhaps he simply wouldn't answer it.

Marvik's fingers played irritably with it and then drummed the window ledge. The taxi driver, after making one attempt to chat and getting no response, drove in silence. It seemed to take an age to get to East Dean but finally the car pulled up a short distance from Meryl's house. Marvik paid the driver and ran towards the house, rapidly scanning the road around him. There were no cars or motorbikes parked in it and no one loitering suspiciously. As he entered the driveway, he saw that Karen's Mini was parked outside the front door. There was no sign of Karen or the baby. There was also no sign of Stephen's car or Meryl's Audi. With a racing pulse and a sinking feeling in the pit of his stomach, Marvik made his way towards the house. He only hoped and prayed that he wasn't too late.

# CHAPTER FIFTEEN

With his stomach knotted hard and his senses on full alert, he tried the front door. It was locked. He scanned the windows. There was no sign of movement. Unlatching the gate, he swiftly and stealthily made his way around to the rear. Could this bastard have killed a child? Was there so much at stake? Had he failed by not being quick enough or by not being hard enough? The answer to that had to be yes if he'd let a child die.

He was at least half an hour behind Karen, forty minutes at the most, and a hell of a lot could happen in that time. Would he find her, Stephen and the child dead inside? But this killer couldn't risk it looking like murder. A chill ran through him. Not unless he could make it appear as though Stephen Landguard, confronted by his wife's infidelity with Ian Bradshaw, had killed her and the baby and then taken off in his car and killed himself. And this killer was good at framing people.

He tried the rear door. It was open. Holding his breath, he entered and caught the sound of a child's cry. It was coming from upstairs. His relief was tempered with the fear that, although the child was alive, Karen might not be. Racing up the stairs two at a time, he burst into the room from where the cries were coming and drew to an abrupt halt with an overwhelming sense of relief as Karen Landguard spun round and gave a startled cry. The child was in her arms.

'Jesus, you scared the life out of me! What are you doing here?' she demanded, alarmed, her expression hardening, but he heard the fear in her voice. She stepped away from him, tightening her hold on the child who continued to grizzle, the tears mingling with the snot from his nose.

'How long have you been here?' Marvik asked sharply, crossing to the window and looking out. They were still alone, but for how long?

'About five minutes.'

He turned his bewildered expression on her. 'Danny said you left well over half an hour ago.'

'I had to get some petrol and then I got stuck in a traffic jam.' Marvik thanked God for that as she continued, 'Why are you here? Why did you ask Danny where I was?' She stepped further away from him, obviously afraid he was behind everything that had happened.

'I'll explain later. Where's Stephen?'

'I don't know. He said he'd be here but I found Charlie alone.'

'We need to get away from here.'

But she refused to move. Clutching the squirming, crying boy, she eyed Marvik warily. 'Stephen said—'

'He's not coming back, at least not to here,' Marvik quickly amended for her sake. He didn't think Stephen was ever coming back and neither was Meryl. 'Karen, you're in danger and so is Charlie. We don't have much time.'

'But why? This can't be because of Stephen's dad.'

'We haven't got time to discuss it. I'll explain in the car.' He made towards the door. 'Please, Karen. I'm mixed up in this, yes, but I'm not a killer. I'm trying to protect you. You have to take me on trust.' He held her frightened stare. Maybe it was the urgency in his voice that persuaded her or his expression, but she took a breath and nodded.

They made for the car. Marvik quickly surveyed the area. All was quiet. What to do next? How much peril were

Karen and her son in? What would have happened to them if she hadn't needed petrol and hadn't been stuck in a traffic jam? The fact that the killer hadn't waited for her to arrive, though, indicated to Marvik that he hadn't known she was on her way to the house. That meant Stephen had called her before going to his mother's.

Marvik resisted the impulse to snatch the car keys from Karen, sensing that would only alienate her. The child had stopped crying and was playing with a soft toy as Karen drove through the village towards the main road. Marvik was banking on them not being followed. Stephen might be unconscious or gagged. His abductor might still be interrogating him to establish how much he knew about Ian Bradshaw, Gavin Yardly and the *Mary Jo*. Marvik knew that, under pressure, Stephen would mention him and their previous visit to Meryl Landguard's house. Stephen didn't know of his visit to Moorcott or to Stapledon but either one of them or both might be in the killer's pay. And Stapledon now knew where Marvik was based. That meant he had to rule out taking Karen to his boat. He could hope to cast off and get away before Royden showed up, but it was a gamble he wasn't prepared to take. If someone came for him on his boat, he could handle it but there was a chance he wouldn't be able to keep Karen and Charlie safe if they were there with him. But if he allowed Karen to return home and Stephen told the killer of his wife's affair with Bradshaw, the killer might believe that Bradshaw had whispered sweet nothings in Karen's ear and confessed his darkest and deepest secrets, which meant that her and Charlie's lives were at risk. The scenario he'd envisaged earlier — a woman and child murdered by a jealous man followed by his suicide — would be arranged.

'Where shall I take you?' she said as though reading his thoughts.

'To your home.'

She flashed him a glance. The alarm was back in her eyes.

'You'll need to collect some things. It won't be safe for you and Charlie to stay there.'

'Look, is this really necessary?'

'Yes. Tell me what happened with Stephen. What did he say when he called you?'

She indicated on to the main road. 'He asked me to meet him at Meryl's house. He said she had sent him a text to say she was on her way home and was sorry for alarming him. There was something she wanted to talk to him about.'

'Only him, not you?'

'That's what Stephen said but he told me he wanted me there.'

'Why?' Marvik asked sharply, checking the wing mirror. There was a white van behind them but it didn't look as though it was tailing them.

'He said it was about time we all discussed matters and it was important that I also heard what Meryl had to say.'

'Did he say what matters?'

'No.'

There was a slight flush under her skin that betrayed her thoughts. She'd considered the fact that her husband wanted to expose her affair with Bradshaw in front of her mother-in-law.

'We argued. I accused him of being scared of mummy and wasn't it about time he stood up for himself. He said that was exactly what he was doing. I reminded him I was working but he said that I had a lunch break and with Ian dead no one was going to sack me for taking some extra time out. He told me to be there. He sounded different.'

'How?'

'Upset, disturbed. I was worried about Charlie. I said I'd go.'

Did Stephen have some sixth sense that he was walking into a deadly trap? But if so, why involve his wife? The van stayed behind them.

Karen continued, 'When I got to the house, there was no sign of his car or Meryl's. I let myself in and called out. There was no answer, then Charlie started crying. I raced up the stairs to find him in his cot. Stephen had just left him,' she added angrily and disbelievingly. 'I tried to comfort Charlie while I thought what to do. I wondered if Stephen had taken the car to the cliffs and done something stupid. Perhaps Meryl had gone after him. I didn't know what to think, then you showed up.'

'I don't think Stephen went voluntarily,' Marvik said quietly.

She flashed him a frightened glance before quickly putting her eyes back on the road. Her skin had paled and her hands gripping the steering wheel whitened. The van turned right. A dark blue Mercedes was now behind them with a fair-haired woman at the wheel.

Marvik said, 'The text from Meryl was a hoax designed to get Stephen to the house with the intention of abducting him, probably, as Meryl has been abducted. Are you OK to drive?'

She nodded grimly.

'Whoever did so couldn't have seen Stephen arrive with your son. Stephen, finding no sign of his mother or her car, got suspicious. He took Charlie upstairs and put him in his cot, then perhaps crossing to the window he saw someone watching the house or someone walking up the drive.' And was that someone he knew? wondered Marvik. 'Stephen went down to meet this person, was forced into his car and told to drive away. He had no choice and he certainly wasn't going to tell this person about Charlie being in the house and you on your way. But he might be persuaded to talk. His abductor will see that he called you on his mobile unless Stephen wiped his call log clean beforehand. I need to get you and Charlie to safety.'

'But—'

'Stephen knows about your affair — no, I didn't tell him but under pressure he'll tell his abductor about it and that puts you in danger. This person might believe you know about Ian Bradshaw's past and what he was involved in.'

'But I don't,' she insisted. 'This is mad. It can't be happening.'

'How far now?'

'What? Not far. We live on the western outskirts of Old Town.'

No one had followed them. 'You can't stay in the house. Stephen or Meryl will tell them where you live. I can't leave you there, Karen. You and Charlie need to go somewhere no one knows about, not to your friends or family. I can get you to a hotel.' But even then the killer could check out the hotels and bed-and-breakfast places. 'You'll have to stay put inside until I tell you it's safe.'

'Why don't we call the police?'

'Because they can't protect you.'

'Why not?' she demanded.

'You have to trust me, Karen,' he added solemnly and earnestly. When she still looked doubtful, he said, 'Ian Bradshaw is dead. His throat was cut in a brutal murder. Gavin Yardly has also been killed, his body dumped at the bottom of a cliff. Your mother-in-law contacted Ian Bradshaw shortly before his death and after Gavin Yardly had confronted her about the loss of the *Mary Jo*. Now she has gone missing, along with your husband. I'm trying to find out why Bradshaw and Gavin Yardly were killed. That's all I can tell you.'

She pulled up at a set of traffic lights.

'If you stay in your own home, I can't protect you and neither can the police.'

Maybe she saw something in his eyes or heard his sincerity. She took a breath and nodded.

Marvik breathed a silent sigh of relief. 'Tell me when we're close to your house.'

He needed to dump this ruddy great signpost of a car with Medlowes sprawled all over it. They were a sitting target. And there were two places he could dump it: one was outside the office, the other outside Karen's house. He'd plumped for the latter. Both might be being watched if this killer had resources, but would he have got there or sent someone there this quick? Possibly. Marvik hoped not. He asked her for any landmarks close to the house.

'It's just past the recreation ground.'

As Karen negotiated the residential streets, Marvik consulted his Ordnance Survey map and found where her house was situated. Charlie had fallen asleep. Marvik instructed her to park where she usually did, which was across the road from the small end-of-terrace house. He checked the road for any sign of a suspicious vehicle or motorbike cruising, or any vehicles parked with darkened windows, or a man or men sitting in them. There didn't appear to be anyone watching the Landguards' modern house but he wasn't going to take any chances. Marvik was out of the car before Karen and, releasing the harness on the child seat, he lifted Charlie, who stirred but didn't wake. It was mid-afternoon.

Marvik nodded at Karen to head for the house. She let them in. So far, so good. No one was watching the house and it hadn't been broken into. The killer, though, would get Stephen's keys from him. Marvik didn't think there had been time for that yet but it would be close. Karen's mobile phone rang, startling her.

'It's Danny at the office. He's probably wondering where I am.' She made to answer it but Marvik prevented her.

'Switch it off,' he commanded. She hesitated for a second, then did so. Marvik said, 'Your location can be traced and from now on we don't want that.' Her face was drawn. 'Have you got a rucksack and a baby harness, the type I can put on my back?'

'Yes, it's in the utility room.'

'Pack some things for both of you for a few days. Put on some warm clothing and flat shoes, walking boots or trainers, and a rain jacket.'

'We're walking?' she asked, dazed.

'Yes.'

'But the car—'

'It's too easily recognized. Get some warm clothes for Charlie.' Marvik still had hold of the child. 'Be as quick as you can. Pull the curtains in your bedroom and in Charlie's and switch on the light.' When it grew dark hopefully the killer would believe Karen and her son were in the house.

But she paused on the stairs. 'There is somewhere we could go. It's a small, two-bedroomed cottage just outside the village of Jevington. It's not far from here. It's a holiday let, one of the few we have on our books. It was Ian's latest business venture. No one's booked in it for the next fortnight. I can turn on the water and the heating but I haven't got the keys — they're in the office.'

Lack of keys wouldn't pose a problem for Marvik. 'Does it belong to Bradshaw?'

'No. The owners live in London.'

'We'll head there.'

She ran up the stairs. Marvik entered the lounge and put Charlie down on the sofa. He stirred and moaned but didn't wake. Marvik crossed to the window and surveyed the road from behind the curtain. Everything looked in order. Removing his Ordnance Survey map from his rucksack, he again swiftly consulted it while listening for noises outside and from upstairs. He found the village of Jevington. It lay about five miles by road and four miles by foot over the South Downs.

His ears pricked up at the sound of a car driving slowly past. He heard it pull over and the engine running softly. It could be nothing. On the other hand . . . He looked out, making sure to keep behind the edge of the curtains and out of sight. There was a high wall in front of the modern end-of-terrace house screening the road. He couldn't see the vehicle.

He could hear Karen moving about upstairs. Stuffing the map back in his rucksack, he went through to the kitchen where he opened the fridge, extracted cheese, some ham, butter, milk, a bottle of water and a small orange juice and thrust them into his rucksack. Next, he opened the cupboards and found some tins of baby food, beans and tuna. These, along with a packet of biscuits, half a loaf of bread, some tea bags and a small jar of instant coffee, he pushed into his bag. He hoped that he could find a shop or farm shop close to the cottage to buy more food. But in case he couldn't, this would keep them going.

Then he made for the utility room and unlocked the back door. It was raining again but not heavily. There was a side gate to his left. From the hook in the small lobby he removed a rain jacket — Stephen Landguard's. He also retrieved the baby carrier.

Returning to the hall, he called up to Karen to hurry. Then he lifted Charlie into the harness and draped Stephen Landguard's waterproof around and over him. He was already dressed in outdoor clothes. It would be awkward carrying that and his rucksack but the latter he quickly adapted to wear over his chest after taking out the Ordnance Survey map and encasing it in the plastic holder, which he lifted over his head so that he could easily read it while walking. He pulled the curtains and switched on a table lamp and the television set.

Karen appeared in the doorway, carrying a large black rucksack and wearing jeans, trainers, a rain jacket and a scarf.

'Ready?' Marvik asked.

She nodded. Her face was drawn but her expression was set and determined. He'd finally got through to her how serious this was. Now that she'd made up her mind to trust him and believed in what he was saying, he saw a different woman to the petulant, short-tempered and sharp one he'd witnessed earlier. She kissed what she could see of Charlie's head and her fingers brushed a strand of his hair. Marvik donned the baby carrier. 'He'll be OK and so will you,' he reassured her.

'I hope so.'

He had failed to protect Sarah. He wasn't going to fail to protect Karen and her son.

# CHAPTER SIXTEEN

Marvik led her through the tiny garden to the side gate and out into Bramble Close. They couldn't risk walking along the road; they'd be spotted immediately. But the map had shown him that at the end of the close was a footpath which led into a dense area of hilly wood. A light, drizzling rain was falling as they strode out around the curving road of the small close of detached modern houses. The rain was keeping the neighbours indoors and that was a good thing. No one to stop them and no one to report their progress. Charlie woke and grizzled but Karen quickly soothed him and soon he was burbling away quite happily. Marvik had made sure to stuff the little soft toy in with him. The child was a heavy weight on Marvik's back but much lighter than what he'd carried in combat and on covert operations. He'd only once had a cargo like this: a young Afghan child he'd found wounded and abandoned. He didn't know whether the child had lived or died after he'd got him to the field hospital. He'd had to move on. He'd always been moving on.

Ahead was the public footpath sign. Marvik drew to a halt in front of it and glanced behind them. They were safe. No one was watching or following them. He wondered if the car with the idling engine was still parked down the road from the house and the killer, or his accomplice inside it, waiting for his chance.

He turned right and led the way along a narrow, muddy path bordered by trees in bud. Karen followed but she didn't complain and neither did she speak, except to direct the occasional reassuring remark to her son. At least the trees sheltered them from the rain but soon they would be in the open on the Downs.

He was surprised how fit Karen was. As though reading his thoughts, she smiled and said, 'I don't pay gym membership for nothing.'

He smiled back. The rain had thankfully stopped by the time they began to climb the steep ascent to the top of the Downs. Only then did she begin to breathe more heavily. He eased back for her.

Charlie seemed to be enjoying himself judging by the sounds he was emitting. The view at the top of the rolling Downs, stretching for miles with small outcrops of houses dotted in some of the dips was breath-taking. The mist and rain had cleared, leaving a fine late afternoon. There was no one in sight and Marvik could see for miles, right across to the silver sea in the distance.

'I'd forgotten how lovely it is,' Karen said with sadness. 'It's been ages since I walked up here. Stephen and I used to do it regularly before Charlie was born.' She fell silent as they walked along the ridge, slightly northwards. After several minutes, she said, 'Do you think Stephen will be OK?'

'I don't know,' he answered but he suspected not.

'It's all my fault,' she said forlornly.

'No, it's not, Karen. Even if you hadn't been involved with Ian Bradshaw, Stephen would still have been in danger.'

'But who could be doing this?'

That's what he was desperate to know. They turned down towards the small group of buildings he could see in the distance — the village of Jevington.

'Tell me what happened when you showed Gavin Yardly the flat?'

'I said it was a large room which doubled as a bedroom and a sitting room with a kitchenette off it, and a shared bathroom with a shared separate toilet down the hall. Shared between two of the flats — the one at the rear on that floor has its own bathroom and toilet, so do the two basement flats. I told him that perhaps it might be too large for one person but he barely looked round it. He stepped inside, said it was fine and he'd take it. He didn't even want to look at the bathroom and toilet.'

'Did he ask about the other tenants?'

'No.'

'How did he get the job at Aquamarine Cleaning?'

'He must have approached Ian directly. I didn't mention Gavin Yardly to Ian.'

'But he was unemployed when he took the flat.'

'No. He wasn't on housing benefit. He told me he was a freelance IT consultant. You said he'd been killed — why? He must only have been a teenager when the *Mary Jo* went down. Was he related to one of the crew?'

'Not as far as I know.'

After a moment, she said, 'What do I call you?'

'Art.'

She nodded. The strain of the last four days was beginning to show on her face. She looked exhausted.

Marvik said, 'Didn't Stephen ever try and confide in you about his father and how he felt after the tragedy?'

'He's not the confiding type. He keeps everything inside. That's half his trouble. He's shut it out. I tried to get him to open up when we used to walk like this on the Downs but I just got the silent treatment.' She tossed him a slightly defiant glance. 'He has days when he hardly says a word, not even to Charlie. I never know what he's thinking. If I ask him what's wrong he says nothing and clams up. Even when I shout at him he just looks blankly back at me. It drives me mad. I've often wished we could have a full-blown argument to clear the air, but Stephen doesn't do confrontation,' she added with a touch of bitterness.

Perhaps Stephen suffered from depression and Karen hadn't or didn't want to recognize that.

'Where was Stephen on Monday night?' he asked.

She looked at him, confused, but answered, not making any connection that it was the night Bradshaw had had his throat cut.

'At work.'

'All night?'

'They had a big campaign to finish. He stayed up in London. He came home Tuesday night at the usual time.' Which was what Stephen had told him.

Karen said, 'There's the property, just at the end of that lane.'

Marvik could see it — a small, detached flint cottage. Its nearest neighbour was a large house about half a mile to the south. A lane led from the cottage towards a group of buildings about a mile away, obviously the village of Jevington. It was secluded and yet not too isolated, and there was no reason to suspect that whoever had abducted Stephen should find his wife and child here. But he asked her if Stephen would know of the cottage. The answer was no.

'Danny knows about it because it's on the books, but he wouldn't have any idea I'm here. I'll have to call in sick for tomorrow. Will I still need to be here on Tuesday?'

'I don't know. And you mustn't call him. You could give away your location. I'll do it.'

She frowned, concerned, but was prevented from saying more as they drew nearer and Charlie became restless and irritable. 'He's hungry and he probably needs changing. Let me take him.'

Marvik slipped off the harness. They were almost at the rear of the cottage anyway. He asked her for the alarm code and instructed her to wait. He approached the cottage confident that there was no one about and no one to see them. Opening the gate, he stepped into the small, neat courtyard garden and crossed to a set of double-glazed patio doors. They could be easily opened but Karen had said the alarm box was just to the right of the front door, so he'd enter that way and deal with that first. Not that he believed anyone would hear the alarm from where the cottage was situated. It seemed pointless having one and any burglar worth his salt would have sussed that out.

It was a solid wooden door but with a lock that he could easily manipulate. He inserted the metal device from his penknife into the lock. A few seconds later the door gave way and the alarm rang out. Swiftly, he keyed in the code and it fell silent. There were bolts on the inside of the door, and a safety chain as well as a peephole. Good. The lock would still work, though — he hadn't forced it.

He rapidly checked through the house just to make absolutely sure it was empty and there were no surveillance devices inside, which there shouldn't be but always best to be certain. Everything was fine. Leaving the door open, he gestured to Karen who, with Charlie in her arms and the rucksack on her back, headed towards him. She told him where the stopcock was and the central heating system, and while Marvik tackled both she saw to Charlie in the bathroom, which was upstairs between the two small bedrooms.

Marvik entered the kitchen and emptied his rucksack of the provisions he'd brought with him. He placed the perishables in the fridge, filled the kettle and switched it on. He had a good view from the kitchen window of the lane that led to the village. It was deserted save for a couple of blackbirds.

Karen returned with Charlie, who was still grizzling, in her arms. Marvik said, 'I've brought some food but you'll need more.'

'There's a shop in the village; I can get some tomorrow. I've got my debit and credit cards.'

'No. You're to see and speak to no one. Don't switch on your phone. Tomorrow I'll bring you a phone that can't be traced and some provisions.'

'You're not staying?' she said, surprised but with a hint of relief, Marvik thought.

'If you do as I say, you and Charlie will be safe here. Is that understood?'

She nodded, her expression deeply troubled. 'Where will you be?'

'I don't know yet — that depends.' He didn't say on what and she didn't ask him.

'Are you leaving now?'

'After I've made us something to eat.'

He left before it got dark and took the same route back to Eastbourne, over the Downs. He didn't like leaving Karen and Charlie alone. Not because they weren't safe in the cottage — they were, as long as Karen did as he had instructed, but he wasn't certain she would. She was strong-willed and intelligent, but if she couldn't resist switching on her mobile phone then a call from Stephen pleading with her to do as she was asked by his abductor or he'd be killed, or a strongly worded text, which she felt compelled to reply to, might be enough to draw her out of the cottage, or certainly give away her location. Alone, as night drew in, brooding over all that had happened, maybe she would also consider she must have been mad to leave her home with a scarred stranger and be stuck in a cottage with little food, minimal clothing and only the television and her son for company. 'Not even a bottle of wine,' she'd joked over their beans on toast. But she had sounded as though she'd have dearly loved a drink. As the minutes and hours ticked by and the adrenaline of their escape over the Downs wore off, he wondered if she'd grow more fractious and more sceptical so that by morning she'd believe she must have imagined the danger and that he was a nutcase. She'd leave and return to her home. She might even try Stephen's number, or her mother-in-law's, either of which would seal her death. It had been foolish of him to leave her but he couldn't stay there. He had to get back to Newhaven Marina. He was expecting a visitor. Had Alec Royden already tried to find him there? If he had, Marvik knew he would return, or maybe he was waiting. Marvik was convinced that Stapledon would have told him about their conversation and that Royden wouldn't want anyone stirring up the past and besmirching his company's reputation even if he had nothing to hide, not with a major deal going down. And everyone had something to hide.

Marvik came out into the road where the Landguards lived. The light was shining in the upstairs bedroom and in the lounge. Cars were parked along both sides of the road but there was no one sitting inside them. Nothing looked suspicious. He could enter the house, despite not having a key, but he didn't see any need to. According to Karen, Stephen wouldn't have kept anything that could help him find the truth behind the *Mary Jo*'s disappearance. The same applied to Meryl Landguard's house. Except in the latter case he might return and find mother and son dead, or one of them dead inside it.

Forty minutes later found him outside Eastbourne railway station. Before taking a taxi back to Newhaven, he called Strathen on the mission mobile. Quickly he relayed all the salient points of what had occurred during the day and his concerns about Karen Landguard staying put.

Strathen said, 'I'd go there myself but I can't take Helen. Karen probably thinks Helen's mixed up in Gavin's murder. She won't trust Helen and seeing her might only confirm that you're the abductor and killer. And I can't leave Helen here alone. I'm sorry, Art, I can't help you out this time. We'll just have to hope that Karen does what you tell her.'

Marvik could hear the tension in Strathen's voice. He could sense, even down the line, Strathen's frustration at being hindered by Helen's presence.

Strathen continued, 'This mystery crew of the *Mary Jo* still bothers me and, from what you're saying, they seem to bother Stapledon.'

'Maybe Royden will throw some light on them.'

'Landguard could have set sail for Canada alone. Perhaps his intention all along was never to reach Newfoundland. Duncan Helmslow, Ian Bradshaw and Meryl Landguard all had something to gain from the *Mary Jo* not doing so.'

'Would Duncan Helmslow have sacrificed his boat, though?'

'His company was going down the pan. The *Mary Jo* was his first and only love and he was damned if he was going to let Almbridge get hold of it, or let it be sold off for a profit when Royden got his hands on Helmsley's. Perhaps Timothy Landguard is still alive and Meryl Landguard knows full well where he is. She could even be with him abroad, with a passport under a different name.'

'But would she keep that from her son?'

'He could have gone to join them. No, I don't believe that any more than you do, Art, and *I've* never met him. But Timothy Landguard could have wanted to disappear and start a new life somewhere *without* his wife and that suited Ian Bradshaw and Meryl Landguard. He could have a woman in another country and money stashed away in an overseas account. He made arrangements to be collected by another boat while at sea and scuppered the *Mary Jo*.'

'Hence no distress signal. Maybe Alec Royden is on the level then and his donation to the memorial fund was a genuine generous gesture. Perhaps he'll confirm that when he responds to my message delivered by Stapledon.'

It was just after nine thirty when the taxi dropped Marvik off by the public conveniences and recreation ground outside the marina. There were two cars parked in the lay-by and another one further along the road but no sign of any drivers. It had been a long day, his head was throbbing and the wound in his leg was beginning to play up but he blocked out both. He had to stay alert.

He crossed the road to the marina car park. Moorcott's boat was in its allotted berth and in darkness. So the accountant hadn't taken off in fright — not unless he'd driven away in his Aston Martin.

Marvik once again went over his boat. All was secure. No one had entered it. He swallowed a couple of strong painkillers, then froze as he felt a movement on the pontoon. He steeled himself in readiness. His cabin lights were on. He couldn't see who it was, only an outline of a dark-clothed figure. There was nowhere to hide. Besides, he wouldn't hide anyway. This was what he anticipated. He knew who his visitor was. Had he come alone, though? Had he come with the intention of killing him?

Marvik's senses were on full alert for the smell of petrol, the placing of an explosive or the thud of an incendiary device which could be lobbed on to his boat, resulting in a massive fire. He might just have time to leap off the side into the sea.

His heart was beating fast, the adrenaline pumping. He'd left the cabin door open but he didn't go outside. Instead he climbed silently and swiftly on to the fly bridge, keeping low. Here he had a good view of the pontoon. There were two of them. The bulkier one wore a peaked sailing cap rammed low down over his forehead, dark trousers and a sailing jacket. He nodded to the leaner, bare-headed man beside him, also dressed in dark clothes. The lean man climbed carefully on to the rear of Marvik's boat and stealthily made his way around to the cabin door while the other man stayed on the pontoon. Marvik saw him glance nervously in both directions and back at the pontoon from where he'd come, towards the car park.

The boat rocked gently as the man entered the helm. Marvik could hear him breathing and sensed him searching it. Was he armed? Then he heard the soft footfall on the steps that led to the upper helm where Marvik crouched. As the head appeared, then the upper torso, Marvik launched himself on it and within a second had the man's neck in a tight arm lock before the bastard could blink or cry out. The heavy duty torch in the man's right hand — not brought for illumination, Marvik thought, but for striking — clattered to the deck.

'You really should get some practice in,' Marvik growled in the man's ear as he gripped his arm and wrenched it up his back. 'Now, do you want me to break your neck or your arm, or shall we go down and invite your mate to come on board?'

Marvik's grip tightened. The man's eyes bulged in a face which was rapidly turning blue as the oxygen was being severed. He managed to blink acceptance of the offer and Marvik picked up the heavy torch then thrust the man down the stairs ahead of him on to the deck, still holding him by the neck and in an arm lock. Marvik called out to the bulkier man on the pontoon who had already seen them and had started nervously. 'You'd better come on board, Royden, or would you rather I break your mate's neck?'

'No. I'm coming,' Royden hastily replied and scrambled on board.

## CHAPTER SEVENTEEN

Royden held up his hands to show he was unarmed. His face was pale and his expression alarmed.

'Take off the cap,' commanded Marvik. Royden instantly obeyed and Marvik found himself studying a round, rugged, strong boned face with a wide mouth and dark brown, fearful eyes. He was in his late fifties. 'Inside.' Marvik jerked his head and Royden eased his way around them. Marvik, still keeping a firm grip on the thin man, kicked the cabin door shut behind Royden. 'Now that we're all nice and cosy, shall we talk? Sit down, Royden. Hands on the table.'

Royden did as he was told. Marvik recalled saying the same to Stephen only two days ago. If Royden, and the man in his grip, had abducted Stephen and killed him, Marvik vowed he'd make them both pay. But he was doubtful they were the culprits. He could tell these two were amateurs — they just thought they were tough guys.

He thrust the man he'd been holding away from him so that he fell to the deck. He looked up at Marvik, terrified, coughing. He was younger than Royden but only by about five years. His narrow face was heavily lined and his complexion sallow.

'Get up. Sit beside your mate and put your hands on the table,' Marvik commanded. 'And don't even think that you can join forces and get the better of me because it would be child's play to take you both out.' Marvik thudded the heavy torch into his palm. They'd have a job to extract themselves from behind the table, and by the time they did Marvik would be ready for them. 'Right, let's start with names. Yours I know — Alec Royden, Managing Director of Almbridge. Who's your mate?'

'Geoff Bowman. He works for me,' Royden answered as Bowman was trying to clear his throat after almost having his air supply cut off.

'Doing what? Killing people?'

'No!'

'Tell that to the police.'

'I never killed no one,' Bowman croaked, moving his right hand.

Marvik brought the torch crashing down on the knuckles of the left one, still on the table. Bowman squealed in pain and put his other hand over the swollen knuckles.

Royden went white. 'You've broken his fingers.'

'Shame.'

'You can't do this,' Royden protested.

'Why not? Isn't it what you did to Gavin Yardly?'

'I never touched him!' Royden exclaimed, 'And neither did Bowman.'

'But you know him?'

'I know his body was found at the foot of the cliffs, close to the Birling Gap, but I don't know how he died.'

'Bollocks.' Marvik moved forward. Bowman shrank back but Royden stayed put, though Marvik could see it cost him an effort.

Rapidly, Royden said, 'I know the police think he was involved in Ian Bradshaw's death only because I saw that on the news.'

'And you know he was killed, as was Bradshaw, because of the *Mary Jo*.'

It looked for a moment as though Royden was about to deny it, then, holding Marvik's cold hostile gaze, he exhaled and said, 'I suspected it might be connected but I don't know how or why and only because Yardly came to see me. He wanted to ask me some questions about the *Mary Jo*. I told my secretary to tell him I was unavailable.'

'When?' rapped Marvik.

'Three weeks ago last Friday. I swear it. I was on my way to London. I thought he'd gone but he was waiting outside for me by my car. He was muttering on about the *Mary Jo*, talking nonsense about sabotage.'

'So much nonsense that he is now dead and so is Bradshaw. And Meryl Landguard and her son have been abducted and probably killed.'

'But that can't be right.' Royden sounded bemused. He made to rub his hand over his face but remembered what Marvik had done to his companion's knuckles, which were swelling up. Bowman's lined face was creased with pain. 'Look, what the hell's going on?'

'I'm waiting for you to tell me.'

'I don't know anything about why the *Mary Jo* was lost at sea or what happened on that last voyage. I swear it,' he added when Marvik made as if to threaten him.

'Then why did Stapledon warn you that I'd been around asking questions and why come here and try to scare me off?'

'It's complicated.'

'We've got all night.'

'Let Bowman go?' Royden threw a glance at the man next to him. 'He has nothing to do with the *Mary Jo*. He didn't even work for me then.'

'He stays put. Why are you and Stapledon so worried? Are you scared I've discovered that you and he stole money from Helmsley Marine in a fraudulent deal and that was why Gavin had to die?'

'I've stolen nothing,' Royden hotly denied. 'Hugh Stapledon was only trying to protect me because I can't afford any questions being asked now.'

'Because of the acquisition by Drakes Marine. What's so big a deal about it?'

'They're a major international marine company. I'm to be CEO of the UK operations.'

'So it's a lucrative deal.'

'Yes.'

'But if the bosses of Drakes discover you deliberately wrecked a salvage vessel and killed four men, so that you could eliminate the competition and sell off what remaining assets there were in Helmsley when you acquired it for a knockdown price in a fraudulent scam you participated in with Ian Bradshaw, they'd run a fucking mile,' Marvik sneered.

'I haven't killed or wrecked any boat,' Royden pleaded. 'I wasn't involved in any financial scam and I bought Helmsley fair and square, but if rumours like that get around it would scotch the deal and we're within days of finalizing it.'

'And that was why Gavin Yardly had to die — you couldn't have him running around spreading rumours. Then I showed up and Hugh Stapledon tipped you off so you and your pathetic mate here thought you'd come and silence me.' Marvik moved threateningly forward. This time Royden cowered back and Bowman licked his lips nervously.

Royden's face was ashen as he obviously visualized his precious deal going down the drain. 'It wasn't like that,' he whined. 'I've done nothing wrong. I just wanted you to go away.'

'And your incompetent thug here was hoping to see that I did,' Marvik spat scathingly. 'I'm not Gavin Yardly. You'll have to try a darn sight harder than that to get rid of me. OK, so let's have the truth and maybe I'll keep quiet.'

Defeated, Royden said, 'What do you want to know?'

'Everything, starting with the *Mary Jo* and the phoney crew.'

Royden stared at him, confused.

Marvik elaborated. 'The crew that Bradshaw supposedly recruited.'

'I don't know what you're talking about. I can assure you they were genuine.'

'You met them?' Marvik rapped.

'No. But—'

'You saw them go on board?'

'No. But they *must* have been on board. Tim couldn't have managed the job on his own.'

'He never got to the job. Maybe that was the intention all along. Maybe he wanted to disappear and start a new life somewhere. His wife could claim the insurance money, Helmslow could get the insurance on the boat and Bradshaw his share of the insurance money on the phoney crew and their wages, which he shared with Meryl Landguard because they were having an affair. And you got Helmsley Marine and the contract to salvage the *Celeste*.' Royden's eyes widened. The blood drained from his face. Bowman was looking baffled. His knuckles were turning a deeper blue.

'That's just not possible,' Royden protested. 'Tim would never have taken off like that or deliberately scuttled a boat. I knew him well; we'd worked together at sea. He was scrupulously honest and thorough, and so too was Duncan. In fact, we all worked together — me, Bradshaw, Landguard, Helmslow, Elmsley and Stapledon — on the same car carrier years ago on the Japan to Southampton route transporting cars. And Duncan certainly wouldn't have sacrificed his beloved *Mary Jo*.'

'Bradshaw worked with you all.'

'Yes.'

Stapledon hadn't mentioned that. Why had he omitted Bradshaw? Could he simply have forgotten he worked with him? Unlikely.

Royden continued, 'I took over the contract for the *Celeste* because Duncan could no longer meet the commitment to scrap her, and he was only too willing for me to do so and to buy his company.'

'And you felt so guilty that you gave a whacking great wad of money to the *Mary Jo* memorial fund.'

'OK, so I did, but not for the reasons you've said,' Royden was stung to retort. 'I originally pitched to buy the *Celeste* along with Helmsley and we were all set to get it when the owner decided to sell to Helmsley, thanks to Ian Bradshaw. I hoped it would go wrong. I wanted it to be one gigantic cock-up, even though I knew Tim Landguard and he was a damn good salvage master, but I never sabotaged the *Mary Jo*.'

'Bradshaw was involved in some kind of side deal.'

'I couldn't prove it. He said he'd bring the *Celeste* to Britain for recycling, which didn't sound a bit like him, because not only would that cost more but Helmsley would get less on the salvage value. India was a much better location for scrappage, for getting maximum value, along with lower overheads and cheaper wages.'

'So it didn't make good business sense to bring it to Britain.'

'Not unless you were going to be *paid* to do so.'

'Bradshaw took a bribe from the company who would recycle it?'

'Either from them or from someone in government who had an interest in boosting our fledging ship recycling industry, which is still struggling to get off the ground.'

'He was crooked even when you worked with him at sea?'

'He was always looking for a chance to make money.'

'Like you.'

Royden's lips tightened. 'No. Not like me,' he said stiffly. 'All my deals have been strictly legal.' But his shifting eye contact said something else. 'I was amazed Duncan took on Ian Bradshaw. They were total opposites and never really hit it off at sea. Bradshaw was flashy and crass, and a womanizer, which was why he loved working on the cruise liners. It didn't suit Tim, who did a stint on them but left to go into the salvage industry and then to work for Duncan, who like him was serious and played it straight. I stuck to the cruise ships for a while but, like Martin Elmsley, I wanted to be my own master and not of a ship. Bradshaw was a good talker, though, and probably persuaded Duncan and Martin to take him on. When Martin died Duncan was completely lost. Bradshaw was running the show. By the time we got hold of the *Celeste* no one was remotely interested in where the thing was scrapped.'

'So you did a deal directly with Bradshaw, who sold it on to you for one price but told Duncan you'd paid less. He falsified the invoices to cream off some money. Or perhaps you agreed a figure and shared the cut.'

'No. The deal was done through the same broker Ian Bradshaw used the first time, Marcus Kiln, and it was simply a case of transferring the contract to us on the same basis. Helmsley bought the *Celeste* "as and where seen", selling everything there was to sell on her when she was stripped down and broken up to earn back the outlay and gain a profit. As I said, India is very good for getting the best prices for metals and other equipment on board ships.'

'And did you profit?'

'Yes. Nothing wrong in that,' he declared defensively.

Marvik recalled what Crowder had told him. 'There was some valuable property on board: aluminium, bronze, ornamental balustrades, murals, gilt, gold, even.'

Royden looked taken aback by Marvik's knowledge.

'Must have swelled Almbridge's coffers or was it your own personal bank account that got a boost in a deal you did with this Marcus Kiln?'

A cloud crossed Royden's eyes. 'It was all properly recorded and accounted for.'

'Was it?' Marvik scoffed. He doubted that. Someone had overseen the dismantling of the *Celeste* and, judging by Royden's body language and expression, some of that profit had most probably found its way into an offshore account under Royden's name.

'Where can I find Marcus Kiln?' Marvik asked.

'I don't know. I haven't heard from him since then. It's true,' he hastily added. 'He must have left the shipping industry right afterwards. We did the deal and that was it.'

Marvik eyed him disbelievingly. It sounded too convenient. Was Royden making this up? Did this Kiln really exist? Had Royden invented him in order to divert attention from himself and his profiteering on the side and his attempts to escape the taxman?

'What did he look like?'

'I don't know. I never met him. All our negotiations were conducted by email and phone. It was a very straightforward transaction.'

Marvik studied him. Was that a lie? Royden was looking increasingly frazzled.

'But he oversaw the dismantling operation in India?'

'No. We liaised with the manager at the Indian recycling plant.'

'You trusted them not to cream off anything?'

'Yes.'

Marvik wasn't too certain about that.

'I swear we had nothing to do with the loss of the *Mary Jo*.'

'But you came here mob-handed. Not sure I believe you, Alec.'

'We just wanted you to stop asking questions.'

'Afraid I can't do that.'

'Then at least wait another week and the deal with Drakes will be done. Their chairman, Terry Keydell, is very strict on ethics. If there is one sniff of anything untoward in the history of a company he wants to acquire that's it, he drops the deal.'

'Even if it's profitable?' Marvik said incredulously.

'Yes. He's eccentric, reclusive and principled.'

'Then you'll just have to hope it doesn't reach his ears, or the fact that you've fiddled the taxman.'

'Fat chance of that,' Royden scoffed. 'It's a small industry. Everyone knows everyone.' He paused and took a breath as his brow furrowed in thought. 'And we don't know you,' he added decisively. 'Just why *are* you so interested?'

'Because I'm eccentric and principled. Out,' he commanded. Royden slid out of the seat, followed by Bowman. 'If either of you try anything I'll break more than your knuckles. And I'll start spreading stories so fast that you'll be lucky to get so much as a contract to salvage a rowboat. Where can I find Stapledon?' Royden hesitated. Marvik took a step forward.

'He lives just off the Old Willingdon Road in Friston.'

Not far from Meryl Landguard's house in East Dean, just the other side of the A259.

Royden gave Marvik Stapledon's address.

'I take it you said you'd phone him after this visit?'

Royden nodded.

'Then pass the message on.'

Royden looked puzzled. Marvik elaborated. 'I'm not sure his donors and the Charity Commission will be too pleased when I start telling them how one of their fundraising directors has been pocketing the funds.'

'But that's a—'

'Lie? Is it? Where can I find you if I have more questions to ask?' Marvik added threateningly.

Royden's face fell. 'Either here, on my boat—'

'What kind?'

'A Sealine F46 motor cruiser.'

The same make of boat that Colbourne had been on but the marina night-duty manager had said that Colbourne had been heavy-set, muscular, about forty. The description didn't fit Royden, although he was bulky. But if Royden had been one of those men in Eastbourne Marina talking about taking out a 'target' then why go to Eastbourne Marina, enter via a lock and be seen when he could have met his accomplice here in private?

'Name?'

'*Bayrisca.*'

Boat names could be easily changed. 'And if you're not here or in your office, where will you be?'

Royden shifted uneasily. 'At home. Dukes Haven, Alfriston.'

Which Marvik knew was only a few miles north-east of Seaford and about ten miles to Eastbourne.

'But don't come there. My wife's pregnant and I don't want her bothered and upset.'

Marvik said nothing. He watched them climb off the boat. Royden turned before heading down the pontoon back to the shore. Marvik didn't need to see his expression in the dark, wet night because he knew it would be troubled. But how deep was he in?

He quickly locked up and followed them through the car park to the road that bordered the recreation ground. The two men were so deep in animated conversation that Marvik doubted they would have noticed or heard him if he'd been directly behind them. Bowman was nursing his bruised hand and possibly broken fingers and complaining vociferously about it. They came to a halt beside the two cars parked in the lay-by, still arguing. Marvik stepped back into the shadows. Bowman zapped open one of the cars but he didn't climb in. Marvik couldn't hear what they were saying but by Bowman's gestures and catching the occasional raised word, it sounded as though Bowman was insisting on Royden driving him to hospital. Royden was refusing. Then he looked as though he was pleading with Bowman who, after a moment, zapped his car shut and stormed off in the direction of the sea, but Marvik thought his destination was the pub at the end of the road, close to the beach, and a stiff drink before calling for a taxi to take him to Accident and Emergency.

Royden climbed into his car and reached for his phone. Swiftly, Marvik tailed Bowman and as he reached the curve in the road at the entrance to the fort car park, only sixty yards away, where Marvik had directed Moorcott. Marvik struck him on the back of his head with his torch, enough to make him fall and pass out but not enough to kill him and dragged his body into the shrubs. The streets were deserted and Royden wouldn't have seen him because of the bend in the road.

Deftly, Marvik searched the pockets and, retrieving a mobile phone and car keys, ran back towards Royden's car in time to see its taillights in the distance. Marvik climbed into Bowman's car and followed. Royden could be going home; he could be reporting back to Stapledon but Marvik was guessing he had already done that on the phone. He was curious to see what he would do next, and there was that driving instinct deep inside him that said Royden could lead him to some answers as to what had really happened to the *Mary Jo*.

Royden headed east out of Newhaven on the A259 towards Seaford, in the correct direction for his home. Marvik hung back. There were two cars in front of him. The road wasn't busy. Instead of turning off for Alfriston, though, Royden drove on towards Eastbourne. He crossed the narrow bridge over Cuckmere Haven, an area of floodplains where the River Cuckmere led down to the English Channel and the beach. It had been very popular with smugglers over the centuries. The car in front of Marvik pulled off to the left. They were almost on the road that turned off to Friston, but instead of indicating into it, Royden continued. He wasn't going to visit Stapledon then but Marvik saw him indicate right, taking the road to East Dean and the Birling Gap. He followed, keeping his distance. Royden was driving fast, taking the wet country lane at speed. They'd already passed Meryl Landguard's house. Soon they would be at the entrance of the car park at the Birling Gap, which at this time of night and in this weather would be deserted, as was the road.

The dark shape of the Downs loomed on Marvik's right and lights from a handful of houses on the approach to Crowlink glimmered through his rain-spattered windscreen. Still keeping his distance, Marvik registered a large black four-wheel-drive vehicle ahead on the edge of the car park almost at the same time he saw Royden approach the bend. It happened in a flash. The vehicle pulled out right in Royden's path. Instinctively, he swerved to avoid it. His car spun round, left the road, flipped over and rolled several times until it struck a tree with force. Marvik quickly pulled over and was out of the car running towards Royden while noting the four-wheel-drive vehicle's tail lights disappearing up the hill in the distance. Only the wind and the rain drumming on the roof of the upturned vehicle now disturbed the night. There were no houses close by and no other vehicles on the road.

Marvik reached the upturned vehicle. He shone his torch inside it at the same time as trying the car door, but it was locked and his beam picked out the grey, immobile, strong-featured face and staring eyes of Alec Royden, the blood running from his nose. Royden was dead.

He took a breath and remained motionless for a moment. Whoever had been driving the other vehicle had taken a chance that Royden would be killed. He could have survived such an impact, albeit seriously injured, but that would have been enough to have put him out of action for some time and maybe even in a coma for many days or weeks. Maybe if the driver hadn't seen Marvik's lights he would have stopped to make sure Royden was dead, and if he wasn't he'd have finished him off.

Marvik turned away and climbed back into Bowman's car. He swung it round but instead of making for Newhaven he made for Friston and Hugh Stapledon.

# CHAPTER EIGHTEEN

The lights were showing from behind the curtains in the detached house on the small estate but that didn't mean Stapledon was at home. Marvik pulled up outside and walked up the short driveway where a new saloon car was parked. He hadn't expected to see the four-wheel-drive vehicle that had forced Royden off the road because he didn't believe Stapledon had been driving it, but he could have instructed an accomplice to do so. Except if Stapledon was the killer, why wasn't he living in greater luxury than in this modest 1980s detached house? Had he really sabotaged a boat and killed seven men just so that he could live like this? The same applied if Stapledon had been fiddling the charity's funds. Marvik would have expected a much larger and more prestigious property. But then, for all he knew Stapledon could have huge debts. He could be a gambler or a drinker or both. He could be paying his ex-wife a very hefty alimony, not to mention having to cough up for his son's wedding. He could have money stashed away and be living a double life. And there *was* a shiny new car on the driveway.

Marvik pressed his finger on the bell and kept it there until the door was opened by a haggard Stapledon, who hadn't changed out of the suit Marvik had seen him dressed in that morning at the wedding. It seemed incredible that it was less than eleven hours ago.

Stapledon's bony face registered alarm, then fear and he made to close the door, but Marvik thumped the flat of his hand on it and pushed it open.

'I've got nothing more to say to you,' Stapledon said stiffly.

'But I've got plenty to ask you.' Marvik stepped inside, roughly pushing Stapledon back so that he hit the wall. Marvik couldn't hear anyone moving about, only the sound of the television. And no one came rushing to see what had caused Stapledon to cry out.

'What did Alec Royden tell you when he phoned an hour ago?' Marvik demanded.

'He hasn't phoned me.'

Marvik stepped forward and balled his fist. The colour drained from Stapledon's narrow face.

'He hasn't. I swear it.'

'Give me your mobile phone.'

'It's in the lounge.'

'Then let's get it.' He grabbed hold of Stapledon and roughly pushed him into the room on their right where the television was on. There was a half-empty bottle of whisky and a glass on the table in front of a tired-looking sofa, along with the mobile phone. Marvik grabbed it and scrolled through Stapledon's last calls. There was nothing from Royden, or at least his name didn't flash up. The last call Stapledon had received had been earlier that morning from a woman called Eileen Jepson. Marvik ignored it. And the last call Stapledon had made had been shortly after Marvik had left him that morning. It was to Alec Royden. Stapledon watched on nervously.

So, who had Royden called from his car? He should have retrieved the mobile phone from Royden's body. That had been a mistake. But he swiftly told himself that even if he had, he was certain the number would lead him nowhere. It would be disconnected by now. This killer was no fool. And the police would discover the same when they checked it or Royden's mobile phone records, except they had no reason to do so because they would believe his death was an accident. It would be assumed that Royden had taken the bend too fast and swerved to avoid an animal. Stapledon hadn't killed him or arranged to have him killed, but Marvik was certain that Stapledon had something to hide just as everyone connected with this mission seemed to have.

Marvik reached for the television remote control, pressed the mute button, threw the device on the sofa but kept hold of the phone.

'Tell me about the *Mary Jo*.'

'I've already told you everything I know,' Stapledon cried with exasperation.

Marvik stepped forward.

Hastily, Stapledon gabbled, 'I don't know anything more about it.'

Maybe he didn't. His fear and protest sounded and looked genuine.

'Marcus Kiln. You know him?'

'I know he was a ship broker,' Stapledon quickly answered.

'Describe him?'

'I can't. I've never met him.'

Marvik looked for the lie but he couldn't see it in Stapledon's expression.

Stapledon, looking fearful and bewildered, hastily continued, 'I've heard of him. He brokered the deal between the owners of the *Celeste* and Helmsley and then between Helmsley and Almbridge. Alec will know more about him than me.'

'Alec Royden is dead.'

'Dead? What do you mean? My God, you've killed him!' Stapledon said, horrified, his skin turning ashen. He stepped back fearfully from Marvik.

'*I* haven't but someone has, even though his death was made to look like a car accident. It's the same man who killed Ian Bradshaw and who by now has probably killed Meryl and Stephen Landguard.' He thought of Karen Landguard and her son and prayed silently that they were still safe in the cottage at Jevington.

'But I don't understand.' Stapledon sank down heavily on the chair. 'Why would anyone want to kill them? How can it be connected with the *Mary Jo*?'

If it was an act then it was a very good one. Stapledon looked genuinely distraught and confused.

'Why did you bullshit me about Gavin Yardly being Stephen Landguard?'

Stapledon went so pale that Marvik thought he might see right through to his bones. He rubbed a hand over his perspiring forehead. 'I don't know. It just came into my head. I'd heard that Ian was dead and I thought . . . I don't know what I thought.' Stapledon's hands now played nervously in his lap.

'You thought I'd discover you embezzled money from Duncan Helmslow's estate.'

'That's a lie. I've never done that.'

But the protest sounded half-hearted to Marvik. Stapledon wasn't squeaky clean, of that Marvik was convinced. Everyone connected with the *Mary Jo* seemed to have had their hands in the till — Bradshaw, Meryl Landguard, Moorcott, Royden and Stapledon. Sick of him, Marvik marched out and drove as fast as the speed restrictions allowed back to Newhaven. Stapledon wasn't the only person who knew where his boat was moored. Had Royden told the killer his whereabouts in that phone call? If so, he'd soon find out. And it wouldn't be anyone as inept as Bowman and Royden, who would descend on him next time.

He turned into a side street close to the marina and wiped the car of his fingerprints, tossed the key in a hedge and ran back to his boat. There was no one in the street or in the boat yard and no one on his boat. On board, he removed the SIM card from Bowman's phone and threw the phone into the sea just as he had done with Bradshaw's. He pushed the card in his own phone and scrolled through the numbers.

Alec Royden had called Bowman earlier that evening. There were no other names Marvik recognized. He wondered if Bowman had recovered from the blow he'd given him or if someone had found him and called an ambulance. He didn't think Bowman would tell the police about his escapade on board the boat because he would have to admit to entering it unlawfully and he'd be shit-scared Marvik would come after him. But when he learned of Royden's death would he go to the police? Bowman would believe he had killed Royden.

How long would it take for Royden's body to be found? It could be early morning when the coastguard chaplaincy did his rounds. It was almost morning now but Marvik thought he had a few hours' grace yet. And there was still Karen Landguard to deal with before he moved the boat out of Newhaven. He wouldn't be able to return to Eastbourne because the moment he entered the lock the police could be alerted and there were very few places to put into on this coast. Even Brighton Marina to the west was locked and if Bowman went to the police — Marvik knew Stapledon wouldn't — then they'd put a call out for him there.

Marvik's thoughts were interrupted as he felt the pontoon rock. He tensed. Maybe it was already too late. This could be the police or the killer. He prepared himself for either as the footsteps grew nearer but then he relaxed and went on deck. It was a tread he knew well and he was pleased and relieved to see Strathen.

'You look as though you could do with a drink,' Strathen said, climbing on board.

'You don't look so bright yourself.'

Marvik reached for a beer from the fridge and handed it to Strathen, who dumped his rucksack on the deck and eased himself down on the seat Royden had vacated earlier.

'Where's Helen?' Marvik asked.

'At Eastbourne police station.'

Marvik raised his eyebrows and, helping himself to a beer, took the seat opposite. His news about Royden could wait.

Strathen took a long draught which almost drained the glass. 'She overheard me talking to you on the telephone and took umbrage.'

'As you knew she would.'

Strathen pulled a face. 'You saw through my ploy.'

'You knew I would.'

He nodded. 'I feel bad about it but—'

'You had no choice. What happened?'

Strathen tossed back some beer. 'She packed her rucksack, said she knew when she wasn't wanted and stormed out, even though I told her not to be so melodramatic.'

'That must have gone down well,' Marvik said, grimacing. 'You followed her.'

'After a while, yes. I'd sewn two tracking devices into her clothes while she was sleeping and placed one inside the lining of her rucksack, just in case they were needed. One is in the hem of her jacket; the other in the hem of her skirt. The one in the hem of the skirt is so tiny and light that she won't even feel it there, and she hasn't found it or the others.'

'And you phoned the police anonymously to tell them where she was and to pick her up?'

Strathen nodded and drained the glass.

Marvik rose and fetched him another beer.

Strathen resumed. 'I called the Eastbourne cops because it's their case and said that I'd spotted her at Hamble railway station. I reckoned they'd send a local police unit to apprehend her. She was on the platform heading east. The next train to Brighton wasn't due for an hour. I parked the car outside the station and waited until the cops arrived. She didn't look too pleased when they escorted her to the car.' Strathen added with a grimace, 'I feel a heel for putting her through this but we both know that the police station is the best place for her at the moment, despite the pressure and stress of being questioned. I followed her to Eastbourne and made sure she got where I intended. The tracking devices are still working and I saw her enter the police station. Helen will handle it. Besides, she rang me from there.'

'Her one permitted phone call.'

'She's not been charged, only assisting them with their enquiries, as the saying goes. But she insisted she wasn't going to say a bloody thing without a lawyer present and as she didn't know any smart arsed lawyers, and couldn't trust the slimy toads anyway, she rang me, as I knew she would. It had to be either me or you and she chose me because I was the sod that had put her there in the first place, she said.'

'She knew you'd called the cops?'

'She's not daft. On the contrary. I told her she was in the best place, which didn't go down very well, as you can imagine. And that I had to go to help you. She was hurt that I hadn't thought highly enough of her to leave her alone in my flat and that I didn't trust her with all my equipment.' He left a short pause. Marvik could see he was mentally replaying the scathing comments Helen must have hurled at him.

Strathen swallowed some beer. 'I said I'd ring my lawyer in London, who would liaise with the police. I gave Helen her name and her telephone number but said I wasn't sure if she would get there, it being Saturday tomorrow. Today,' he corrected, glancing at his watch. 'You can imagine how she greeted that particular bit of news.'

Marvik could.

'I told her that if she was released she wasn't to return to her flat but to call Colin and Amy Chester in Arundel on a pay phone and Colin would come and collect her. I would warn him to expect her call.'

The Chesters were friends of Strathen. Colin was an amputee like Strathen, but ex-army rather than Marines. They'd met at the military rehabilitation centre at Headley Court in Surrey. Marvik had met the Chesters on his first mission for the National Intelligence Marine Squad when Helen had needed safe refuge and Strathen had supplied it courtesy of the Chesters and their bungalow on the outskirts of the small West Sussex historic market town with its eleventh-century castle, the family home of the Dukes of

Norfolk, perched high on its hill. Marvik knew that Helen liked the Chesters and trusted them.

Strathen said, 'She didn't promise me she'd do as I asked; in fact, she said "I am quite capable of looking after myself". She's tough, clever and independent but we both know that up against the cold-blooded bastard we're after she wouldn't last five minutes. She's disposable. I know where she is and I'll take care of her, but we don't work in a threesome and we are on a mission. I'll make it clear to her when I see her.'

'If she'll let you.'

Strathen drank his beer. 'My lawyer, Karina Fording, called me after she'd spoken to the officer-in-charge. At the moment they're holding Helen for questioning in relation to assisting in the murder of Ian Bradshaw. Karina said that she would be at the police station as soon as she can. She's in Cornwall at her holiday and weekend place. Yeah, I know it's not the end of the earth and there are roads and trains from Cornwall to East Sussex but I told Karina not to hurry. Helen will be fuming at spending a night in the cells but I'd sooner have her there than wandering about the streets. I've set up an alert on my laptop and mobile phone. If Helen starts walking I'll know about it.'

'Will she tell the police about us?'

'Me maybe but not you. I told her if pushed to say that I went to Eastbourne to pick her up and brought her back to my flat. I persuaded her to stay. We had a row and she walked out. I think she'll stick to that. Meanwhile, you said you needed to get a non-traceable mobile phone to Karen Landguard and persuade *her* to stay put. I've brought a phone with me — the rest will be down to you. I feel bad about Helen but I couldn't risk bringing her here. I know you won't say I didn't have to come because I did. We can operate remotely for some considerable time but not for all of it, especially when things start to hot up, as they seem to be doing.'

'Even more so. You just missed my uninvited guests.' Marvik told him about his recent visitors, ending with the information about Royden's death. 'According to Stapledon, Royden didn't call him but Royden was on the phone to someone when I saw him sitting in his car, and that someone is the killer or under instructions from the killer. Royden can't have told the killer where I am or he'd be here by now but Bowman might tell the police, which means I will probably need to move the boat in a few hours. We need to make sure Karen Landguard is safe first and get that phone to her. You can't go to her alone, Shaun. I've told her to admit no one.'

'Then we'll do it at first light. If the police come crawling over your boat while we're away then we'll know about it. I've come equipped.' He nodded at the rucksack beside him. 'I'll rig it up with alerts so that we'll know if so much as a fish moves under it. We get the phone to Karen Landguard — make sure she's safe. Then we need to find out more about a woman called Jemma Duisky. I think she's the reason Gavin asked for a flat in that road. And it could be why Helen, once she'd walked out on me, decided she'd return to Eastbourne — not because she has a flat there but because she found the lead to Jemma and perhaps had the idea that she could show me she was capable of following it up.'

Marvik brushed off his fatigue and sat forward eagerly.

Strathen said, 'Helen trawled through the Internet for anything untoward that had occurred in Harold Road in 2003. She found press reports on two robberies in April and a vehicle accident in July. There was also some debate over a planning application in May to knock down a crumbling Edwardian house and replace it with a block of flats. Maybe that hasn't happened.'

'Could be the block of flats opposite.'

'It's immaterial. Then she came across an article and a few online references to a Jemma Duisky, aged nineteen, found dead of a drug overdose in her rented flat above a cycle shop in Harold Road in September 2003. Her body was discovered by the flat's owner, Wilfred Palgrave, who also owned and ran the cycle shop.'

'It's still there,' said Marvik, recalling it. 'It looks as though it hasn't changed in years. It could still be owned by Palgrave.'

'The article says that Palgrave, after receiving no answer to his knock, let himself in and discovered her body on the bed. It was believed she had been dead for twenty-four hours.'

Marvik rapidly thought. 'She was the same age as Gavin at the time.'

'Yes, and that's not all they had in common. They attended Hastings College and were on the same A-level computer science course according to the alumni records, which fortunately were online.'

'So Gavin went to Eastbourne this year because of Jemma, but why did he wait so long?' Marvik mused.

Strathen shrugged. 'I've found a record of her burial and a notice in the local paper asking for any relatives to come forward. It was placed by the Eastbourne Polish Society. I also found a small article on the inquest that said a high number of barbiturates had been found in her system but there was no evidence that she had been an addict. There was also no suicide note, or if there was either Palgrave took it or someone else did. Helen knew that what she'd discovered could be significant even though I tried to say it might be nothing. Call me old fashioned or politically incorrect or any damn label you like but both you and I know that Helen is easy bait for this professional and ruthless killer despite what you read or don't read in romantic crime fiction.'

Marvik agreed. She'd not get the better of him. He'd just witnessed the grey face of Royden with blood trickling from his nostrils. He couldn't bear to think of the same end result for Helen. He recalled the pictures he'd seen of Sarah's body, the strangulation marks around her neck and the dead, staring eyes in the purple face.

Strathen said, 'I've also managed to get some background information on Alec Royden. He's been married twice and is currently on wife number three, who's nearly thirty years younger. Claims she's a former model but if she is I can't find her in any photoshoots except the ones she's put on the Web of herself at Ascot and Goodwood and the likes. Very glamorous and very expensive. He has two kids from his first wife, now both in their late twenties, and one from his second, who's in her teens.'

'He was about to become a father again, according to him.'

'He was taking, a very generous dividend from the company to fund an expensive lifestyle. The Drakes Marine deal would have made him a very wealthy man.'

Marvik rose. 'I'll call Crowder.'

'It's nearly two a.m.'

'So?'

Strathen smiled, and as Marvik rang Crowder Strathen began to rig up the boat with surveillance, tracking and security alarms which would only sound at his end on his mobile phone and laptop computer.

Crowder answered within four rings. Marvik didn't think he sounded tired or as though he'd been woken from his sleep. He asked if anyone had come forward to identify Gavin or if the police had found any of his next of kin.

They still hadn't. Marvik told Crowder about Gavin Yardly's connection with Jemma Duisky and where Helen was currently located, adding, 'We'd like her to stay there as long as possible.'

'How long?'

Marvik took a breath. He didn't know. 'Until Monday night, at least.'

'There are certain conditions that have to be met.'

'I know.'

'I can't interfere.'

Marvik knew that too. He told him what they suspected about the fraud and the possibility that the *Mary Jo* was being used for smuggling, about Stephen Landguard's disappearance and that he had got Karen Landguard and her child to a place of safety. Then he relayed the fact of Royden's death.

When Marvik finished, Crowder said, 'Things are moving,' which Marvik knew was about as close as Crowder would get to admitting they were making progress. At a terrible cost, though, he thought bitterly, ringing off. Crowder had neither confirmed nor denied it could be fraud on a massive scale, or drugs. Marvik hadn't expected him to. Maybe Crowder really didn't know what had happened in 2003. It was their job to find out. But they could do no more that night. They were both exhausted. They would grab a few hours' sleep but Marvik knew that, like him, Strathen would be on the alert for unwelcome visitors and attuned to the slightest movement or sound on the pontoon.

# CHAPTER NINETEEN

*Saturday*

It was just after dawn when they started for Jevington and Karen Landguard. No one had disturbed their fitful light sleep, but even given the early start when they reached the cottage Marvik saw, with a sinking heart, that there was no sign of Karen or Charlie. Equally, he thought with slightly raised hopes, there was no indication that the killer had discovered her whereabouts. The cottage hadn't been forcibly entered and if Karen had willingly gone to meet her abductor then she'd packed her bags before doing so and emptied the fridge. It was as Marvik had said the previous night to Strathen, and as he'd speculated after he had left her alone: Karen had had serious doubts about the validity of staying put and his credentials and had cleared out.

'Let's check her house in Eastbourne. She might have returned home.' Marvik hoped not. She hadn't. There was no answer to his knock and no sign of anyone watching the property. The curtains were still drawn and he and Strathen went to the rear where Marvik broke in. 'Just to be sure,' he said to Strathen, hoping the neighbours weren't too vigilant and wouldn't report seeing two strange men breaking in.

The house was empty and it didn't look as though Karen had returned and collected more clothes or personal belongings because the lights were still switched on. Marvik left them that way. He could call her mobile but he wasn't certain she would answer given the fact she hadn't called him to tell him she was on the move. And if he did call her then he might betray her whereabouts. Perhaps she'd gone to her mother's or a friend's. And perhaps she'd call the police and tell them her husband was missing and why. If the police put that with what Bowman might tell them they would certainly put a call out for him and he was easy enough to identify given the scars on his face.

Strathen made for Harold Road and pulled over outside the cycle shop. There was no one inside the dark and cluttered interior and the sign on the door said it would open at ten o'clock. Marvik peered up at the grimy windows of the flat above the shop. 'Looks like a pretty depressing place to live.'

'Perhaps it looked better in 2003.' Strathen gave a cynical smile. 'I doubt it too. Doesn't look as though it's been painted since 1983. But it does have its own entrance.' He nodded at the scratched and scuffed black door to the left of the shop window. It was also a short distance from the building where Gavin had lived and where Bradshaw had died. Strathen drove there and again pulled over. It was still early, and the weekend, so the street was quiet.

'Do we search it?' Marvik asked, nodding at Gavin's flat where the curtains were still drawn across the window. The police would have done so but they would have been looking for evidence of Yardly's guilt over Bradshaw's murder and not his investigations into the secrets of the *Mary Jo*. 'Could Gavin have hidden a backup somewhere in the flat containing his findings?'

'It's far more likely he backed up using an online provider but if this killer is as clever as we think he is, and we know he's ruthless, then he might have got that information out of Gavin before killing him, along with his encrypted password.'

'According to Crowder, Gavin wasn't tortured but the threat of torture could have been enough. Perhaps the killer threatened to throw him off the cliff, or more likely off a boat unless he coughed up. And he'd have kept him alive until he checked it out.'

'But Gavin wrote a good old-fashioned letter to GCHQ so perhaps he also recorded in long hand what he'd discovered and stored that in a safe place off the premises. It might not even have crossed the killer's mind that there could be written evidence of Gavin's investigations, so he never asked him and Gavin never volunteered the information.'

Marvik's thoughts flicked to his father's notebook and the disk taped to it, wondering where else his father and mother had recorded information which hadn't been found. He didn't have time to consider that now.

Strathen was saying, 'Perhaps Gavin's visit to the library, which Helen witnessed, was to take his backed-up USB with him and use one of the library's computers to send it to an online provider so that he left no trace of it on his own computer's hard drive for the killer to find.'

'Now that we're here, we might as well look it over.' They'd also search for surveillance devices but Marvik thought if any had been planted by the killer then he or his accomplice would have removed them just before or after killing Bradshaw. Marvik voiced this to Strathen.

'Unless the killer wants to see who comes knocking.'

'Then let's give him a floor show.'

'I'll do the soft shoe shuffle; you can do the conjuring.'

Marvik smiled. He still had Helen's keys which would get them into the building but not into Gavin's flat, the door of which was secured with a bolt and padlock, the work of the locksmith called by the police after they had affected an entry. Strathen kept watch as Marvik manipulated the lock and pushed open the door. No one stirred and the only sound was the baby crying again in the basement flat.

The large, high-ceilinged room was what Marvik had expected from what he'd seen of Helen's flat and from Karen's description. It was furnished with cheap plywood furniture that looked as though it might collapse if used, a grey corded carpet that needed cleaning and cheap rust-coloured curtains at the windows, which allowed enough light for them to search. Their torches would get into dimmer parts. To the right was the small kitchenette with off-white units, a black Formica-type worktop and the usual kitchen appliances, a kettle and toaster. There was a fridge and an electric cooker; the fridge had been emptied. The flat was very neat. The police might have tidied the place after they had finished with it but Marvik thought that perhaps Gavin had been meticulous in his habits. There was nothing of a personal nature — no photographs, letters or documents. If they had existed the police had taken them. Gavin's clothes remained. They were cheap and worn. Marvik went through them, not expecting to find anything because the police would have gone through them. Strathen was checking all the nooks and crannies and the ceiling for the usual places to plant a listening or surveillance device, and with a shake of his head declared the place clean. There was nothing taped to the back of the drawers or under the bedframe. No hidden disk, notebooks or anything else remotely connected to the *Mary Jo*. Marvik hadn't really expected to find anything.

He pulled back the curtain a fraction. No one appeared to be watching the flat but he could see that the killer would have had a good view of the street in both directions and would certainly have seen Helen approach along the road and leave by the side alleyway, and he'd have seen Bradshaw arrive. Gavin also had a view of the cycle shop which was further down to Marvik's left on the opposite side of the road.

He crossed the room and looked out into the hall. No one was about. The baby was still crying and there was music coming from upstairs. He relocked the padlock.

Outside, Strathen said, 'Breakfast?'

Marvik nodded. Leaving the car parked, they walked a short distance along the road before turning south in the direction of the seafront where they found the Italian ice-cream parlour and coffee shop Marvik had noted on his first journey to Harold Road when he'd been with Helen. Forgoing the ice cream, Strathen ordered coffees and breakfast and they found a seat in the corner overlooking the road and the promenade. The sea glistened in the distance. It was just on nine and still quiet, with only one other couple at a table at the opposite end of the café.

First Strathen searched the Internet for news of Royden's car accident and shook his head. Marvik knew that didn't mean he hadn't been found, just that the police weren't releasing the news until his pregnant wife had been informed. Perhaps an early morning walker had made the gruesome discovery. If so they hadn't yet broadcast it over the jungle drums of social media.

Marvik drank his coffee. 'Royden mentioned someone called Marcus Kiln, the broker who did the *Celeste* deal with him and Bradshaw. But he said he hadn't seen or heard of him since. Stapledon says the same and that Kiln is probably no longer in the shipping business. See if you can find him.'

Strathen began a search for Marcus Kiln. Their breakfast arrived, delivered by a dark-haired, smiling half-Italian half-English woman in her mid-twenties.

Marvik ate hungrily while Strathen tapped into his computer and put the occasional fork of food in his mouth.

'Nothing showing up for a Marcus Kiln but I can check him out more thoroughly after I see what I can find on Jemma Duisky. I'll stay here and overdose on caffeine while you visit the cycle shop.'

Marvik finished his breakfast before returning to Harold Road.

He wished he knew if Karen and her little boy were safe.

There were five minutes before Wilfred Palgrave officially opened to the cycling public of Eastbourne but, through the grimy windows, Marvik could see a stout, scruffily-dressed man in his sixties with long, thinning grey hair and a straggly grey beard. Not exactly Sir Bradley Wiggins, he thought, knocking loudly on the door. Palgrave ignored him, or perhaps he hadn't heard. Marvik rapped louder and kept doing so until the man shambled to the door. Looking at his watch, he pointed at the sign in the window.

'I need to talk to you. It's important,' Marvik shouted. 'You open in five minutes anyway.'

'Then you can wait five minutes,' Palgrave shouted back.

Palgrave was obviously not raised in the school of customer care. 'It's about Jemma Duisky,' Marvik said, this time keeping the volume of his voice normal. He could see at once that Palgrave had heard or lip-read. He looked taken aback before his flabby, slightly ruddy face creased up with a frown. He unlocked and opened the door.

Marvik stepped into the shop crammed with bicycles, most of which would end up on the pavement where Marvik had seen them on his second visit to the street. Wheels hung from the ceiling; old metal shelves were stacked in a haphazard fashion with cycling accessories: helmets, inner tubes, clothing, bags, bells, bottles and cycle pumps. The air was filled with dirt, grease, dust and cobwebs, and Palgrave's loose-fitting trousers and pullover contained a great deal of the first three. In his podgy, grimy hands was a very oily rag. He closed the door but didn't lock it and studied Marvik with open curiosity. Marvik kept a discreet distance, hoping he wouldn't have to get closer to force information out of the man because his halitosis was almost overpowering — the cause of which was explained by the few teeth Marvik could see, rotten and yellow.

'Why do you want to know about her? That was years ago,' Palgrave said warily.

Perhaps he was wondering if Marvik had come to sue him for causing her death in some way. Marvik introduced himself as a distant relative of Jemma Duisky who had only just heard the news of her death. 'I wondered if you could tell me about it,' he said.

'Not much to tell.' Palgrave looked relieved. 'Poor kid. It was a bit of a shock to find her like that, dead on the bed. Drugs. She took an overdose. Quiet girl, nicely spoken, didn't go out much.'

'How do you know that?'

'Because I was here in the shop like I am now and I was most days back then — not on a Sunday, though. I only started opening on Sundays three years ago to keep up with the competition. People expect it now. I rarely saw her. Heard her moving about sometimes. She might have gone out at night, I suppose. And she could have had friends over but I never saw anyone visit her. Spent all day on her computer. Leastways, that's what I thought she was doing. She was on it when I called on her a couple of times. I asked if I should put my stuff on a computer and she smiled and said I probably wouldn't know where to find it if I did but she said I could have a website and sell stuff from it. I told her she was nuts but she wasn't. Look at what they sell on it now — everything and anything. Maybe I would be making more money but who cares.' He shrugged and his body wobbled.

'What happened to her computer and belongings?'

'Don't know. I don't think she had much personal stuff. The flat was let fully furnished, as it is now, to a West-Indian, nice man who works for the council. The police sent someone round to clear it out. I think it was a woman from a local charity shop who came. I don't remember it being a relative. Well, no one came to me and said they were related to her. No, that's a lie — a woman did come from the Polish Society, asking if Jemma had ever mentioned any relatives. I didn't know Jemma was Polish — she never spoke with an accent but then the name does sound foreign. The police handed back the key to me and said I could re-let it. Took me an age to do so. Not many people want to live in a place where someone has died, although they'd be hard pushed to find a house or flat, particularly an old one, where someone hasn't died.'

'Did you attend the funeral?'

He looked dumbfounded. 'Of course not.' But he refrained from adding that she was only a tenant, perhaps because Marvik was eyeing him with slight distaste.

'How long was she here?' Marvik asked.

He scratched his head. Marvik could see the flakes of dandruff fall in the dusty air. 'She took the flat in March 2003 and died in September 2003.'

'And her references checked out.'

'Didn't take any. She paid six months in advance, cash. Poor girl died just as her rent was due.'

Marvik's antennae twitched. Why six months? Why die before any more rent could be paid? Was that because she'd run out of money and was destitute and depressed? Like hell it was. The timing fitted with the period of the *Mary Jo*'s disappearance.

Palgrave said, 'I never had any complaints about her and she never complained about anything to me,' he added slightly defensively. 'She was as quiet as a church mouse. There is only the one flat above the shop and she had her own entrance — the door to the left of the shop gives on to the stairs.' Marvik had seen it.

'Did she say why she came here?'

'No, and I never asked.'

'Did she work?'

'The police said they couldn't find an employment record for her, not for the last year of her life. She told me she worked freelance on the computer for folk but I don't know who.'

The shop bell clanged and a man dressed in luminous orange Lycra with a cycle helmet perched on his large head entered.

Palgrave addressed him. 'Need any help?'

'A puncture kit.'

Palgrave served him and returned to Marvik after a few minutes. 'That's all I know. No one's been here to ask about her except you . . . No, again I tell a lie. There was someone.' Marvik's ears pricked up at this.

'Young chap, ginger hair, turned up about a year ago. Said he'd been a friend of hers, at college and had only just heard she'd died.'

'Did he give a name?' Marvik asked.

'No, or if he did I don't remember it.'

But Marvik knew who it was. Gavin Yardly. A year ago. Had that been when he'd started to look into her death and had discovered something mysterious about the *Mary Jo*, or was it the other way around or no link at all? He dismissed the latter. He was convinced of a connection.

'What did he ask you about her?'

'Just the usual, like you. What happened to her stuff? How long had she been here? I couldn't tell him any more than I'm telling you, except that she got packages from abroad. I only mention that because he asked me if she'd received anything from overseas, or if anything from abroad had come for her after her death. I told him I'd never sent anything back to the post office or turned away a courier after she died.'

Marvik felt a frisson of excitement. If Gavin was keen on this then so was he. 'Did she get any packages?'

'Two that I know of, about the size of a few books. But they weren't books. She didn't have any. It was cosmetics or women's things,' he said vaguely as though he had no idea what those might be, and Marvik thought that was probably true given his rampant halitosis. Women in Palgrave's life must be very rare indeed or not particularly fussy.

'Where were these packages from?'

'No idea. I just saw a load of foreign gibberish on the label.'

'Could it have been Polish?'

'Could have been Klingon for all I'd know.' He grinned toothlessly — or almost.

Marvik resisted the impulse to step back. 'You told this other man that?'

'Yeah. He more or less asked the same as you. Wanted to know how many packages had come here. I told him I hadn't a clue, only that I took two up to her. The first time the delivery driver might have knocked and she didn't hear him; the second time I was just turning up at the shop.'

'Why did you think it was cosmetics or feminine products?'

'It was from a laboratory — I saw that on the label. I can't remember the name, though.'

'But both were from the same laboratory?'

'Dunno.'

'Did this ginger-haired young man ask you anything else?'

'No. I saw him about two weeks ago, though, walking along the street. And he looked right through me.'

And why was that? wondered Marvik as he took his leave of the halitosis cycle shop owner. Because he was being watched or followed? Or because he no longer needed Palgrave's information to piece together the last days of Jemma Duisky's life or the reason why she had died.

He hurried back to the coffee shop, his mind racing with thoughts. Had Jemma Duisky been working for Ian Bradshaw? Had Gavin Yardly suspected Bradshaw of killing her? Maybe Bradshaw had murdered Jemma. Was that why Gavin had wanted to be in one of Bradshaw's properties and in the road where Jemma had lived and died? But there was more. Gavin had discovered what Jemma had been working on just before her death. And it had something to do with the disappearance of the *Mary Jo* because aside from knowing one another, attending the same college and both being computer experts, that was what she and Gavin had in common. So what did being an IT specialist have to do with a salvage vessel that had mysteriously vanished before it could reach Newfoundland and the SS *Celeste*?

Marvik's footsteps slowed as his mind mentally raced through what he and Strathen had discovered and what he'd just learned: a crew with no dependents; a clever IT specialist installed in a flat with no neighbours, fellow tenants, friends or visitors and who had paid cash; packages being delivered from a laboratory; a salvage vessel that had disappeared without having time to send out a distress signal; another clever computer specialist, Gavin, who had written to GCHQ saying he had located it; the dates Jemma had been here — 'she took the flat in March 2003 and died in September 2003'; his earlier conversation with Strathen about smuggling — 'drugs, arms, stolen art, artefacts, diamond smuggling . . . take your pick'; 2003 . . . And suddenly Marvik had it. He knew exactly what the *Mary Jo* had been smuggling.

# CHAPTER TWENTY

'It was chemicals,' Marvik said, keeping his voice low despite his excitement. Swiftly he relayed to Strathen what he'd learned from the cycle shop owner. 'Palgrave said the packages were *from* a laboratory. They might also have been sent *to* a laboratory, a fake one Jemma created with a fake website, and she used the flat address to get deliveries. She was unlikely to be disturbed as there were no nosy neighbours to see the packages arrive. It was just her bad luck that Palgrave intercepted them on two occasions but she soon learned he wasn't suspicious. I know this is all supposition but it fits, especially if you put it with Gavin's interest, his letter to GCHQ and the year, 2003.'

'The invasion of Iraq.'

Marvik nodded and sipped his coffee. It was a year that neither of them would forget. They'd been engaged in combat, working covertly in a conflict that had begun in March 2003 when a combined force of troops from the United States, Great Britain and smaller contingents from several other countries had invaded Iraq and rapidly defeated the Iraqi military and paramilitary forces in April 2003. The first phase of the Iraq War was over by the time the *Mary Jo* was lost, but the conflict continued with the United States-led occupation of Iraq opposed by an insurgency; an insurgency that would have been only too eager to get their hands on lethal chemical weapons. It wasn't until 2007 that the violence began to decline and the United States gradually reduced its military presence, withdrawing completely in 2011.

Marvik continued, 'I think Bradshaw, and whoever he was working with, was engaged in supplying lethal chemicals to terrorists.'

'Was Meryl Landguard involved?' asked Strathen.

'I don't know. Maybe. Perhaps Timothy Landguard also knew what he was carrying. If not him then someone on the *Mary Jo* did, and maybe more than one person.'

'The phoney crew.'

Marvik nodded. 'The *Mary Jo* was engaged to rendezvous with the buyers, as we'd already speculated, not to collect drugs but to deliver a toxic chemical — one which could have wiped out that crew swiftly and silently, causing the *Mary Jo* to drift and disappear into the ice of the Arctic. Maybe the chemical package got damaged in transit, or one of the crew accidentally tampered with it before they could deliver it. Or perhaps they delivered one consignment successfully and didn't realize there was another on board which killed them before they could head on to Newfoundland.' Marvik sat forward. 'Bradshaw and his accomplice, the killer, could have hoped they'd found a new way to smuggle chemicals to terrorists but perhaps the fact that it went wrong persuaded them to shut down that route and particular trade. Bradshaw stayed put and made his money out of the insurance and accounting fraud, along with Meryl Landguard, but the third man with them in this took off.'

'Or never returned because he was on the *Mary Jo*.'

Marvik could see what Strathen was driving at. He said, 'You could be right. The other man involved in this collected the money, then got off the *Mary* Jo and vanished into the sunset, leaving the boat to drift with the remaining crew dead on board. Could it be Timothy Landguard?'

'It's possible.'

'Did Gavin discover this and tell Bradshaw that Landguard was still alive and where he was, and Bradshaw thought he was owed a lot more than he'd got and demanded it?'

'He was an idiot, then.' Strathen swallowed his coffee and pushed down the lid of his computer.

Marvik frowned in thought. 'Did Royden know who it was or did he discover it after our conversation on my boat? Maybe I jogged his memory enough to get him killed as a result. Did Jemma know the extent of what she was involved in?'

'Bradshaw, or our killer, could have told her the chemicals were needed for a beneficial project, or perhaps she didn't care about the war and the damage it would wreak on humans. The challenge to obtain them might have been enough for her not to bother asking too many questions.'

'Or perhaps he spun her a line that she was working for British intelligence on a covert IT project to help flush out terrorists.'

'That would fit,' Strathen said, digesting this.

'But why didn't Gavin write to MI5?'

'Because GCHQ monitor conversations and pick up intelligence via the Internet. Gavin would have considered them a natural home for his information. Or perhaps Jemma had sent Gavin a message to say she was testing IT intelligence on behalf of someone working for GCHQ. He thought nothing of it at the time, not until last year when he started to look into her death. Whoever hired her could have said he'd heard about her talents and that he needed someone with excellent computer hacking skills, and that if she proved her worth she'd be recommended for more projects with GCHQ.'

'I wonder how Bradshaw, if it was him, or the killer, located her,' Marvik mused.

'I've managed to contact the secretary of the Polish Society, Mrs Monika Podanski. She says she remembers

Jemma Duisky, and the manner of her death. She took responsibility for burying her.'

'Did she dispose of her personal belongings, including her computer?'

'We can ask her. I've arranged to meet her at Jemma's grave at eleven o'clock.'

Marvik rose; Strathen followed suit. Outside, as they made for the car, Strathen said, 'Our killer is clever, scheming, manipulative and probably has others working for him who will do as they're told. If we're right about the chemicals then he must have known something about them, which could indicate he has a military background or that he worked for the intelligence service.'

'Perhaps he worked as a pharmacist, chemist or . . .' Marvik paused as something Royden had said flashed into his mind. He rapidly put that with what Stapledon had told him. Eagerly, he continued, 'Or he worked *with* chemicals, transporting them by sea or salvaging them from a marine casualty, which brings us back to Timothy Landguard or another member of the crew on the *Mary Jo*. Perhaps there was a chemical incident at sea that triggered the idea of smuggling.'

'I can check out the marine casualties via the marine accident investigation reports, but it couldn't have been a major disaster or chemical spill because I'd remember it.'

Marvik would also have but nothing rang a bell with him.

Strathen started the car. 'Let's hope Mrs Podanski can tell us more about Jemma.'

Marvik didn't hold out much hope of that. How could she when all she'd done was bury the poor girl?

For the second time in a week, Marvik found himself staring at the gravestone of a young woman, only this time it was one he had never met. The first had been Sarah's grave in the cemetery in Southampton, on the same day he'd visited Nigel Bell and asked him about his parents' belongings and papers. Jemma's grave told them nothing about her save the year she was born and the year she died, but heading towards them was the squat figure of a woman in her late sixties with a bunch of white chrysanthemums in her hand, windblown silver-grey hair and a broad smile on her friendly, fair face. She threw Marvik a surprised glance as her eyes flicked over his scars and then took in Strathen.

'You lads look as though you've been in the wars, literally,' she said, concerned rather than fearful.

'We're not terrorists,' Strathen replied with a smile, extending his hand and making the introductions.

'Didn't think you were.' She returned the smile. 'Army?'

'Royal Marines.'

'Why are the Marines interested in Jemma?'

'They're not — we are. We're no longer in the armed forces. It's complicated and confidential.' But Strathen didn't get the chance to elaborate, which Marvik thought was a good thing, because Monika Podanski was keen to talk — another plus factor, he thought.

'Is it to do with Jemma's mother, Elona Kadowski?' she said slightly breathlessly. 'Her being Russian?'

Marvik threw Strathen a look. 'We're not sure,' he answered evasively and truthfully. 'Perhaps you can tell us what you know.'

'Of course.' She placed her flowers on the grave and straightened up.

'Shall we sit down?' Strathen indicated the bench between two blossoming trees. They crossed to it.

When seated, Monika Podanski began. 'Elona Kadowski was a very talented Russian artist. Famous in her early days and even more sought after following her death, but that's often the way with the creative arts, isn't it, sadly. She was commissioned to paint murals in public buildings and her work was also exhibited and bought by Russian officials. She was a futurist. Do you know what that is?'

Strathen answered, 'It's a twentieth-century art movement. Futurists loathed ideas from the past, especially political and artistic traditions. They loved speed, noise, machines, pollution, cars, cities, the industrial town.'

'Yes.' She beamed at him as though he was a pupil who had just answered a difficult question. Marvik wondered if she had been a teacher — perhaps she still was one. He liked her enthusiasm. It reminded him of Sarah when she had spoken to him in that steamy café on Swanage seafront about her passion for marine archaeology. He pushed the thought from his mind and put his full attention on Mrs Podanski.

'It was largely an Italian phenomenon,' she was saying. 'Although there were parallel movements in both Russia and England. Elona, at first, imitated to a certain degree the work of Natalia Goncharova who left Russia in 1915 and died in poverty in Paris in 1962. She was a major figure in early twentieth-century Russian art and is now one of the most highly priced Russian artists in history.'

'You've done a lot of research,' Marvik said.

'I enjoyed it, or I would have done if the reason for it hadn't been so tragic. If only Jemma had contacted us. We would have helped her not to feel so alone.' Her face fell and, in the silence she left, a blackbird squawked and chirped noisily as someone invaded its territory. Marvik looked across in its direction to see a man in his seventies pause by a grave.

Mrs Podanski resumed. 'Elona fell out of favour with the Soviet government in 1967 because her work became too futuristic. She began to portray Soviet Russia as it really was. Her paintings were seized and burned and her public murals were taken down and destroyed. She fled to Poland, which was then Soviet-backed, where she met Edward Duisky, Jemma's father. He was a Polish Jew and a mathematics lecturer at Warsaw University. He was also a very talented musician, but in March 1968 events at Warsaw University — the banning of the performance of a play by Adam Mickiewicz at the Polish Theatre on the grounds that it contained anti-Soviet references — was used by the authorities to launch an anti-intellectual and anti-Semitic, anti-Zionist campaign, and about twenty thousand Jews lost their jobs, including Edward. He and Elona were forced to flee Poland and came to England. Jemma, their only child, was born in 1983. By then Edward was sixty-eight and Elona forty-one, very old for first-time parents in those days, not quite so old nowadays. They never married. Edward died in 1987 and Elona thirteen years later in March 2000. I couldn't trace any living relatives and I asked both the Polish and Russian embassies for assistance. Whether they tried to find any I don't know, but no relative contacted me and nobody attended Jemma's funeral, except myself and a few other members of the Polish community here.'

'Did you contact anyone in the art world?' asked Strathen.

'Yes. Sotheby's put me in touch with the Tate gallery in London. They have one of Elona's paintings, which they bought at an auction in Moscow in November 2000, only eight months after Elona had died. It was one of three paintings found in the basement of a government building in Moscow, which was being demolished. The person I spoke to said they had discovered that Elona had died in England but they weren't aware of any child. Jemma's birth was registered in her father's name and, although Elona is named on Jemma's birth certificate as the mother because there was no marriage certificate, they didn't look for any offspring. Elona and Edward are buried in Hastings where they lived. I don't know who attended their funerals. Of course, Jemma was only four when her father died and only seventeen when she lost her mother. Perhaps she handled her mother's funeral alone or had friends and neighbours to help her but no one in the Hastings and District Polish Society knew of it, or of Elona and Jemma. I got the impression that Elona and her family kept a very low profile. Edward was a lecturer at Hastings College. If Elona continued to paint when she arrived in England then the pictures have either been destroyed or are lingering in people's houses — the owners totally unaware of who she was. The person at the Tate seemed very taken aback when I said there was a daughter.'

Did Jemma know of her mother's fame, Marvik wondered, and want no part of it, or had she been completely ignorant of it? Surely someone like Jemma would have searched the Internet for background on her mother. But if her mother had never revealed her surname then Jemma had no reason to look for it; it wouldn't have been until Elona died that Jemma would have discovered her name, but even then she might not have been curious, and her mother had kept the fact she was a painter from her. Something nagged at the back of his mind but he couldn't pinpoint it.

He said, 'Were the paintings dated?'

'No, but the experts believe they were painted in the mid-sixties, sometime between 1964 and 1967.'

Again, something jarred with Marvik. Was it the date?

'When I saw how Jemma had been living in that squalid, poky flat I felt very angry and upset. She should have had something from the sale of those paintings. That money might have prevented her from ending her life in so dreadful a way.'

Keenly, Marvik said, 'You went to her flat?'

She nodded. 'The police checked her family background and, discovering her father was Polish, contacted me. I said I would do all I could to help. They didn't know her mother was a renowned artist — neither did I, not then. We also helped with the costs of burying her from our funds.'

'Was there a computer among her belongings or a mobile phone?'

'No. Nothing like that. Just a few clothes, shoes, a couple of photographs of her mother and father, which were buried with her, and that was it. So sad.'

Marvik couldn't help his thoughts returning to Sarah. She'd had no living relatives and her funeral had been a depressing affair with a handful of former colleagues and a few friends, which was more than Jemma had had.

'Was there any correspondence in Jemma's flat?'

'Nothing. And no personal papers. I'm sorry but I must be going.' She rose and they followed suit. 'I'm not sure I've helped you much,' she said, turning towards the cemetery entrance.

Strathen answered, 'You've helped a great deal.' She beamed at him. He said, 'How much were those paintings in Moscow sold for?'

'That's the sad thing, when you think of how Jemma died. They fetched four million pounds.'

Marvik saw Strathen's astonishment, which he knew must be mirrored on his own face. His mind whirled with thoughts and at last what had been eluding him crystallized into a conversation he'd had five days ago at the start of this mission on board his boat with Crowder. And with it came the realization that they'd been looking for explanations and motives in completely the wrong place.

## CHAPTER TWENTY-ONE

'Nice lady,' Strathen said as they climbed into his car.

'And a nice fortune Jemma's mother would have left behind if she had died after those paintings had been found and auctioned and Jemma had been located. The authorities in Russia didn't bother to search for any relatives, they just wanted the money from the sale. The art galleries didn't bother either, but I think someone looked very hard to find Jemma Duisky, or rather to see if there were any living dependents of Elona.'

Strathen eyed him curiously.

Marvik eagerly began to relay the thoughts that had rushed through his mind. 'They might not have been the only paintings Elona left behind. Crowder said the *Celeste* started life as the MS *Lyudmila,* a small Russian cruise ship built in East Germany in 1961 for the Soviet Union's Baltic Shipping Company and launched in 1964. When she was withdrawn from service in 1979 she sat in the Murmansk shipyard for six years with everything inside her intact, including ornamental structures and balustrades made of bronze and silver, and that's not all. He said there were murals on board. When I mentioned that to Royden he looked surprised. I thought it was because I knew more about the *Celeste* than he'd anticipated but perhaps it was the fact that he hadn't heard about any murals being on board. But whoever handled the dismantling of the *Celeste* had.'

'This Marcus Kiln who doesn't exist as far as I can find,' Strathen said. 'There is nothing on him, no register of birth or death.'

'Another phoney, who nobody saw. I've nothing to say for certain that Elona painted those murals on the *Celeste* but I'm betting she did and that they survived the refit by the Norwegian owners. I wish we had pictures of the interior of the *Celeste*.'

'I might be able to find some online and those paintings of Elona's that were auctioned.' Strathen started the car. 'I can get a faster connection to the Internet on the seafront.'

Marvik's mind was racing. As they headed there, he continued, 'Royden told me that Bradshaw had served on cruise liners — maybe one of those was the *Celeste*. But if he'd known the true worth of the murals he wouldn't have risked bringing the *Celeste* back to Britain to be scrapped. Here they might have been recognized. And as I said, I don't think Royden knew about them, otherwise he could have retired on the money he got from the sale of them.'

'He could have it stashed away in an offshore account.'

'Then why was he killed?'

'Because he was in league with Kiln, who helped him to sell the murals from India. Much easier to offload them there on to private buyers from Hong Kong, Russia and Singapore than over here.'

'Must have taken a lot of planning.'

'And time to locate and build relationships with buyers who not only had the money and the desire to own such paintings but who were also as unscrupulous as the seller and didn't care how they were acquired.'

'And Royden only got the contract for the *Celeste* after the *Mary Jo* disappeared. He said he thought he was going to get it first time round and Kiln was counting on it, but Bradshaw did a private deal with someone to switch bringing the *Celeste* to Britain. And that meant the *Mary Jo* had to be taken out.'

'Hence the purchase of the chemicals. Not to smuggle to terrorists but to wipe out the crew of the *Mary Jo*. Whoever is behind this could have told Jemma it was the only way she could get her hands on her inheritance.'

'Yes, and the loss of the *Mary Jo* meant Duncan Helmslow wouldn't be able to fulfil the contract so it was taken over by Royden.'

Strathen turned on to the seafront. He parked up and was soon engrossed on his computer interrogating the Internet. Marvik left him to it. He needed air and time to think. So much seemed to be happening and their enquiries were leading them into new and unexpected territory, but he felt instinctively that at last they were on the right track. He was only sorry that it had taken so long to get there and had incurred more deaths — Royden's — not to mention Marvik's concerns about Meryl and Stephen Landguard. Then there was Karen and the child. He hoped to God they were safe. Should he call Crowder and ask him to find them? But he couldn't because that would involve alerting the police and scaring off the killer who, if he hadn't already silenced them, wouldn't hesitate to do so. Who else did he have on his slaughter list? Stapledon? Or was Stapledon their killer? If he was then he was damn good at hiding the proceeds from the sale of those murals and living as though he depended only on his salary from the charity. At least Helen was safe in Eastbourne police station.

Marvik crossed to the beach. He watched as the waves crashed on to the stones. The sky had grown overcast and dark clouds were gathering out to sea and over the cliffs of Beachy Head to his right. Was the *Celeste* the key to what had happened in 2003 and recently? Bradshaw had known nothing about the murals, not until Gavin had come along. He and Meryl had believed their fraud would be exposed but perhaps Bradshaw suddenly realized what had really happened and recognized who was behind it. If so, that would have given him enormous scope for blackmail, which he'd tried with disastrous consequences. It had to be someone he had worked with. And someone who knew those murals were on the *Celeste*. Royden had said that Landguard had done a stint on cruise liners. *It didn't suit Tim . . . who did a stint on them but left to go into the salvage industry and then to work for Duncan.* Convenient then for him to have been the master on the *Mary Jo*. And had Royden finally realized what had happened and been taken out because of that?

Marvik's mind flicked back to the chemicals acquired by Jemma Duisky which could have been used to wipe out the crew of the *Mary Jo*. A deadly chemical that acted swiftly and silently and could kill within an instant so as to prevent the master or any of the crew sending out a distress signal. But perhaps Timothy Landguard hadn't wanted to send out a distress signal. Perhaps he'd worn a protective mask because the chemical had to be something that could kill when breathed in and not on impact, causing an explosion which would have wrecked the boat and killed them all. And Landguard would have had to get off the *Mary Jo* and aboard another craft he'd arranged to rendezvous with.

He watched two children playing on the beach and a dog leaping around their feet as they threw stones into the sea for it to retrieve. It was a chemical that Landguard had come across during his time at sea. Not one involved in a marine casualty because that would have been big news, as Strathen had said. Perhaps it was a consignment of chemicals which, not necessarily lethal on their own, when exposed to air could be deadly. It could be a chemical used in a manufactured commodity. Had an incident on board a container ship Landguard had worked on contained this chemical, which had given him the idea of how he might dispose of the crew of the *Mary Jo*?

Marvik stared out at the horizon, where he could see in the far distance a large car carrier making for the Continent. Strathen hailed him and Marvik hurried back to the car.

'Take a look at these — they're the paintings Mrs Podanski said were found in the basement of the government building in Moscow.'

Marvik found himself firstly studying a brightly coloured picture with an elongated figure working over a giant piece of machinery. There was a kind of fury about it, an obsession that at all costs the job must be done but, instead of liberating the worker, the machinery looked to be dominating him. He said as much.

'You'll make an art critic yet. But you're right. And that's one of the reasons why the authorities came to dislike her. Her work came to represent the slavery of the Soviet citizens. Take a look at the other two.'

They were both in the same style. One was of a tall, thin woman with a sharp-featured face in front of a fast-moving train that gave Marvik the impression of someone being swept along in a direction she didn't want to take. The other was of a giant ship and a man with a small hand tool and a tiny bench in front of it. He was dwarfed by the ship, possibly representing the common man being overshadowed and subdued by the state.

Strathen said, 'Mrs Podanski was right — they were sold at auction for just over four million pounds. The shipbuilding picture is in the Russian Museum in St Petersburg, the factory one is in the New York Art Gallery and the train one is at the Tate in London. And there's more which could confirm that the murals on the *Celeste* were Elona's work.'

Marvik listened keenly.

'I haven't been able to find any images of them but what I did find was that Yakov Borislov was the state official responsible for commissioning ship building in the early 1960s, including the *Lyudmila*.'

'The Soviet defector, or rather he hoped to be.'

Strathen nodded. 'Yes. Officially, and conveniently, he died of a heart attack on board a cruise ship, not the *Lyudmila*, in 1967 before he could jump overboard and get picked up by the US coastguard. Someone shopped him and I don't think it was Elona because I suspect she might have been his mistress in return for the commission and in the hope that she could follow him to the West, except he failed to tell her when he was going. So we have three possibilities. One, our killer worked on the *Celeste* as part of the crew as you said, and when he read about the find and the auction of those paintings in either one of the broadsheets or the art magazines where it was fully reported, he realized their potential worth.'

'Possibly Landguard.'

Strathen nodded. 'Two, our killer was a passenger on the *Celeste* and after reading the newspaper articles remembered what he'd seen on board and set himself up as a ship broker in order to acquire them. Or three, he had a mission to carry out — to terminate Borislov, which he successfully completed. And if that's the case then he would have full knowledge of Borislov's affair with Elona Kadowski and that she was an artist engaged in painting those murals on the *Celeste*. He thought nothing of her or her work until he read how much her paintings had been sold for. And he knew that Borislov had commissioned her to paint the murals on the *Celeste*. If he's our man then we're looking for someone in his early to mid-seventies.'

'It fits with the language Helen overheard those two men, Colbourne and Marwell, using on the pontoon about taking out the target, although from the lockkeeper and marina duty manager's description neither of them were old enough to be our agent, or rather one certainly wasn't. The other man could be. Nobody saw him. Would someone who was once an agent engage others to do his dirty work?'

'He's getting older and made a fortune out of flogging those paintings. Maybe he got tired of soiling his hands and hasn't got the health or energy to take anyone out now but he'd know all about deadly chemicals. He could have been a double agent back then and possibly has been for years. And he could easily have traced Jemma Duisky. He would have had access to information on Edward Duisky, Elona Kadowski and Yakov Borislov. Edward Duisky and Elona Kadowski were granted asylum here and naturalization because of the fact they could have had information that could be helpful to the government. Their communications and movements would have been monitored for a while on the grounds they could have been spies. Or perhaps Elona Kadowski was working for the British long before she arrived here. She might have been detailed to get close to Borislov and while working in East Germany managed to get certain information, which she'd extracted from him, to one of our agents. She had to get out of Russia when Borislov's defection failed because she was in real danger of being arrested as a spy. Edward Duisky could have been her contact in Poland and then it got too hot for them there. When she came here she brought with her valuable information, which means her identity could have been protected for some time afterwards.'

Marvik rapidly digested this. 'The killer, after reading that her paintings were now worth a fortune, traced the *Celeste* to Newfoundland where he found the ship waiting to be salvaged. He made certain the murals were on board. Then he had to check there were no living relatives but why bother with that if he was going to steal them?'

'Maybe he was hoping he'd discover more of her paintings.'

'And he found Jemma completely ignorant of her mother's fame. He also discovered she was something of a genius when it came to computers. But he didn't need her expertise in that field — not until Bradshaw messed up his plans to get the *Celeste* to India. Whoever the killer is — an agent, former crew member of the *Celeste* or passenger, how would Bradshaw have got hold of him recently, *if* he did, in order to blackmail him?'

'Maybe Gavin had tracked him down and told Bradshaw.'

Marvik considered this. 'Gavin could have just given the name to GCHQ but he didn't. Why?'

'Perhaps he didn't know it then. But he finally made the connection and confronted the killer.'

Eagerly, Marvik said, 'Bradshaw could have been the key to giving Gavin the identity of the killer. According to Karen Landguard, Gavin insisted on a flat in that road. There were others vacant with other landlords but it had to be one of Bradshaw's and he went to work for Bradshaw. Why?' Marvik asked, his mind working furiously. Then answered his own question. 'Not just because it was where Jemma had died but because he needed to pump Bradshaw for background information about his former career and his time with Helmsley's.'

'Gavin could have discovered from Jemma's files her boss's name — phoney, no doubt — but maybe she also described him. She could have backed up her files online and those are the files Gavin managed to locate and open.'

'In 2003?'

'Of course. Remote backup came into being in the late 1990s with the dot-com boom so it's perfectly feasible she backed up all her research online but with whom and where would be the question. Whoever she used might have gone out of business by now but it's far more likely they've been taken over or merged with another provider. If anyone could locate them then Gavin stood a good chance of doing so having known her from his college days and being something of a computer genius. He would still have needed the password to gain access to the encrypted files, but again that would have been child's play for someone like him.'

Strathen's words brought Marvik up sharply. He'd never considered the fact that his parents might have backed up their projects and their research findings online. Their deaths had occurred in 1997; he'd thought it was too early for online backup of computer files, but not so, it seemed. It was possible that they had used both offline backup, such as the floppy disk he had found in Sarah's possession, and online backup. He wouldn't even know where to begin looking for the latter unless there was some reference to it in his parents' papers in the safe-deposit box at the bank or on that disk. Could the password his father had used be *Vasa* — the name he'd written on that disk?

'Are you OK, Art?' Strathen asked, concerned.

Marvik tried to bring his mind back to the job in hand but Strathen, who knew his background and the manner of his parents' deaths, deserved to know what had momentarily distracted him from the mission. 'I was just wondering if my parents had used an online back-up service in the 1990s.'

'Would you like to find out?' Strathen asked.

'If you had asked me that a month ago I would have said no, but Sarah's death, and Crowder's belief it was as a result of something my parents were occupied on at the time of their deaths, has changed that.' Marvik told him about the disk he'd found and how he had placed it in the bank without looking at it. He gave no more than the facts. He didn't explain how he felt or relay details of his visit to Bell, the solicitor's clerk, on Monday. There was no need for that.

Strathen listened in silence. When Marvik had finished, he said, 'When and if you're ready to look into it, let me know. I can try opening the disk for you using the ancient hard drives I have, which will take that format, but that doesn't mean to say I'd be able to read what is on the disk. After all this time, it could be corrupted.'

Marvik knew that could be the case. And if Strathen couldn't retrieve information from the disk then no one could. Crisply, he said, 'To get back to Gavin, he knew it was someone that Bradshaw would recognize or know from the past.'

'And once Bradshaw told Gavin who it was without perhaps realizing it, Gavin then set about locating him.'

Marvik's mind teemed with thoughts. 'Gavin couldn't have told Meryl who it was because according to Stephen Landguard his mother thought Gavin had discovered their fraud. Meryl Landguard phoned Bradshaw after Gavin had met her. No one saw him after Helen did. Maybe Bradshaw sussed out what Gavin was after once he'd met up with Meryl on his boat and went directly to the killer to confront him and blackmail him over it. Bradshaw told the killer what he knew and what Gavin had unearthed. The killer promised to cut Bradshaw in if he'd remain silent, while we know what his real intention was. Gavin was taken somewhere by boat, possibly even Bradshaw's boat.'

'Or the killer's or his accomplice's.'

Marvik nodded. 'Gavin was held somewhere alive, probably drugged, as the autopsy shows no evidence of him being bound and gagged. Bradshaw was killed after Gavin had seen Meryl. Gavin could have known who the killer was when he met Meryl and was seeking confirmation of a fact that would prove he was correct but didn't say anything to her about it. He put what she said with what he'd got from Bradshaw and knew who it was and where he could find him.'

'Timothy Landguard?'

'Perhaps that's why the discovery of the *Mary Jo* is so interesting, because instead of four bodies on that vessel there are only three: Warrendale, Chale and Goodhead.'

'Gavin would have needed to have crystal clear images of the intact bodies including facial images to know that, and have photographs of them all in order to be able to identify them.'

'But they had been frozen in ice so it's possible, especially if they didn't die from an explosive device, which is unlikely if the boat was found intact. And if it had been struck by a freak wave, then it would have sank or overturned. The chances of all four crew being swept overboard, while not impossible, is unlikely.'

'But how would he know what the crew looked like? I can't find anything on them.' Then Strathen quickly added, 'But he discovered what Timothy Landguard looked like.'

'And he wasn't on board.'

'Or the *Mary Jo* was a ghost ship with no bugger on board.'

'If so then why were we called in?'

'To find out what happened to the crew.'

'No.' Marvik shook his head. 'I don't think the Squad, GCHQ or MI5 would have bothered if that was the case. If the crew sent their CVs to Jemma then it's possible she had pictures of them on her backed-up files.'

'And Meryl Landguard could have described her husband to Gavin.'

'I'm not sure about that. From my meeting with her, she'd have told Gavin to leap off a cliff.'

'Which he was supposed to have done but didn't. Bradshaw might have shown Gavin a photograph of Timothy Landguard or described him and the crew to Gavin.'

'Maybe. And maybe Stapledon did too. Gavin Yardly visited Stapledon, only Stapledon pretended to me that it was Stephen Landguard who came to see him. He said he panicked when I asked him questions but there was a reason why Gavin needed to question Stapledon and a reason why Stapledon lied to me. He gave me Moorcott to put me off the scent, or strictly speaking to divert me to the fraud, which means he knows a great deal more about all this. Gavin could have spun him a line about his research and tricked Stapledon into talking about Timothy Landguard and the crew and, despite Stapledon telling me he hadn't met the crew, maybe he had. He's had time to think about Royden's death. Let's go and talk to him.'

# CHAPTER TWENTY-TWO

But Hugh Stapledon wasn't at home. His car had also gone. Marvik peered through the windows and letter box. He didn't expect to find Stapledon inside. He cursed silently. They could wait for him to show but they didn't have the time for that, and besides, there was the possibility that he'd taken off if he was their killer — which Marvik had already mentally discounted and did so again — or perhaps the killer had got to him ahead of them. As he was considering his next move a neighbour, spotting him, obviously curious and suspicious, came out and asked if he could help.

Marvik explained that he had been given Stapledon's address by the charity he worked for and needed to speak to him urgently about a marine matter. The man's expression cleared then looked sorrowful. 'You mean the death of Hugh's friend. Hugh told me about it on his way out about an hour ago. He was very distracted and upset. I could barely understand what he was talking about. He said something about having worked with him on car carriers, transporting Japanese cars and how he couldn't believe it had happened the way it must have done.'

'How what had happened?' Marvik asked, trying not to sound too sharp and frightening off the neighbour, but his heart skipped a beat as the thought that had been niggling at the back of his mind suddenly crystallized.

'I'm not sure. The accident, I guess. He took off in his car saying he needed to think.'

'Any idea where he was heading?' Marvik asked without much hope.

'He said his friend had been killed by the Birling Gap, so I suppose he could have gone there. People often wish to visit the scene of the tragedy, don't they? To pay their respects.' Marvik thanked him and climbed into the car.

'According to the neighbour, Stapledon could have gone to the Birling Gap. It's only two miles from here. If he has then his car will be there.'

'He could be anywhere on the Downs.'

Marvik knew that and, if so, it could take an age to find him.

As Strathen headed for the Birling Gap, Marvik rapidly relayed what had occurred to him. 'I think Stapledon's finally realized who the killer might be and he's worked out what happened on the *Mary Jo*. So have I.'

Strathen threw him a look.

'Sodium azide.' Marvik let Strathen digest this. He knew it wouldn't take him long.

It didn't.

'Used as a chemical preservative in hospitals and laboratories, in agriculture for pest control and in detonators and other explosives,' Strathen said.

'Yes. And we both know how highly explosive it is if it comes into contact with heavy metals such as silver, gold, lead, copper or brass, or if there is friction as a result of heat or a shock. In such cases sodium azide changes into a toxic gas called hydrazoic acid. Breathing that in a confined space would have killed them rapidly and silently. The *Mary Jo* didn't explode though because, according to Gavin Yardly, he found it in the ice. There is the possibility there might have been a minor explosion on board in a small, confined space where the crew were assembled but there is another way that sodium azide can kill and that is if it comes into contact with water.'

'It blocks the oxygen to the heart and brain and kills swiftly.'

'Yes, and before any of the crew of the *Mary Jo* could send out a distress call. I think Jemma sourced it for our killer, hence the packages from a laboratory,' Marvik continued eagerly. 'And I believe I know why it occurred to our killer to use it. Sodium azide is used in car airbags. An electrical charge triggered by the car collision causes the sodium azide to explode and convert to nitrogen gas inside the airbag. Stapledon and Royden worked on car carriers, transporting Japanese cars to Southampton. They'd know about sodium azide and so too would Bradshaw, Landguard, Helmslow and Elmsley. The only one of that crew who is alive is Stapledon.'

'Or Landguard if he faked his death.'

Marvik nodded. 'And there could have been someone else on the car carriers with them at one time or another, who could also have worked on the *Celeste* and Stapledon's gone to meet him.' A thought stirred in the back of his mind but before he could pursue it they drew into the car park. Stapledon's car wasn't there and they hadn't seen it parked anywhere on the approach to the Birling Gap. Marvik said, 'He might be parked in one of the lay-bys on the road to Eastbourne or at the Beachy Head car park.'

Strathen turned the car round and they headed east. It had started to rain heavily and the wind was strengthening. If Stapledon had been foolish enough to contact the killer then he was dead. He said as much to Strathen.

'How would Stapledon know where to find him?'

Marvik considered this. 'Three options: Bradshaw told him, Royden told him or the killer contacted Stapledon and asked to meet him.' Then he paused. 'There might be a fourth option. The killer must have made a fortune from selling Elona's murals, so what did he do with the money?'

'Spent it on wine, women and song?'

'Or used it to live in the lap of luxury abroad as a tax exile. And maybe he reinvested it to make more money.'

'In an offshore account, which is hard to trace, or at least the assets are.'

'And maybe he donated to charity.'

'I'd hardly think he'd have much of a conscience.'

'No, but he'd want to make very sure that nobody ever found him or came asking questions about the *Mary Jo* or the *Celeste*, and there is one way he could have done that. He's been donating to Stapledon's charity, and perhaps also making sure that Stapledon got something out of it personally in return for informing him if anyone came round asking about the *Mary Jo*.'

And into Marvik's mind flashed the spare, ageing figure of Nigel Bell, the solicitor's clerk who had bagged up and catalogued his parents' papers. Had he or the solicitor, Colmead, been instructed to let someone know if he or anyone else ever came around asking questions about his parents' deaths? Had Sarah visited Bell or Colmead? Was that why she had to die? But surely neither man would have told her anything. Maybe the mere fact she asked and was then seen talking to him in the café in Swanage was reason enough to kill her. He thought it time to have another talk with both Colmead and Bell, to retrieve that disk from the safe-deposit box and to look through his parents' papers. After this was over he would. He wouldn't even countenance the fact that he might not be alive to do so. Failure was not an option. And neither was it an option regarding Sarah's murder and his parents' deaths. He'd find the truth, no matter what it entailed. And, relieved he'd made the decision, he brought his sharp attention back to the job in hand.

'Stapledon was probably spun some yarn that the tragedy had touched this killer. He wasn't going to ask too many questions and nobody had come sniffing around about the *Mary Jo* for years until Gavin contacted him just over two weeks ago. That was why Stapledon lied to me about it being

Stephen Landguard. He had to inform his paymaster. Now, after all these deaths, he's running scared.'

'And he's right to be.'

The lay-bys were empty of vehicles of any kind — so too was the waterlogged and windswept road — but as Strathen came to the Beachy Head car park and turned into it, there was Stapledon's Nissan.

'He could be in the pub next door?' Strathen said, climbing out.

Marvik threw him a cynical look.

'Yeah, I know, unlikely.'

They checked it out. He wasn't inside. The wind and rain buffeted them as they crossed to the cliff edge. The weather was keeping everyone away.

Strathen said, 'Stapledon could be walking the Downs.'

'He could be lying under them.' Or his body could have been swept out to sea. Strathen headed east along the cliff edge while Marvik went west. They agreed to search for about half a mile each way. Marvik didn't think Stapledon would have walked further to rendezvous with his killer or walked far in his company.

There had been two deaths along this stretch of coast, stretching from Eastbourne to the Seven Sisters chalk cliffs. Correction: two people had been brutally murdered — Gavin Yardly and Alec Royden — one made to look like suicide, the other a car accident, and now Marvik thought they would need to add another to that death toll. And what of Stephen and his mother? Would Stephen also end up dead along here somewhere? Had Meryl Landguard already been dumped at sea or was she lying dead in her home, ostensibly killed by her son whose body would then be found on the beach, just as Gavin's had been? So many bodies discovered along here in a short space of time sadly wouldn't create any curiosity because this stretch of cliff-lined coast was notorious for jumpers. The coastguard chaplaincy had its work cut out trying to talk people down who were threatening to throw themselves off the cliffs and gently cautioning people not to go too near to the cliff edge which could crumble at any time. This bastard liked to stage-manage his killings. The thought pulled Marvik up sharply. He hurried back to Strathen, who had arrived at the car with a shake of his head. But before Marvik could express what had occurred to him a loud and continuous bleeping emanated from Strathen's phone.

'Shit!'

'What is it?' Marvik asked, climbing in the car, noting Strathen's concern.

'It's the tracking devices on Helen.' Consulting his mobile phone with a troubled frown, he said, 'That's interesting. Helen's in three places at the same time. She's heading north towards London, east towards Dover and west towards Brighton. I'll call Karina.'

Marvik sat with his thoughts while Strathen spoke to his lawyer. 'Karina's phoning me back,' he said, coming off the line within a couple of minutes. 'She hasn't been informed that Helen's been released. I'll call Colin Chester in case Helen has contacted him as I instructed. The westward direction could mean she's heading for Arundel.'

But if that was the case, Marvik knew as well as Strathen did that all three would have shown her going in that direction. His concerns deepened as Strathen's short conversation progressed.

'Colin hasn't heard from Helen,' Strathen announced, clearly anxious. 'If Helen is on her way there under her own steam and is perfectly OK then why the hell does one of the signals show she's making for London and the other Dover?'

But Strathen knew what it meant. He was just expressing his frustration.

Strathen continued, 'One of this killer's operatives must have been keeping a watch on Eastbourne police station, waiting for her to be apprehended. It's no secret the police were looking for her. I should have considered that.'

'We both should have,' Marvik said solemnly.

'She must have been bundled into a car the moment she left the police station and searched. They found two tracking devices — I'm guessing the ones in her coat and rucksack. Let's hope that they believe they're the only ones and they've missed the one in the hem of her skirt.'

Strathen's phone rang. It was his lawyer. When he came off the line, he said, 'Helen was released without charge. That's all anyone knows.'

'The correct signal has to be the one heading west,' Marvik said. 'Why would they take her to London or Dover? OK, if they intended leaving the country it's a possibility but they wouldn't want Helen with them. This is where all the deaths have occurred. They think they've found all the trackers and that it was me who planted them unless Helen tells them about you. She'll know it was you. But she might not tell them that. She can tell them I took her to the Hamble by boat and that she's been staying in a flat I own. They won't have had time to verify that yet. She can say she got bored and decided to come back to Eastbourne but a member of the public spotted her and the police arrived. She's not stupid. She'll think on her feet.'

'Unless she's forced to tell the truth.'

Marvik took a breath. He knew that it was a possibility. She could be terrified or tortured into saying more and telling the truth.

Strathen, following Marvik's train of thought, said, 'I have to follow the one heading west.'

'We'll both go.'

But Strathen was staring at his mobile phone screen. 'Not you, Art, you've got visitors?' he said solemnly.

Marvik tensed. 'On the boat.'

Strathen nodded.

'It could be the police. Bowman's told them about his and Royden's encounter with me.'

'On the other hand, it could be the killer. Either Stapledon or Helen's told them about your boat, which could back up your theory. It wouldn't be hard to trace once she gave them the name and description. And Stapledon knew you were moored there. You'll need me with you.'

'No. You have to follow up Helen. If it's the police on my boat I'll duck out. If it's the killer, I'll deal with it. He might be alone.'

'You know he won't be. This is a mission,' Strathen said tersely.

'And Helen's at risk. We have no option. *You* have no option.'

Strathen's worried gaze searched Marvik's face, then he gave a brief nod. He pulled out of the car park and headed west back to Newhaven. They didn't speak. They didn't need to. They each knew the other's thoughts. Marvik didn't want to think the worst but he knew they had to.

The fort car park, which Strathen pulled into thirty minutes later, was deserted as Marvik had expected given the weather, and it was getting dark. Strathen consulted the monitors on his phone. 'She's still heading west. And it's not the police on your boat.'

'You know what to do?'

Strathen gave a curt nod.

Marvik watched him turn the car round and head back towards the town centre. From there he would make in the direction of Helen's tracking device, pick it up and follow it to its destination. He only hoped the killer hadn't discovered it and it wasn't also a decoy.

He crossed the road in the slanting, stinging rain and walked through the marina car park towards his boat. There was no hurry and Strathen needed all the time he could get in order to reach Helen. Marvik could see his boat moored up on the pontoon at the harbour end of the marina. There was no other boat alongside it and no lights were showing. He couldn't see anyone on board but they were there. How many? One? Two? Maybe three? Would this killer have such reserves? Marvik thought so. Two operatives must be decoying them with the two tracking devices. One must be with Helen. Marvik thought he'd find two people on board his boat. One would be the man who had sabotaged the *Mary Jo* and stolen Elona's murals from the *Celeste*. The other would be one of his accomplices. For someone to have such resources indicated he was wealthy, powerful and influential, and aside from it being a former intelligence agent, which Marvik discounted, and given all that he had learned, there were only two men it could possibly be. He was about to discover which of them it was.

# CHAPTER TWENTY-THREE

Facing Marvik in the cabin was a sturdy, casually and expensively dressed, suntanned man in his mid-fifties with greying dark hair and deep-set brown eyes. Beside him was a younger, burly black man. He was carrying a gun. It was pointing at Marvik.

'Where's Helen?' Marvik asked.

'You'll find out soon enough,' the older man answered.

Marvik's mouth tightened. 'Is she still alive?'

'For the moment.' He addressed his accomplice. 'Give me the gun and take the boat out.'

Marvik's fists clenched.

'It's OK, we'll take good care of your boat. Paynton is a very experienced helmsman. Sit down. We might as well make ourselves comfortable while we wait.'

Marvik didn't ask for what.

'Keep your hands on the table,' the man instructed just as Marvik had instructed Stephen Landguard, Royden and Bowman.

Marvik obeyed as the boat's engine throbbed into life and Paynton left the cabin to cast off. For a moment, Marvik was alone with his captor. He could have taken him then and dealt with Paynton but there was too much that

Marvik needed to know first, including Helen's whereabouts. Returning to the helm, Paynton eased the boat into the choppy waters of the harbour. There was no one to stop them. Why should they? Marvik's brain was swirling with thoughts not just of how he would extricate himself from this but with everything he had learned over the last six days, putting the pieces together and arriving at the true identity of the man who was pointing the gun at him.

'Colin Prior, the man whose boat Gavin Yardly and Helen Shannon cleaned on Thursday when it arrived in Eastbourne Marina, and Marcus Kiln,' Marvik said evenly. 'Both false names but not the one you go under now. What is it, by the way?'

'You don't know?'

Marvik shrugged. 'I could guess. I'd say the eccentric, reclusive and principled owner of Drakes Marine, Terry Keydell.' He saw the flicker of annoyance in the man's dark eyes. It was the man Royden had called because he'd connected the murals Marvik had mentioned as being on the *Celeste* with one of Keydell's interests — art. But it wasn't only that which had made Royden realize who he was dealing with. He'd rapidly put it with Keydell's reclusiveness, his reluctance to be in England, particularly on the south coast where he might be recognized, and what he knew of the men he had served with at sea, and suddenly he knew who was behind the killings. But Royden had got it wrong. It wasn't Timothy Landguard who had become Terry Keydell.

Marvik said, 'You look remarkably well for a corpse swept out to sea in 2001 while trying to rescue a stricken fishing vessel out of Newhaven.' Marvik registered Martin Elmsley's surprise with some satisfaction.

'How did you know? Did Yardly tell Helen Shannon? I know he didn't tell Bradshaw, Royden or Stapledon.'

'I worked it out all by myself,' Marvik said coolly. 'It had to be either you or Timothy Landguard who had masterminded his own disappearance because it was someone who had worked in the shipping industry and knew about the ship recycling business. It also had to be someone who had served on the *Celeste.* Stapledon told me you had been on cruise ships, not which one but Royden also said that he, Landguard, Bradshaw and you had all served on cruise liners. He knew, but didn't tell me, that two of those men had served on the *Celeste* — Timothy Landguard and Martin Elmsley.'

'I see you've got a long way.'

'Even further. It also had to be someone who likes stage-managing deaths, and while Landguard could have arranged his on the *Mary Jo*, there was also one other person who could have stage-managed his. And no doubt you've already worked out a nice little scenario for me. What's it to be, Elmsley? Make it look as though I killed Helen and then killed myself? Is she somewhere along this coastline and both she and I are going to end up on the shore with a bullet through our heads?'

'I don't think you need worry about that,' Elmsley said, smiling. But Marvik could see by the slight narrowing of Elmsley's eyes that he was right.

'And will you then return to your lucrative life in your nice safe tax haven, which is where?'

'The Cayman Islands.'

In the western Caribbean about a hundred and fifty miles south of Cuba. A tax-neutral offshore jurisdiction, where any investment assets, no matter where they were in the world, property, art, jewellery, cash, securities and more were all protected from income tax, estate tax, inheritance tax and capital gains tax. All perfectly legal, although some would say immoral, and all very private.

'Where's Hugh Stapledon?'

'The cliffs and sea are dangerous places.'

It was as he and Strathen had thought. 'And Meryl and Stephen Landguard?'

'That's no longer your concern.'

Elmsley looked unperturbed. This man had ruthlessly plotted and killed. He would continue to kill. He had no compunction over what he'd done. 'And Karen Landguard and the child?' Marvik asked with dread. Had they been added to his slaughter list?

Elmsley shrugged. Maybe they were safe, Marvik thought with hope.

Elmsley said, 'I'm not sure why you've stuck your nose into this business but I'd like to know. And we have time before we need to part company.'

The boat swung eastwards, out beyond the breakwater along Seaford Bay where, away from the shelter of the harbour, it began to roll and buck in the height of the waves. The sea spray exploded over the for'ard and the slanting rain hit the decks like machine-gun bullets as Elmsley's henchman steered the boat as close to the shore as he could get without it being dangerous. They had the sea to themselves.

Marvik said, 'Jemma Duisky.'

Elmsley's dark eyes narrowed. His brow knitted with puzzlement. 'She had no relations.'

He was clearly trying to place Marvik. 'And of course you checked, thoroughly. Were her mother's murals worth all those deaths? Four on the *Mary Jo*, then Jemma, Ian Bradshaw, Gavin Yardly, Alec Royden, Hugh Stapledon, Meryl Landguard and her son. That's a hell of a lot of killings. And I trust a bullet for me and for Helen, not sodium azide?'

Again there was that shadow of irritation in Elmsley's eyes.

Marvik said, 'You enlisted Jemma's help in getting hold of it — how?'

But Elmsley didn't answer.

'Then let me tell you. You spun her some bullshit story about being from British intelligence or GCHQ and said you needed her expertise to test the robustness of the chemical manufacturers' IT systems and that of the marine salvage industry, who get called out to marine casualties carrying dangerous chemicals.'

Elmsley tried not to react but Marvik, watching him closely, saw the hardening of his mouth. Elmsley didn't like his plot being so transparent. Marvik continued, 'You also told her that you needed to source a specially trained crew for the *Mary Jo* who had expertise in the shipping industry and the marine salvage business but no relatives to come nosing around and kicking up a fuss after they disappeared. She set up a fake recruitment website and posted the jobs, requesting CVs and details to be sent confidentially to a false ID you'd set up, which you then passed on to Bradshaw, who couldn't care less where they had come from. And after the *Mary Jo* vanished, when he realized they had no next of kin or relatives, he was only too pleased to keep his mouth shut and take the insurance money, their wages and a share of the memorial fund, which he spilt with Meryl Landguard and Stuart Moorcott.'

Elmsley was frowning hard and Paynton at the helm was increasingly throwing him troubled glances, maybe because he was learning something new about his boss, but more probably because he, like Elmsley, was becoming concerned that if Marvik knew all this then others might also. Good; Marvik wanted them rattled.

Evenly, he persisted. 'It was the Iraq War, there was a lot of news about the possibility of chemical weapons being used and the increasing danger of bio-terrorism. Jemma was to set up a fictitious laboratory and see if she could get hold of sodium azide because from your experience in transporting cars you knew that car airbags are fitted with the chemical. You knew how toxic it could be and how rapidly it reacted when it came into contact with water or a shock. Had there been an incident at sea with Stapledon, Royden and Landguard on board a container ship?'

'You tell me — you seem to have all the answers,' Elmsley snapped. The boat was rocking in the stormy sea but for a man who had spent a career travelling in all kinds of weather and sea states, Marvik knew this was nothing to disturb Elmsley's equilibrium. He remained firmly rooted and the gun stayed steadily pointing at Marvik.

Marvik continued, 'Maybe the master was notified that a consignment had faulty airbags and that it had to be contained at all costs. Stapledon finally made the link. He knew it couldn't be Royden because he was dead — that left you or Landguard. He wasn't sure which of you had faked his death because in both cases there had been no body to identify and bury. But one of you had been paying generously into his charity and giving him a little on the side with instructions to report back if anyone came asking about the *Mary Jo*. He thought back to when he had lived and worked at sea for weeks on end with both men. He knew them intimately — their personalities, interests, strengths and weaknesses.' And Marvik recalled what he'd been told by Stephen Landguard about his father, and by Stapledon and Royden.

He said, 'Landguard was a planner, methodical, thorough and clever. He loved art and spent his leisure time sketching. He was also ambitious. He'd reached the summit of his career as master but he had a crumbling marriage and a scheming, grasping wife who would take him to the cleaners if he divorced her. He could easily have planned the whole thing and created a new life for himself as a reclusive, eccentric businessman operating a thriving marine business — Drakes — which would eventually acquire Almbridge. It's what Royden believed.

'Then there was you. Also clever and ambitious but more outgoing than Landguard. You felt stifled at sea. You liked company so you switched to working on the cruise liners, as did Landguard for a time, but he soon found it wasn't to his liking. You probably enjoyed it for a while but you were desperate to be your own boss, and when you met up again with Duncan Helmslow and he said he was thinking of setting up his own business, you went in with him. But Duncan was too cautious for you. You, unlike Landguard, are much more of a risk-taker and far more ruthless. Did Stapledon guess correctly before you pushed him off the cliff?'

A wave hit them sideways. Marvik rocked in his seat. Elmsley staggered but rapidly recovered himself, saying, 'No. He was, shall we say, struck speechless.'

'By you or your mate there?' Marvik rejoined sourly. Stapledon must have suspected it to be Timothy Landguard, just as Royden had done.

'He stepped back and got too close to the edge.'

'No doubt backed up there by you or Paynton, with the gun you're now pointing at me.' Was Strathen at this moment facing a thug with a gun? Had he found Helen?

Without betraying his concern, Marvik pressed on. 'The sodium azide was planted on the *Mary Jo* and one of the crew you had especially selected was instructed to ensure it reacted with water to make it highly toxic and deadly. What did you tell the man who thought he was working for you? That he'd be protected when he made sure that the chemical was exposed to water? That he'd be OK because you'd issued him with a gas mask to protect him, only what you didn't tell the poor sod was that it was faulty. You didn't want any witnesses to your evil.' Marvik addressed Paynton. 'I'd watch out if I were you. When he's finished with me he'll arrange a suitable death for you.'

'Silence,' Elmsley tersely commanded and the gun came perilously close to Marvik's forehead. Marvik didn't move. He held Elmsley's hot, angry eyes.

'OK, shoot me and throw me overboard. The blood on the boat will mean I shot myself on board. But I haven't reached Helen yet, unless you think the authorities will believe that I killed myself on returning from her. But then the timing will be wrong.' The gun remained pointed at Marvik's head for a moment longer. Then Elmsley lowered it, only fractionally, though. With relief, which he hid, Marvik knew that meant Helen was still alive.

'Was it by chance you found the press articles on Elona Kadowski's paintings in November 2000 and realized the murals on the *Celeste* were her work?' he asked. 'You had to check it out and you found the *Celeste* was lying at Newfoundland waiting to be scrapped with all the interior, including the murals, intact and no one any the wiser that they were worth a fortune, not even Landguard who had also worked on the *Celeste*. But you must have made sure of that. Landguard might have read the articles. He had an interest in art. Bradshaw might also have seen the news and known that murals were mentioned on the ship's itinerary, the same for Duncan Helmslow and Alec Royden.'

'They didn't. Landguard was too concerned about his marriage and his new job with Helmsley's. Royden only ever read the business and sports news and was far too preoccupied with getting his business off the ground. Bradshaw was ignorant about everything except how he could screw women and make money,' scoffed Elmsley.

'And after you realized you could make a fortune if you could get your hands on the murals, you set about tracing any relatives just in case there was some written evidence, a diary or letters, which mentioned them. There wasn't and Jemma was blithely unaware that her mother had been a famous Russian artist. You began to plan how you could get hold of them and sell them.'

'I didn't see why the Norwegian owners should benefit.'

'Or Jemma. Which meant you had to disappear as Martin Elmsley. A death at sea was arranged. How did you do it?' Marvik wasn't sure if Elmsley would answer but he did, maybe just to demonstrate how clever he had been.

'I planned to be swept overboard from the RIB we owned but when I heard that a fishing vessel was in danger I thought that might be the perfect opportunity to die a hero. I didn't know how it would pan out but I thought it worth a try. And I wasn't bothered if it didn't because, as I said, I had planned another death. I rushed to the call before Duncan even knew of it and before anyone could stop me. On the way, I rapidly donned a wetsuit under my clothes, leaving off my socks and wearing canvas shoes. I wasn't sure if I'd reach the vessel in time or before anyone else but I did. I'm a trained diver. I knew exactly what to do and I could react quickly.'

'But you couldn't have worn an aqua lung or had one stashed on the sea bed. And you couldn't have got back to the RIB and put it on without being seen.'

'No. I planned on going under and then being swept out to sea.'

'You took a hell of a risk.'

'Taking risks is my business, always has been, and it's paid off.'

'So far,' muttered Marvik.

'And it will continue to do so,' Elmsley said supremely confidently. 'I attempted to fix the line. I could see assistance heading towards us in the shape of the lifeboat. I slipped and fell into the water. I made to swim and put up a show but let the tide take me inshore and there was also an inshore wind. The fishing vessel was sinking, the lifeboat crew were busy rescuing them and the RIB was drifting. By the time they started looking for me I had reached the shore. All I had to do was get dry clothes and get away. That was easy.'

'You had already pre-arranged all that ready for the accident you had planned. Where had you kept the clothes and the new ID?'

'You'll find out soon.'

It was where Elmsley was taking him.

'It was hard work getting there but I did it,' Elmsley said cockily. 'There was always the chance that someone would see me and report me. If they did, though, then I would just show up as Martin Elmsley, the hero, as long as I could ditch the wet suit, but then I thought why not ditch the clothes and keep the wet suit. If anyone did see me they'd think I was a loony surfer or windsurfer who had lost his board. But nobody saw me or, if they did, they didn't report it. It all went swimmingly.' He smiled at the cleverness of his pun.

'You became Marcus Kiln.'

'Eventually, but before that I became Terry Keydell, not then the owner of Drakes Marine but an independent marine consultant working abroad.'

'And you had contacts worldwide from your years of working in the shipping industry who came in very useful for the fake passport and for helping you to build relationships in the art world with collectors who wouldn't be fussy where the murals had come from. You had two years to set it up, from the time you disappeared as Martin Elmsley in March 2001 to when Bradshaw got the contract for the scrapping of the *Mary Jo* in March 2003. It must have taken a lot of planning and patience.' Which was why Stapledon and Royden had thought it was Landguard, whose personality suited the scam better than Elmsley's.

'And nerve. Someone could have discovered those murals in the meantime. But they didn't. As Marcus Kiln, the ship broker, I had to persuade Bradshaw to buy the *Celeste*, and he had to persuade Duncan that it was a good deal. Bradshaw was easy enough when he realized there could be some money from the scrap value for him, which Duncan and the company didn't need to know about.'

'And by then Duncan was ill and the company was going down the pan thanks to Bradshaw's embezzlement. You were banking on Helmsley taking the *Celeste* to India to scrap, where you could get the murals offloaded no questions asked, but Bradshaw did his own side deal to bring the *Celeste* to Britain, which didn't suit you at all. The only way you could change that was to make sure the *Mary Jo* never reached Newfoundland. And that was where Jemma came in. Who did you become to her?'

'It's not significant.'

'Her death is, though, and the fact that you used her and then killed her.'

'I wouldn't have needed to if that idiot Bradshaw hadn't been so greedy.'

'I think that's a word which fits you more aptly,' Marvik said acidly. 'You knew she was a very clever computer programmer and you knew that Bradshaw was crooked.'

'I discovered Bradshaw fiddling at Helmsley's, which wasn't surprising. He always had some deal going on and there was always money, cargo and equipment missing when we were at sea together. He was about to be sacked from the shipping company when I offered him the job at Helmsley's.'

'Which was in January 2002, and you'd have a corrupt man in your pocket when the time was right.'

'I threatened him with the sack if I found him doing it again and said I'd tell Duncan. Knowing Bradshaw as I did, I knew he'd be very relieved when I died. And Meryl Landguard was no saint. She was having an affair with Bradshaw and cooking the books at the brokerage where she worked, siphoning off money, not to mention being involved in false invoicing.'

'Bradshaw and Meryl Landguard weren't the only crooks,' Marvik rejoined.

Elmsley shrugged. The gun was still pointing at Marvik. They couldn't be far from their destination now, surely.

Marvik said, 'When you learned that Bradshaw had done one of his side deals to bring the *Celeste* to Britain you had to think fast. As Marcus Kiln you suggested to Bradshaw that you would oversee recruiting a crew for the job. He accepted and Jemma helped you set up a fake recruitment operation to engage a crew who would disappear with no relatives to keep stirring things up by asking awkward questions and going to the media.'

'I knew Duncan would jump at it. The last thing he wanted was to be involved in interviewing and that also suited Bradshaw.'

'And when the *Mary Jo* never reached Newfoundland, you then, as Marcus Kiln, resold the *Celeste* to Royden. You knew Royden's weakness for good living and money and told him that if the *Celeste* was scrapped in India some of the money for the silver, bronze and aluminium on board could find its way into a private account which you would set up for him offshore. He went along with that. It's a shame you couldn't have waited before killing the *Mary Jo* crew because the bad publicity over the scrapping of the American warships in Britain meant Duncan would have switched the recycling of the *Celeste* to India.'

'It was too late for that. I had buyers lined up. How far?' Elmsley addressed Paynton with a note of irritation in his voice. He was getting jumpy but Marvik didn't underestimate him. This man was clever and ruthless.

'We'll be at Cuckmere Haven in about four minutes.'

Marvik rapidly recalled the locale — the natural wildlife haven with a beach that was at the opposite end of the Seven Sisters chalk cliffs to where Gavin's body had been found. And perched on the eroding clifftop was a row of coastguard cottages in danger of crumbling over the cliff edge just like the ones at the Birling Gap.

'You're holding Helen in one of the coastguard cottages.'

'Yes, but you'll never reach there.'

'You'll force her to walk down to the shore? You'll have to because if you kill her and move her body the autopsy will discover that and it won't fit with me murdering her on the beach. She has to reach there alive before you shoot her.'

'The details don't concern you.'

Marvik's mind was racing. He knew he was correct. The police would believe she had gone to meet him, and he, her lover, discovering that she had betrayed him with Bradshaw and Yardly, had shot her. Mentally, Marvik played out the scenario. They would anchor his boat and use the tender on the rear to get to the shore. They'd order him into it. Helen would be brought down to the shore. They'd shoot her, then shoot him in the head to make it look as though he'd shot himself, throw his body into the sea and let the tender drift. They would take off in a car parked somewhere close to the coastguard cottages. The police might see tyre tracks but conclude they had nothing to do with Helen's murder and his suicide. And clearly Elmsley wasn't worried about Strathen being there because he believed that Strathen was following one of the tracking devices they'd discovered on Helen to another destination — *if* they knew about him. Perhaps Helen had said nothing about Strathen.

Paynton throttled down. It was almost time. 'Was Paynton watching Helen's flat waiting for her to return, and when she did with me he called the police?' Elmsley nodded.

'And he killed Bradshaw or did you do your own dirty work?' Neither man answered. Marvik continued as Paynton, at the helm, brought the boat to a halt. 'I don't think you'd have got blood on your own hands, Elmsley, but there's a lot of blood on your conscience, or there would be if you had one.'

'Up,' Elmsley commanded, waving the gun at Marvik. He slid out of the seat.

'Killing Meryl Landguard, Stephen and now Helen and me — don't you think the police are going to become suspicious over the high number of murders followed by suicide?'

'I'll be gone by then and so will you, but not to the same place.'

Marvik addressed the man at the helm. With a sneer, he said, 'I'd watch your back if I were you, Paynton. Loyal you might be, but an accidental fall in the sea could be easily arranged.'

The gun whipped across the right-hand side of Marvik's face. Marvik's head reeled but he made no sound and neither did he raise his hand to stem the blood. He held Elmsley's eyes.

'Did Gavin tell you he'd found the *Mary Jo*?' Marvik said tautly. 'Obviously not from your expression. So he held out on you even when you tortured him. Oh, yes, she's been found all right and intact with her crew on board,' bullshitted Marvik. He didn't know that for certain. 'Gavin worked out that the *Mary Jo* with its dead crew on board could have drifted into the Arctic and that one day the ice might reveal her. The Arctic is a gigantic mortuary and often yields frozen bodies years after the ice has devoured them. Gavin accessed the government's satellite and found her. He told GCHQ where to look. It's why I am here. You killed him too late. He'd already sent them a letter by good old-fashioned and efficient snail mail.'

'That's bollocks,' Elmsley scoffed, but Marvik saw with satisfaction that he looked annoyed and uneasy. Elmsley addressed his henchman. 'Hurry up with that tender.' The man slipped past them and left the cabin. Marvik could take Elmsley now but the timing wasn't right.

He felt the sticky, warm blood run down on to the collar of his jacket. 'There's the online backup that Gavin made of his own research along with Jemma's remote backup, which he managed to trace and access. Didn't you know she had backed up everything with an online provider? Yes, even then in 2003, plus the letter he wrote to GCHQ giving them the log-in details and the encrypted password revealing everything you did.' It was a lie but Elmsley didn't know that and he was beginning to look agitated; beginning to wonder if his true identity would be exposed and he would be traced and apprehended. 'You'd better start thinking up a new name,' Marvik pressed. 'And quick.'

'I can leave the country easily. No one except you knows I'm here and you won't be around to tell anyone. I came by boat and I'll leave by boat.'

The rain was spitting off the deck and the boat rolling and bucking alarmingly. Marvik said, 'Is that the boat you hired as Colin Prior which you transported Gavin's body on before you dumped him under Bailey Hill with weights so his body would be found?'

'Out,' ordered Elmsley, waving the gun at Marvik. He obeyed, his mind racing, his eyes keenly peeled in the dark, sodden night on the burly figure at the aft lowering the tender into the swollen sea. It fell with a splash. Elmsley ordered Marvik forward and Paynton to climb in and to start the outboard motor. Marvik knew that he wouldn't be allowed to reach the shore. Elmsley would shoot him at very close range, which meant he would get blood and brain all over himself but he wasn't worried about that. He and Paynton would be able to wash it off and destroy their clothes. Elmsley would hold the gun to Marvik's head and press the trigger. The blood splatter in the rubber dinghy would be consistent with Marvik firing the gun at his head and his body falling back into the sea, left to wash up somewhere, if it ever did.

The dinghy would be found drifting. Helen would be shot with the same gun on the shore. She might already be on the shore with another of Elmsley's accomplices. Strathen might not have reached them. If he had, Marvik was convinced he'd have handled any of Elmsley's operatives, unless there had been two or three of them. Marvik knew that once he was in the tender there was no way out.

He tensed and prepared to seize the spilt-second moment between life and death. He was gambling on the fact that Paynton wasn't armed. Paynton stepped down on to the platform. The tender was bobbing about violently in the dark, swirling sea beneath Marvik, the engine running, the wind roaring around them, the waves kicking up spray over the edge, clashing with the rain and soaking them. Elmsley was behind Marvik. He could feel Elmsley's breath on his neck and the barrel of the gun pressed against his skin. But Elmsley wouldn't shoot him in the neck — suicides don't usually aim for that part of the body, although it wasn't completely unknown.

The boat was pitching violently. Marvik scoured the sea, his heart racing, the adrenaline coursing through his veins, the inside of his mouth dry and the taste of salt on his lips. There wasn't much time, just a second, maybe two. Would the sea oblige him? Would it give up what he wanted? Would Elmsley, a man of the sea, know what he was going to do? Would he counter his move?

Marvik watched the black, swollen wave roll towards them. His timing had to be perfect. As the tender and his boat rose alarmingly with the swell of the sea, Marvik rolled back into Elmsley, who swayed and lost his balance. In an instant, Marvik spun round and gave a vicious karate blow to Elmsley's wrist, which sent the gun flying and sliding on to the wet platform. Marvik kicked it into the sea and swiftly rammed a powerful fist into Elmsley's midriff. As he doubled over, winded, Marvik, his hands locked in a vice, struck them down in a violent blow on the back of Elmsley's neck. His body sank heavily on to the platform and the waves crashed over it, threatening to sweep him overboard, while Marvik registered Paynton rise from the tender and make for him, but the sea state was too turbulent for him to do so. He was caught off balance; a wave swamped him. He struggled up, coughing up salt water. Marvik swiftly reached for a lifebelt and line on the rear of his boat, thrust the first over Elmsley's head and wrapped the line tautly around the unconscious Elmsley to prevent him from falling into the sea. The sound of a powerful launch broke through the night. Elmsley's henchman rose again, coughing and spluttering. He dashed a glance at Elmsley's body and turned back towards the engine in the tender. Marvik leapt into the tender.

'Oh, no you don't.' He raised his fist and punched it full force against the man's jaw. His head reeled back, blood spouting from his mouth and nose. He fell back in the tender. Marvik made to strike him again but the sound of the launch was drawing closer. The man eyed Marvik, then, twisting, leapt over the side and into the sea.

Marvik left him and pointed his tender in the direction of the shore.

# CHAPTER TWENTY-FOUR

'What kept you?' Strathen said.

Marvik noted Strathen's light tone and saw his smile.

Helen was safe. Marvik felt a great sense of relief. 'We were engrossed in such a nice little chat on board that I could barely tear myself away. I didn't fancy a swim either but someone did.'

'Elmsley?'

'No. His henchman, Paynton. Maybe Crowder's team will pick him out of the sea.' Marvik didn't particularly care if they didn't. He could see the powerful lights of the police launch heading for his boat and ahead of it a RIB which was making towards them on the shore.

Marvik turned and looked up to the houses shrouded in the rain on the clifftop. 'Which one is she in?'

'The one on the far end. The others are all empty. I broke into them and checked. No one around to hear her shouts for help. She's not bound or gagged. She's OK, Art. I could see her pacing about the room. There's a crack in the shutters. She's probably cursing. Knowing Helen, she must have tried to get out but the door is locked and bolted. She's in a room on the ground floor. There's no one with her so whoever Elmsley instructed to bring her here and leave her was also told to get out.'

Paynton would have fetched her from the cottage and either he or Elmsley would have shot her. Elmsley hadn't wanted any other witnesses to that, and the two of them had probably executed all the other deaths. Elmsley hadn't drugged her because it would have shown up in her blood, and he wanted the police to believe that Marvik had shot her and then himself. He knew that Strathen couldn't have freed her because he couldn't risk Helen being with him on the shore in case he hadn't overpowered Elmsley and Paynton. Marvik wondered if Helen had known there was a third tracking device sewn into the hem of her skirt. He hoped so because then she wouldn't have been so afraid, and he didn't want her to be fearful.

Marvik caught the sound of a police siren in the distance. 'Sounds like reinforcements are on their way. They can have the pleasure of breaking down the door.'

'There's a car parked two hundred yards down the road out of sight, obviously the one that Elmsley and his mate were planning on using to get away after killing you and Helen. Good thing he never found the tracking and surveillance device on your boat.'

'Or the listening device. You heard some of it.'

'Enough.'

It couldn't be used as sufficient evidence in a court of law but Marvik didn't think Crowder would need it to be able to bring a case against Elmsley. He'd be able to get sufficient on which to charge him and Marvik suspected that Paynton would cough.

Strathen had called Crowder the moment Marvik's boat had left Newhaven Marina and had briefed him, as Marvik had known he would. Crowder would have tracked it by satellite, having despatched the launch and RIB, keeping a safe distance until Marvik's boat had stopped. The mission had always revolved around this area and Crowder would have been somewhere close by in readiness. Marvik suspected Brighton because he'd witnessed nothing of Crowder in Eastbourne or Newhaven marinas and Crowder would have been able to summon up police officers more easily from the large coastal town of Brighton, where they had launches and RIBs at their disposal.

Marvik wiped the blood from his face. The cut had almost stopped bleeding. His wet hair was plastered to his skull, as was Strathen's, and their sodden clothes were clinging to them. Marvik's head throbbed with pain but he pushed that aside as the RIB came on to the shore and Crowder climbed off.

'Did you pick up the man in the sea?' asked Marvik.

Crowder nodded.

'He'll tell you where the Landguards are but I think you'll find them back at Meryl Landguard's house. Whether they're alive, though, is another matter,' Marvik said solemnly. Then added: 'I'm not sure about Karen Landguard and her son.'

'They're at her mother's. Safe and well.'

'Thank God for that.'

Crowder gave instructions to one of the two uniformed officers with him to send a unit to Meryl Landguard's house. He turned to Strathen. 'Is Helen Shannon in one of those cottages?'

Strathen relayed where she was. 'She's not harmed.'

The police sirens had stopped. They must be close by, thought Marvik. Crowder instructed the second uniformed police officer to rendezvous with those in the patrol car, to break open the door and to bring Helen down to the shore. Marvik was surprised by that. He'd expected Crowder to request that she be taken back to Newhaven police station or to her bedsit in Eastbourne, not that Marvik thought she'd be able to or want to stay there. But what would she do now? Where would she go? He wondered if Strathen was thinking the same. From a glance at him, he knew he was.

Marvik postponed his thoughts and, in the lights of the police launch, he watched Paynton and Elmsley being escorted on board.

Within a few minutes, Helen was heading down the cliff towards them guided by the powerful beam of a handheld torch of the accompanying police office and a steadying arm on the slippery, wet path. The hood of her sailing jacket was over her purple hair and she was carrying her rucksack. As she drew nearer, Marvik could see that she looked tired, but as her gaze alighted on them he noted the relief on her face.

She swivelled her gaze to Crowder. 'I might have known you'd be mixed up in this,' she said, addressing him, but her tone was friendly. She and Crowder must have liaised fairly closely over the last couple of months since he and Strathen had apprehended the man who had killed her sister.

Crowder said, 'Shall we go or would you prefer to wait for a police car?'

'Boats are fine with me,' she said firmly and climbed into Marvik's RIB, as did Strathen and Crowder, leaving his police officers shore bound to deal with matters. Addressing both Marvik and Strathen, she said, 'You took your time getting here.'

Marvik answered, 'We had a small matter of a few loose ends to tie up.'

She followed his gaze out to the sea where the police launch was waiting beside Marvik's boat.

'Who was it?'

'A man who was supposed to have died in 2001.'

No one spoke for the rest of the short and rocky journey to Marvik's boat. But when they reached it and the police launch beside it, Helen, seeing Elmsley on board wrapped in a silver thermal blanket, exclaimed, 'That's Colin Prior.'

'That's only one of his names.'

She rounded on Crowder. 'I hope you're going to charge him with murder.'

'We will. Will you give evidence?'

'Too damn right I will if it'll send that bastard to jail.'

When safely on board, and after Strathen had fetched some towels to dry them off, he explained to Helen about Jemma Duisky. 'I knew I was right about her being important in this case,' she triumphantly declared. 'So did you and that's why you shoved me out of the way.'

'Sorry about that.'

'I bet,' she replied with feeling. 'You deliberately let me walk out and then called the police.' Although angry and frustrated, her voice held no trace of bitterness.

'I didn't think the police would let you go so quickly.'

'No thanks to your super lawyer, who didn't show. I could have been killed by that goon who pointed a gun at me and told me to get in the van quietly without fuss. He found your tracking devices but not all of them, obviously. Where's the third one?'

Strathen pointed to her wet skirt. She rolled her eyes.

Marvik started up. The police launch swung round in the direction of Newhaven. Marvik followed. As he did, he relayed to Helen and Crowder the news of the discovery of the murals, Martin Elmsley's part in it and the catalogue of deaths as a result of Elmsley's greed.

'Poor Gavin,' muttered Helen.

Strathen made them all coffee. The rain was still hitting the deck but the sea state had eased a little, along with the wind.

Marvik addressed Crowder. 'Did Gavin really send a letter to GCHQ?'

'Yes. It contained information on the location of the *Mary Jo* which could only have been accessed by hacking into one of GCHQ's satellites.'

As both he and Strathen had said.

'Gavin must have been very good,' Helen said with admiration.

'He was.'

'So was Jemma,' Strathen added, 'to have got hold of sodium azide. It's a potentially lethal chemical,' he explained to Helen, who was looking bewildered. 'It was used to wipe out the crew of the *Mary Jo*.'

Crowder said, 'In his letter, Gavin claimed there were only three bodies on board. We weren't able to verify that and we still can't because the *Mary Jo* has been reclaimed by the ice. But she won't stay hidden, not now that we know her approximate location.'

Marvik said, 'Gavin thought the master, Timothy Landguard, was behind the smuggling of sodium azide. Gavin knew nothing about the murals because Jemma was also ignorant of them and there was no reason for Gavin to delve into that. He was trying to find out from Meryl Landguard if she was in contact with her husband. Gavin reasoned if he was right and Landguard was not one of the three bodies on the *Mary Jo* then he might have been killed and thrown overboard by one of the crew — mercenaries who were told they would be handsomely paid for their services.'

The throb of the police launch faded into the distance as it sped ahead of them. Marvik was in no hurry. He gratefully took the mug of coffee Strathen handed him. God, he was hungry. And tired. He knew that Strathen felt the same and perhaps his fatigue was also tainted with something else — thoughts of Helen. She sat sipping her coffee, looking tired but none the worse for her ordeal over the last week. Maybe it would hit her later.

Marvik continued, 'Gavin thought Bradshaw was behind the smuggling.'

'We won't know that for certain unless we can find Jemma's files and access them. And Gavin's backed-up record of his research and his password to access it.'

Strathen said, 'It'll be a variation on Jemma's — NaN3, the chemical equation for sodium azide. I'm sure your experts will find both files and crack the passwords to them.'

'It might be quicker if you did. I can give you access to the letter and any other information we have, plus what you know and what we'll get from Elmsley will help. He might even have been foolish enough to keep hold of Gavin's computer. It shouldn't take you long.'

Strathen's tired eyes lit up at that. He smiled wearily at the compliment.

Marvik said, 'I wonder who Elmsley gave the tampered mask to.'

'We'll discover that once we find the *Mary Jo*.'

With an edge of bitterness, Marvik, thinking of both Gavin Yardly and Stephen Landguard and a child growing up without his father, said, 'You should have protected Gavin. You could have used his knowledge to help locate that boat and to find Elmsley without all the deaths.'

'You know that by the time we were alerted it was too late. As I told you, Gavin was already dead and so was Ian Bradshaw.'

Crowder was correct. But Stephen Landguard had still been alive, so too his mother, Alec Royden and Hugh Stapledon. But dwelling on that achieved nothing, as Marvik knew all too well, and yet his mind momentarily flitted to Sarah Redburn. Curtly, he said, 'The two men on the pontoon who Helen overheard talking were your officers, weren't they? You wanted Helen involved.'

Her eyes widened in amazement and incredulity.

Crowder said, 'We wanted *you* involved.'

'Then why not just give us the mission?' Marvik said with frustration. 'Why rope in Helen and put her life in peril? Christ, Elmsley or his mate could have killed her. They very nearly did and would have done if she hadn't been spooked enough to leave the flat.'

Crowder turned his gaze on Helen. 'It was a risk we had to take.'

'Thanks,' she said cynically.

Crowder continued, 'You don't scare easily, and you can reason things out pretty well. We knew that having been involved with Marvik and Strathen before you'd relate to the language my officers used. You'd call one of them.'

She narrowed her eyes at him. 'And if I hadn't?'

'You would,' Crowder answered confidently. His conviction seemed to please her. Her lips twitched in the ghost of a smile and Marvik noted the gleam in her green eyes. From what he knew of her life she hadn't had a great many people believing in her.

She sipped her coffee as Crowder said, 'Gavin Yardly's letter finally reached my desk because it was a marine-related intelligence matter. There was no hard evidence to back up what Gavin claimed to have found — toxic chemicals having been smuggled out of the country and used to kill in 2003. I ran a check on him and where he lived and found that one of the tenants in that building was you, Helen. I also discovered that you worked with Gavin Yardly. I detailed someone to follow you on Monday and the officer overheard you arranging to meet on Bradshaw's boat that night.'

'How? I didn't see anyone.'

'I'd have been disappointed if you had. I considered it an ideal opportunity to stage something to get you involved and away from danger. We didn't know that Bradshaw was involved or that he would be killed,' he hastily added when Strathen looked about to contradict him. 'I despatched two officers each by boat to the marina.'

Marvik said, 'Colbourne and Marwell — false names like those of their boats.'

'Yes. They were there to stage that little scenario, which they did admirably, and then leave.' To Helen, he said, 'We had no idea how long you would be on board Bradshaw's boat.'

'You should have done,' she retorted. 'You couldn't think I'd let a man like that grope me?'

'You left sooner than anticipated. When my officers felt the movement of the pontoon they began that dialogue. And the fact that you hid on that fishing boat meant you overheard what you were meant to hear.'

Strathen spoke. 'Did you have anyone watching Helen's flat?'

'No. Gavin wasn't there and we didn't know who was involved, why or how. Helen called you, Marvik, and you came to the rescue. You found Bradshaw's body and when we knew he'd been killed I stepped in to make it official. But if anyone was still watching that house, which they were, they'd have seen you with Helen and wouldn't have suspected that you had any connection with the authorities, only that you were there because of Helen.'

'It worked,' Marvik said, thinking back to his conversation with Elmsley.

Strathen, scathingly, said, 'You gambled with Helen's life. She's not part of your team.'

'No, she isn't. Would you like to be?' he addressed her directly.

'Me! I can't do anything. I'm not a Royal Marine Commando.'

'No, but you have other talents.'

'Like what?' she scoffed.

'We can discuss that.'

Helen looked puzzled and intrigued. She shrugged. 'I've got nothing else to do now that I'm unemployed.'

Strathen said nothing and drank his coffee. But Marvik didn't think he was comfortable about that. Marvik examined how he felt about Helen being involved with the Squad. It depended on how Crowder saw her role. But however he did, and whatever Crowder offered Helen, it was nothing to do with him or Shaun. It would be Helen's decision alone.

Marvik watched the white light of the lighthouse on the long stone breakwater, one long beam followed by one short beam. No one spoke as he motored closer to the port and swung the boat into its more sheltered waters. The police launch was mooring up on the visitors' berths of the marina, which he had left two hours ago. He throttled down and eased the boat on to the pontoon. Strathen alighted and tied off. Marvik silenced the engine. Still no one spoke. Crowder's phone went. He stepped out on to the deck to answer it. Returning, his face grim, he said, 'Stephen Landguard and his mother, Meryl, have been found. Meryl in the garden, strangled. Stephen in the house. No visible signs of death. Looks like an overdose.'

Marvik nodded solemnly. Another person he had failed to save.

Crowder turned to Helen. 'We'll get you a hotel room for now.'

'Where?'

'Southampton. Unless there's somewhere else you'd like to go?'

'No, that will be fine,' she said with a glance at Strathen.

There would be a full debriefing somewhere in a neutral and secure location. Marvik knew they'd see Helen again.

She rose and picked up her rucksack. Her eyes flicked between them. She made to speak, then decided that perhaps there was too much to say and she didn't know how to say it anyway. To Strathen, Crowder said, 'There's a car waiting to drop you back to Cuckmere Haven.'

'Thanks.'

Strathen turned to Marvik as they watched Crowder and Helen walk down the pontoon towards the marina car park. 'She'll be OK,' he said. Marvik wasn't certain if Strathen was really reassuring himself.

'Are you coming back here tonight?' Marvik asked.

'No, I'll head home.'

'I'm also leaving. No need to stay here any longer.'

Strathen understood, as Marvik knew he would. There was no need for him to explain that he needed to put distance between himself and the place where so many deaths had occurred. As Strathen walked away, he said, 'Let me know when and if you want that disk opened.'

Marvik nodded. He cast off and swung the boat out of Newhaven Harbour into the black expanse of the sea and headed for the Solent, the Isle of Wight and the solitude of his cottage.

**THE END**

# THE JOFFE BOOKS STORY

We began in 2014 when Jasper agreed to publish his mum's much-rejected romance novel and it became a bestseller.

Since then we've grown into the largest independent publisher in the UK. We're extremely proud to publish some of the very best writers in the world, including Joy Ellis, Faith Martin, Caro Ramsay, Helen Forrester, Simon Brett and Robert Goddard. Everyone at Joffe Books loves reading and we never forget that it all begins with the magic of an author telling a story.

We are proud to publish talented first-time authors, as well as established writers whose books we love introducing to a new generation of readers.

We have been shortlisted for Independent Publisher of the Year at the British Book Awards three times, in 2020, 2021 and 2022, and for the Diversity and Inclusivity Award at the Independent Publishing Awards in 2022.

We built this company with your help, and we love to hear from you, so please email us about absolutely anything bookish at feedback@joffebooks.com

If you want to receive free books every Friday and hear about all our new releases, join our mailing list: www.joffebooks.com/contact

And when you tell your friends about us, just remember: it's pronounced Joffe as in coffee or toffee!

## ALSO BY PAULINE ROWSON

**THE ART MARVIK MYSTERIES**

Book 1: DEADLY WAVES
Book 2: DANGEROUS CARGO
Book 3: LOST VOYAGE

**THE SOLENT MURDER MYSTERIES**

Book 1: THE PORTSMOUTH MURDERS
Book 2: THE LANGSTONE HARBOUR MURDERS
Book 3: THE HORSEA MARINA MURDERS
Book 4: THE ROYAL HOTEL MURDERS
Book 5: THE ISLE OF WIGHT MURDERS
Book 6: THE PORTCHESTER CASTLE MURDERS
Book 7: THE CHALE BAY MURDERS
Book 8: THE FARLINGTON MARSH MURDERS
Book 9: THE OYSTER QUAYS MURDERS
Book 10: THE COWES WEEK MURDERS
Book 11: THE BOATHOUSE MURDERS
Book 12: THE THORNEY ISLAND MURDERS
Book 13: THE GUERNSEY FERRY MURDERS
Book 14: THE RAT ISLAND MURDERS
Book 15: THE LUCCOMBE BAY MURDERS
Book 16: THE SOUTH BINNESS MURDERS

Printed in Great Britain
by Amazon

31667075R00151